She was i

She could not  r. She
had thrilled  first
encounter in  e was
aware that her eyes were constantly searching
hall and courtyard for a single glimpse of him.
She needed to have him in her sight, to watch,
hungrily, every move he made, to discover how
he behaved with friends, his lord the Duke, and
his men at arms and servants.

She knew very little about him. He was still
unwed, but he had lost his father in battle when
he was still a child. Perhaps that was the reason
he had not been pressed into a youthful
marriage. She gave a little secret smile,
hugging to herself the thought that he would
never allow himself to be pressed into anything
he did not wish to do.

Yes, that was true, but it was not possible that
he would wish to wed her, Rosamund
Kinnersley, soon to be homeless and the
daughter of a dead traitor.

Joanna Makepeace taught as Head of English in a comprehensive before leaving full-time work to write. She loves the old romantic historical films, which she finds more exciting and relaxing than the newer ones. Joanna's home town is Leicester.

HER GUARDIAN KNIGHT

Joanna Makepeace

MILLS & BOON®

First published in Great Britain 2003
Harlequin Mills & Boon Limited,
Eton House, 18-24 Paradise Road, Richmond, Surrey TW9 1SR

© Joanna Makepeace 2003

ISBN 0 263 83949 4

Set in Times Roman 10½ on 11½ pt.
04-0204-91395

Printed and bound in Spain
by Litografia Rosés S.A., Barcelona

For Martin Berka,
my dear friend in the Czech Republic

Chapter One

Chapter One

'Mistress Rosamund, Rosa…' The voice was imperative and Rosamund sighed and wiped her hands upon a linen cloth and went to open the door as Martha, her former nurse, now her personal servant, panted along the corridor.

Rosamund had been working since daybreak in her mother's still room, making preparations for the herbs that would be ready for picking and storing later this month or early June. She wiped her forehead on which sweat was already forming, for since the first of May this year of Our Lord 1472, the weather had been unexpectedly hot. Her stepmother, the Lady Sibyl, had never appeared to be particularly interested in the drying of herbs and making of salves and the work had fallen to Rosamund of late. She had welcomed it today, for the manor had seemed dreary since the departure of her father and a troop of men-at-arms just over a week ago. Rosamund knew that the whole household was waiting anxiously to hear news of him and for his return.

Sir Humphrey had fought recently at the battle of Barnet where the Yorkist king, Edward, had defeated Sir Humphrey's liege lord, the Earl of Warwick, and the earl had been slain. Rosamund's father had fled the field and man-

aged to return home to Kinnersley Manor, but his stay had
been all too short. Hearing that Queen Margaret of Anjou
had landed in England with her son, Edward of Lancaster,
and his bride, the earl's daughter, the former Lady Anne
Neville, Sir Humphrey had decided to join her force, in
the hope that she would succeed in defeating the Yorkist
usurper and place her husband, Henry VIth, once more
upon his rightful throne. He had headed for Tewkesbury,
some twelve miles distant from his own manor in the Cots-
wolds, in order to join the Queen's army, which was
marching towards London from the west. Rosamund hoped
that it would not be long before they were able to receive
news of him.

She turned now anxiously to Martha, who had sank
down upon a stool and was fanning herself vigorously with
the linen cloth Rosamund had laid down upon the working
table.

'What is it, Martha? Have we received bad news? There
has been no word from my father?'

Martha shook her head sadly. She was a big woman,
moonfaced, and decidedly overweight. This heat, coming
so early in the year, was laying her low. 'No, no, mistress,
nothing new. What we heard from that wandering chapman yesterday was but hearsay, as you said yourself. Lady
Sibyl stoutly refused to believe it.'

Rosamund frowned. She sincerely hoped that they both
were right. The pedlar, who had called at the manor to sell
his pins and trinkets, had told the servants he had heard
that the Queen's forces were defeated and many great lords
killed in the retreat from Tewkesbury's meadows. That
information had been so uncertain that all had hoped that
the man had heard incorrectly, yet Rosamund was not so
sure. The chapman had said that King Edward had made
a hasty forced march from London and taken the Queen's
force, under Lord Somerset, totally by surprise. If true, the

news could mean disaster for her father's hopes and even endanger his very life, to say nothing of the possible bleak future for their manor. She thrust the untimely fear to the back of her mind. She would not dwell on it. Rumours were rife in these troubled times, yet she feared that there was often a grain of truth in such stories.

'Then why have you come to seek me so urgently?' she asked Martha.

'Well, mistress, it is just to ask if you have seen Master Arthur this morning?'

Rosamund shook her head. 'No, I breakfasted early and came instantly to the still room. There is much to be done and I needed to keep busy. Has Lady Sibyl been asking for him?'

If that were the case it would be unusual indeed. Lady Sibyl, Sir Humphrey's bride of only just over a year, and only four years older than Rosamund, rarely took any interest in either of her stepchildren, certainly none in Arthur, who was only twelve years old. Lady Sibyl considered children's affairs to be a complete mystery. Fortunately she rarely took much interest in what Rosamund did either, a fact which pleased both of them. While Rosamund did not actively dislike her beautiful stepmother, she could not really approve her father's choice of one so young. Lady Sibyl was the daughter of a wealthy Warwick wool merchant. Her radiant beauty had caught the eye of the forty-seven-year-old widower and she had been willing enough to marry him and become mistress of Kinnersley Manor. She had had no training in the running of a manor household, having been indulged by a father inordinately proud of her exquisite fair loveliness, and the management of Kinnersley had fallen upon Rosamund's shoulders. She had needed to take upon herself more of the work of handling the household, especially since her

father had been busied of late with following his liege lord
to war.

She gave a little shrug. 'I expect Arthur has gone off to
visit one of his friends.' She gave a little smile. 'Father
Giles has provided him with books and copying, but now
that Father is away from home he is, likely as not, taking
advantage and has absconded from his studies.'

'Aye, mistress, that is what I thought but—' Martha
frowned anxiously '—his bed has not been slept in. He
ordered his pony saddled and rode off, the stable hands
say, yesterday afternoon. They thought, as we have, that
he had gone to see his friends in the village and gone
fishing or tree-climbing with them; but no one has seen
him since.' Her lip trembled slightly. She had nursed both
Sir Humphrey's children and was deeply fond of them.
Rosamund's mother had died of a tertian fever when
Arthur had been only eight years old and so his nurse had
been very attached to the child. 'He was very distressed
by the chapman's news and—well, I'm afeared that…'

Rosamund was horrified. 'You think that he may have
ridden off to Tewkesbury in the hope of hearing news of
Father? Oh, no, Martha, surely he has not been foolish
enough to do such a thing. If the news is true—and even
if not, and the armies have not yet met—we know that the
Queen's army was heading towards Tewkesbury and there
will be many marauding masterless men about, baggage
train followers and all kinds of riff-raff. Arthur would be
in the direst of dangers. Why did no one seek to prevent
him?'

'Well, you know, mistress, he pleaded long and hard to
go with your father and Master Murton. He has a great
admiration for your father's squire, who has been teaching
him some skill with the sword and bow.' She hesitated,
then pushed on. 'I was busy yesterday with cleaning and
pressing gowns for Lady Sibyl and I took no notice of

what Master Arthur was about. This morning, when he did not appear for breakfast in the hall, I went to his bedchamber to summon him and found that his bedclothes were undisturbed and I am certain he did not sleep in his bed last night.'

Guiltily Rosamund knew that she, too, had had little time for her young brother recently. After hearing the chilling rumours of the Lancastrian defeat, she had ridden into the village to pray in the church for her father's safety. Her mind had been occupied with the fears that, if the worst had happened and the Yorkists were triumphant, the manor might be occupied or even sequestered. If the boy had been absent from his home overnight, then it could be possible that he had ridden in pursuit of his father's troop.

'And you say that Lady Sibyl has not seen him?'

'She has remained closeted in her chamber since yesterday when I carried the news to her from the chapman. I had to get her permission for him to offer his wares to the maids.'

'And have you visited the stables? What does Old Tom say?' Tom was their chief stableman and as fond of Arthur as Martha was. He had helped to teach the boy to ride and often accompanied him when he rode from the manor. Recently Arthur had declared hotly that he was no baby to be so cosseted and been allowed to ride out alone.

'Tom says the boy went yesterday soon after noon and he has not seen him since. Worse than that, the pony is missing from the stable so...' Her voice trailed off uncertainly.

'Then we must assume that Arthur has not been home since yesterday afternoon. Send one of the grooms into the village to enquire of the young boys there if anyone has seen him or knows in which direction he may have ridden.' Rosamund undid her apron. 'In the meantime, I will go to my chamber and change. It would seem that I must ride after him.'

'But, mistress, if what you said earlier is true, about the dangers abroad, you should not go. One of the grooms or Tom could go and—'

'No,' Rosamund declared shortly. 'Arthur would not listen to reason from Tom or any of the servants. I must go. We have no other choice. Tom can go with me. He will keep me safe.'

Martha rose unwillingly. She knew, by her young mistress's expression, that there would be no point in arguing further. At the door she turned and said, 'Will you ask Lady Sibyl's permission?'

Rosamund compressed her lips. 'I think it would be better if she knew nothing about this. Come to my chamber and let me know when the groom has gone into the village. I can follow. Tell the lad to wait for me near the church lych-gate. If he has Arthur with him or knows where he is, then I will not need to proceed further.'

She locked up the still room. Her mother had always insisted that that should be done. There were dangerous herbs and drugs kept there and only those who had herbal skills should be allowed to enter at will. She went up to her own bedchamber next to the solar and looked out a small saddle-bag into which she packed one or two necessities. She took from her clothing chest a plain blue gown of linsey-woolsey and picked up the small glass mirror her father had bought her on her sixteenth birthday. She remembered that he had gone to London to attend a great feast given by the Earl of Warwick. He had been honoured by the invitation and had talked enthusiastically about the great lords he had seen there in attendance upon the earl. Many of them and their retainers had been slain on the battlefield at Barnet. Rosamund sighed heavily. Many more would die in this coming engagement or were already dead, if what the wandering chapman had said was true. It could not be possible that this present had been given to her less than a year ago. So much had happened since.

Critically she stared at her reflection and grimaced. She was almost seventeen and looked much older. There were worry lines between her brows and dark shadows beneath her hazel eyes. Her brown hair, touched with reddish lights, which she had inherited from her mother, was streaked with sweat and she pushed strands of it back impatiently. Her father had loved her hair, had called her his Nut Brown Maid from the ballad he often sang. He had called her mother that when he had first wooed and won her. Rosamund bit down upon her nether lip. Her father had loved her mother deeply. She knew that. He had been lonely and lost for months after her death and, at last, unexpectedly, on a chance visit to Warwick, he had met and fallen in love again with the lovely young woman who was now still lying abed in her chamber. The Lady Sibyl was certainly not the chatelaine he had expected when he had brought her home to Kinnersley. Rosamund hoped, fiercely, that, if competence in household management was missing from the marriage, love and loyalty were strong bonds, which could keep the couple together and happy. Lady Sibyl had wept tears enough at her husband's departure. Perhaps it was the need to keep her fears for his safety well hidden from the household servants that kept her to her chamber in seeming idleness. Rosamund decided to give her stepmother the benefit of the doubt.

Rosamund leaned closer to gaze again at her complexion. Her face was oval, her brows well marked, her nose small and a little retroussé. There was nothing remarkable about her appearance. She was not lovely, but comely enough. Her father had said so often enough this last year when he had begun to talk of finding a suitable husband for her and of marriage contracts. Lady Sibyl would be glad to have her gone from Kinnersley, Rosamund concluded. It was never good for two women to be considered chatelaines of one household.

Martha came in to the chamber softly. 'I have sent the boy. There is no further news, mistress. You are still determined to go then?'

'Yes. I must. Hand me that plain linen coif on the chest there, Martha. In that and this plain blue gown I can pass as some respectable you g matron, a merchant's wife, perhaps. I will take my oldest grey cloak. It is very hot now, but may well turn quite cool this evening and I may have to stay the night in Tewkesbury. Tom is so reliable and competent. I shall be safe with him. You must not worry about us. Has he got my palfrey saddled?'

'He was doing it when I left the stable and saddling up for himself.' Martha watched, frowning, as Rosamund tied up her abundant hair beneath the plain cap. 'What shall I tell Lady Sibyl if you are not back by suppertime?'

Rosamund gave a faint shrug. 'Whatever you must, the truth if you have to. I doubt that she will be over-concerned, except that she might have to account for our leaving, if anything dire happens to me or Arthur or both of us, when my father returns.'

Martha shook her head. 'I'm sure she would not wish you to go, mistress.'

'I am sure you are right and it is for that reason that I wish you to keep silent about my departure until I am well away from Kinnersley.'

'What if you find Master Arthur? Are you sure that you will be able to persuade him to return with you?'

'He will be difficult, no doubt. He has been difficult to handle recently, but I think he will see reason. If not, I shall have to stay in Tewkesbury and try to keep an eye on him. Tom and I should manage that.'

She had snatched up her saddle-bag and her grey, serviceable cloak and was clearly ready to leave. Martha moved from the doorway unwillingly. Rosamund could see a glimmer of tears on the older woman's lashes and, on impulse, she drew Martha to her and hugged her tightly.

'You must not distress yourself. I shall be quite safe with Tom and, please God, Father will soon be home and able to discipline Arthur as the boy needs. His behaviour has been insupportable since Father married again.'

She paused for a moment on the stair outside the main bedchamber occupied by her father and stepmother, but could hear no sound. Obviously Lady Sibyl had taken to her bed or was occupied inspecting the contents of her clothing chest or her jewellery box, as she frequently was. Such close attention to her toilet would prevent her taking interest in any outside matters, which she left to their steward when Sir Humphrey was absent from the manor.

Martha was standing in the doorway of Rosamund's bedchamber. Silently she lifted a hand in benediction and Rosamund thought she could see her mouthing a prayer. She waited for no more but sped down the stairs, slipped through the now deserted hall and out through the screen door without being observed by any member of the household.

Old Tom was waiting near the stable holding the leading reins of his own mount and Rosamund's pony. He made no demur, though she could see by his expression that he was as worried about her decision to go as Martha was. He led her palfrey to the mounting block and assisted her into the saddle, then secured her saddle-bag and cloak behind the saddle. His glance at them confirmed his suspicion that Rosamund had no intention of returning to Kinnersley without her errant brother. He smothered a sigh and mounted up himself.

The ride to the village church lych-gate was without

incident. The lane was deserted. Most of the villagers were
still occupied with their duties on the lord's land and on
their own strips. Spring was an extremely busy time and
the news of a possible engagement of rival armies near to
the manor lands could not be allowed to interfere with
general work. The manor reeve would see to it that they
were all kept busy.

Young Wilf, their stable lad, tousle-haired and his clothing appearing to have been dragged through all the hedges
in sight, was waiting anxiously by the lych-gate as instructed. He was alone. The village boys would be kept
busy by their fathers and Wilf had probably only been able
to find one or two in the fields and question them briefly
before running back to the trysting place. He shook his
head decisively as Rosamund and Tom rode towards him.
He leaned in close as the two drew rein and took Tom's
leading rein.

'Nay, mistress, I couldn't find one of the village lads
what knew anything about Master Arthur. They all swore
as how they 'adn't seen him yesterday at all.' His expression suggested he was alarmed at his failure to please her
and Rosamund shook her head gently.

'Never mind, Wilf. It is as we expected. None of this is
your fault.' She was aware that, often, Arthur rode into the
village and played dice, climbed trees or fished in the
stream with the village lads and some of the younger members of the Kinnersley household. Recently her father had
frowned upon this habit and had warned him against too
great a familiarity with the peasant lads. One day Arthur
would be lord of the manor; now that he had achieved his
twelfth birthday, he should be aware of the fact and begin
to withdraw from such close contact with underlings. Had
matters been more settled in the realm, Arthur would have
been undergoing training as page and squire in some
nearby manor. The wars between the two rival Houses of

York and Lancaster and their supporters had meant that had not been possible. Who knew which of one's neighbours one could trust with one's son and heir in such treacherous circumstances? Both Rosamund and her father realised that the boy was lonely, missing the company of boys his own age and rank, and had allowed the practice to continue, but obviously Arthur had not sought the company of his village friends yesterday.

Tom said briskly to Wilf, 'Get you back to the manor and about your duties. If anyone asks after the mistress, you're to say you don't know where she has gone but that she's safe with me. Off with you, now.'

The boy touched his sandy forelock and raced off towards Kinnersley. Tom's rule in the stables was strict but fair. Wilf would obey his instructions.

Tom rubbed his nose thoughtfully. 'Well, mistress, it looks like Master Arthur were definitely on his way to Tewkesbury town. I could see as how he were fair set on going with your father, and has sulked since he were refused permission. With luck we should find him in the town before he can run into mischief or danger.'

'How could he behave so irresponsibly?' Rosamund raged. 'If Father were here he'd have the skin off his back for this.'

'Aye, mistress, and may God grant that the master be soon home to see to it.'

As they urged their mounts into a trot Rosamund voiced her principal fear. 'Tom, do you think what the chapman said was true and that the outcome of the battle has already been decided?'

The old man pursed his lips. 'There's allus some as says there's no smoke wi'out fire, Mistress Rosamund, but there's bin no signs of men riding by in the rush of pursuit or any talk of roistering men raiding property nearby, which allus follows battles. If it is so, then them men-at-arms 'ave been kept in firm rein by some great lord or other.'

Rosamund's lips trembled. 'My father could well have been taken prisoner, and Arthur...' Her voice trailed off miserably.

'Now, mistress, 'tis unlikely anybody 'ud do the lad 'arm,' Tom reassured her. 'We'll find him, never fear.'

They were riding through a village on the outskirts of Tewkesbury and came within sight of an inn. Rosamund leaned forward in the saddle to distinguish the device upon the inn sign. She had ridden this way often and knew that it would tell her how near they were to Tewkesbury. At that moment a group of men emerged from the doorway and Tom gave a startled grunt. It was clear that most or all of them were reeling drunk as their inebriated yelling could surely be heard for miles. One was still holding aloft a leather tankard and the others were struggling to gain control of it. The sound of the approaching horses gave them pause and, as one, they turned and stared, for a moment stupefied. Too late, Tom realised that his words, uttered only a moment ago, were not prophetic. Clearly, from their leather jacks and salets, these were men-at-arms from one or other of the opposing armies—and out of control. He shouted a warning to Rosamund to spur on her mount, but he had not counted for the agility of the men, despite their drunken state. With a roar of encouragement one of the men started from the group in the riders' direction and two of his companions launched themselves forward to seize their reins. Rosamund lashed out at the delaying hand of one with her riding crop but the man simply roared again, this time with loud laughter, and held on grimly. The suddenness of the attack blinded her momentarily to fear and she continued to try to beat off the man's grasp. Behind her she could hear Tom's mount rearing in terror and fury and knew that soon she would be unable to control her palfrey. She was shouting at the man, incensed, but nothing, it seemed, would deter him from his determination to halt her in her tracks and pull her down from the saddle.

Her palfrey was now rearing wildly and, despite her superb horsemanship and her grit, she was dragged down and found herself sprawling in the dust, while the whooping, jeering gang surrounded her. Blindly she cried to Tom for help, but knew that he was totally unable to come to her assistance. Her skirts flew up and one of the men shouted his appreciation.

'Here's luck, my hearties, not only two serviceable mounts but a little beauty to boot. Come on, lads, let's have her inside the inn and see what she's really made of.'

There was a chorus of appreciation for his lewd suggestion and Rosamund, mortified and frightened now, struggled to stand up, but two of the men had bent down, grasped her arms, and were chuckling as they attempted to haul her to her feet and drag her into the inn. Fortunately for Rosamund and unfortunately for them, they were both unsteady upon their feet and, as she rose, she was able to tear herself free and send both of them staggering.

She turned to find what had happened to Tom and found him grappling with two of his assailants. While their attackers were undoubtedly hampered in their movements by the quantity of ale they'd drunk, they were considerably younger and stronger than the elderly stableman and his efforts were not meeting with much success.

'Mistress,' he shouted hoarsely, 'run, run for your life. Don't take account o' me. I'll manage.'

Even as he spoke one of the men struck him savagely upon the back of the head with the hilt of a heavy dagger and he sank to the ground.

Rosamund stood, petrified, willing and anxious to try to

go to his assistance, but realising that any effort she made would be totally useless. She gave a great sob of despair. At the same time one of her former attackers had recovered his balance sufficiently to give another whoop of raucous laughter and came towards her, intent on grabbing her arm again. She still held her riding whip and lashed out at him so that he gave a drunken soldier's oath and stepped back.

Rosamund could see now that Tom was down on the ground and his attackers were bending down and striking at his helpless body with their drawn weapons and fists. She could hear their obscenities and heavy gasps of breath as they continued to strike. She looked wildly round. Her attacker was sullenly sucking at his bared forearm where her whip had struck him, while three of the other men were struggling to control the stolen mounts.

For one moment no one was attempting to seize her. Again she gave a rasping sob. She knew she could not help Tom. Indeed, he might even now be dead. She must do as he said—run. There was no earthly use seeking sanctuary in the inn. Likely enough these drunken beasts had already raped every inn wench in sight and possibly injured or killed the innkeeper and stolen his ale. She lifted her skirts, tore at them to allow her more freedom of movement and took off while the injured man was still drunkenly weeping over his hurts. Ahead of her she spied a gap in the hawthorn hedge that bordered the road and dashed towards it, hurtling through, heedless of the damage the thorns and branches were doing to her face and hands. She felt her gown tear and raced on across the uneven pasture land. Behind her she could hear the yells of angry men. Whether they were complaining about the loss of a victim or difficulty in controlling the horses she could not tell and dared not heed. Her breath was coming now in terrible gasps and she could feel real pain in her chest, but still she blundered on. Then it seemed that the angry voices faded in the distance and she slowed a little, putting one hand to her side, which had developed a cramping stitch.

To her right she saw a drainage ditch dug from the river some half-mile away to serve the needs of the village barley strips beyond in dry summers. She scrambled over and, finding a dry space between the water and the bank, sank down, hoping that its slight elevation would hide her from the road and, putting her head down on the ground, sobbed out her fear and despair and her terrible grief for Tom.

Sir Simon Cauldwell paused for a moment before the entrance flap of the Duke of Gloucester's battle tent. Before it, on a lance head, its butt stuck in the ground, flew the standard bearing the young duke's personal device of the White Boar. Two men-at-arms in the blue-and-murrey livery of the House of York guarded the entrance and stared impassively at Sir Simon. The young page who had summoned him was allowed into the tent and soon came hurrying back to inform the guards that Sir Simon was to be admitted. They lowered their pikes and he followed the boy inside.

Richard, Duke of Gloucester, the king's younger brother, was seated on a camp chair behind a folding camp table littered with maps and vellum scrolls. He looked up, nodded at Sir Simon and gestured to the page to pour wine into two goblets for himself and his visitor.

'Thank you for your attendance, Simon. I am sorry that I needed to summon you so soon again, but I'm afraid I have a new task for you.' He indicated that his visitor should seat himself on a stool near the table.

Simon bowed and, having known the duke since their days of service together as squires at Middleham Castle in the service of the Earl of Warwick, did not attempt to argue that it was not fitting. Richard of Gloucester might be but eighteen years of age, but he had proved himself a fine soldier and strategist both in the battle of Barnet and the very recent engagement here at Tewkesbury. One did not question his orders, but simply obeyed. Simon Caldwell was the elder of the two by three years and had been a senior squire when young Richard had been trained to arms at Middleham, but he had been honoured by the friendship of the younger boy and did not feel uneasy now in his presence.

He thought that the duke looked very tired. There were lines of strain upon the forehead and round the grey-green eyes. Like Simon's, his dark hair was streaked with sweat and he moved restlessly in his chair to ease his cramped right leg. Simon's lips tightened slightly at the sight. He was aware of the slight difference in the length of the duke's limbs. A childhood riding accident, resulting in a heavy fall, had caused an infinitesimal malformation of the right shoulder and had left the prince with the barest of limps when he was over-wearied as now.

As the duke lifted his own goblet in silent salute, Simon lifted his own and drank.

'You look as tired as I feel, Simon.' The duke's lips twisted in a little grimace. 'Controlling a crowd during executions is not a pleasant duty, almost as distasteful as having to order them.'

Both men had been present in Tewkesbury market square, throughout the morning, where Duke Richard, as High Constable of England, had been responsible for overseeing the execution of the Duke of Somerset and other Lancastrian prisoners. Sir Simon had been in command of the troop of men-at-arms responsible for controlling the behaviour of the townsfolk. There had been no trouble. The folk of Tewkesbury had witnessed the entry of King Edward, his two brothers, the Dukes of Gloucester and Clarence, and his principal commanders into the abbey after the battle to demand the surrender of the Lancastrians who had crowded into the nave to beg for sanctuary. The king had announced imperiously that the leaders of the Queen's force must give themselves up next morning and he had been obeyed. Only a handful of the Queen's commanders had been sentenced to death in a short trial before the High Constable—the lesser knights and men-at-arms had been allowed to disperse without charges. Somerset, in particular, had previously offered his allegiance to King Edward and had later turned his coat. Like the other condemned prisoners he had been judged traitor and had been summarily beheaded. Simon was aware that, though the task of judging and overseeing the executions had been at the king's behest, Duke Richard had found it distressing, though Simon also knew that Richard would never admit it.

He drained his goblet and set it down carefully. 'There is still no news of the queen and the Lady Anne, your Grace?'

A frown crossed Richard's brows and he shook his head. 'Not as yet. We should hear of her capture soon. She must be a broken woman indeed, Simon. Her son, Prince Edward, was killed in the pursuit and will be buried in the abbey. It is as well that the King was not forced to order his execution.'

Prince Edward had been nominally in charge of the Queen's force, though Somerset had been her principal adviser and commander. The prince was too young and inexperienced to really hold the balance between possible defeat and victory. Simon had witnessed his body as it was conveyed into the abbey. He was the only child of Henry VI and Margaret of Anjou, and the Lancastrian heir. A fleeting thought passed through his mind that Warwick's younger daughter and the joint heiress to the Warwick lands and fortunes was now the prince's widow and might, even now, be carrying his child. If so, that would be a misfortune indeed, since the king would find it hard to tolerate any possible challenge to his throne in the future. The Lady Anne, with the defeated Queen Margaret, had fled the district and Yorkist men were searching for them and the handful of supporters who would be trying to assist them. It was unlikely, Simon thought, that either woman would be able to escape the country and their capture would be announced within days or even hours.

He was silent. He remembered that Duke Richard and the Lady Anne had been very close in friendship during the days of the duke's training at Middleham Castle and his mind must be full of anxiety for her safety.

Richard eyed him curiously over the table. 'You are considering that Anne might be in considerable danger?'

'I doubt that, your Grace. All men are aware that the Lady Anne is cousin to the king and sister-in-law to the Duke of Clarence, your brother. When she is once more returned to Yorkist hands she will most likely be handed over into the care of her sister, the Lady Isabel, the Duchess of Clarence.'

The duke's frown deepened and he glanced down thoughtfully at the rings upon his fingers. 'And you think that such custody would be the best possible fate for the Lady Anne?'

Simon's eyebrows swept upwards as he sought to find a discreet reply. He was aware, as Duke Richard was, that the Lady Anne was a great heiress since the death of the earl, her father, at Barnet. The Duke of Clarence might not be anxious to share such a great fortune with his wife's sister.

Duke Richard gave a little harsh laugh. 'I apologise, Simon. I should not have put so compromising a question to you. We both have affection for the ladies Anne and Isabel and we must hope for the best for them at this sad time.'

Simon nodded gravely.

'And now I must come to the reason I sent for you.' The duke's youthful face became clouded once more. 'It grieves me to say so, but I am informed that there is still looting of bodies and those gravely injured still upon the meadow field. This must not go on. I would be grateful if you would take it upon yourself to patrol the battlefield with a troop of men tonight and put a stop to it. Arrest anyone you find busied about such foul work.' He sighed. 'I would do it myself, but I am called to sup with the king and my brother tonight in the abbot's lodging. Rob Percy and Dick Ratcliffe will be in attendance also, which is why I need to call upon you. I feel that this task calls for some-one with innate authority. The men are still celebrating their victory and not easily managed, I fear.'

Simon bowed in answer. 'Certainly, your Grace. You know that you only have to summon me and I shall put myself instantly at your disposal.'

The duke's answering smile was one of real warmth this time. 'I am pleased to count you amongst my true friends from the old days,' he said quietly. 'God grant that all this will soon be over and that we shall be able to return to a measure of peace and stability throughout the realm.'

Simon said soberly, 'Unfortunately there are many who will not see that, your Grace, and plenty of widows and orphans who will need protection.'

'Aye, that, too, we must look to before we leave for London.'

'Is there anything else you require of me, your Grace?'

'No, nothing. I hope this work will be quickly concluded and that you will be able to retire to your tent early for some well-deserved rest.' Again came that wry smile. 'I wish I could do so also, but there are still many plans to be made and the king will want me by him.'

Simon rose and bowed himself out of the tent. He stood for a moment, thoughtful, in the late afternoon sunshine, then turned and moved off to summon a sergeant to call together a troop of reliable men for the night's patrol.

Chapter Two

Rosamund struggled on grimly across ridged pasture land, hoping that she was heading in the right direction. Several times she found herself sobbing with desperation and weariness, and for the fate of poor Tom who she had been forced to abandon on the highway. She had no way of knowing just how late it was now, but she could see that the sun was getting very low in the sky; it would soon set and she would be trying to find her way in twilight. She could not remember whether she was on the right side of the Severn to reach the town. Several times she had blundered across flooded ground; once she believed that she had splashed through a ford, and her shoes and stockings were soaking wet. She stopped for a moment to catch her breath and peered ahead for some indication that Tewkesbury town was ahead of her. A little copse of trees was directly in front of her and the dying sun bordered the tops with red. She hoped that soon she would be able to see the towers of Tewkesbury Abbey.

She sat for a moment on the tussocky grass beneath one of the trees. At least it was dry here. She had not dared to approach the town for what seemed hours. Several times she had heard the sound of laughing voices and hoofs some distance from her, which she judged to be the highway. The sounds of whooping, shouting, swearing men and raucous laughter made her shudder. She dared not risk another encounter, yet how could she proceed if she dared not enter the town? Somehow she had to find Arthur or her father with his squire. Perhaps then it might be possible for her father, with his authority, to make some enquiries about Tom and discover if he still lived and, if so, to find some means of returning him to Kinnersley for tending. If he did not, then his body must be returned to the manor church for decent burial.

She swallowed hard as the realisation dawned on her that the terrible sight of that group of marauding men at the tavern meant that what the chapman had said was now confirmed. The battle was over; he had been convinced that the Yorkists had been triumphant. What hope had she of finding her father alive or free? Surely there would be some measure of control over the men in the town and she must go there.

She knew that pillage and rape were the order of the day for the men celebrating victory, but their commanders, knowing that it was in their interest to keep control of them—for men without discipline were useless when needed—would eventually call them to heel. She had some coin tied in a small bag around her waist, thinking that she would need some to find lodging in the town if any of her kinfolk were injured. Fortunately she had managed to escape from the men before that had been discovered so, if she could reach Tewkesbury before nightfall, she could find shelter and food before setting out to enquire about Arthur. The horses were lost to her and she did not know how she could reach Kinnersley. It was more than twelve miles on foot, but that problem could be faced later. If Arthur still had his pony one of them at least could ride.

There were other, more pressing dangers that occupied her fearful mind.

She pushed herself wearily to her feet. She must press on. As the sun finally sank to rest, the trees of the copse appeared to crowd upon her menacingly. She shivered again and, this time, it was not from fear or revulsion. It was growing cold and her cloak had been lost to her behind the saddle of her stolen palfrey. For the first time she became aware of the unkempt appearance of her clothing. Her serviceable blue gown had been scratched and torn as she had forced her way through the hedge and she had deliberately ripped at the skirt to allow her to run more freely. Somewhere she had lost her white linen cap and her hair was falling about her shoulders. She bit her lip to prevent it trembling. Far from the picture of the respectable merchant's wife she had hoped to present, she now gave the appearance of some loose woman of the town or a member of the baggage-train followers of one of the opposing armies. She shrugged off the thought impatiently. That could not be helped. She must try to persuade some innkeeper to grant her lodging, even if it were only in one of the common rooms he let out to lesser folk. She had good coin with which to pay and her demeanour and speech would surely give the lie to any suspicion he might have concerning her virtue. At all events the difficulties must be faced and overcome.

It was now full dusk. She turned, listening intently for a sound that might betray any follower in the wood who would mean her harm, but all was silent now. Even the birds had gone to roost for the coming night and the small nocturnal creatures had not yet begun their rustlings. She was determined to set aside her fears and push on through the wood with its frightening shadows and darkness.

At last she was clear and she gave a little cry of joy as she saw ahead of her in the gathering gloom across the water meadows, facing her, the towers of the abbey church. She was at last in sight of her goal.

Her courage was renewed now as if sight of the abbey church, where for centuries men had received sanctuary, gave her hope. She began to move towards the towers across the meadowland. Now it was decidedly easier going. There were no raised ridges or unexpected ditches and she hastened on, hoping to reach the town streets before it was full dark. Where there were townspeople abroad, surely she could count on being safe from molestation.

She was so intently looking ahead that suddenly something before her feet tripped her up and sent her sprawling so that she gave a sharp cry of alarm. Fortunately the soft meadow grass had cushioned her fall, so she felt no real hurt and hastily tried to scramble up again. She was anxious to find out for herself what obstruction had lain before her. Whatever it was felt soft and yielding and, as she stood and uncertainly, moved closer to look, made no sign of movement. She stood, gazing down and put a hand to her mouth to stifle a scream. She had tripped over a human body, a man's body.

Her first thought was to take to her heels and run, but it was getting really dark now and surely, if the man was not beyond human help, she should not leave him here. She glanced hurriedly about to see if there was anyone nearby she could call to for assistance, but the meadow was shadowy now; she could glimpse little more than a few yards ahead of her and something warned her not to cry out.

Hesitantly she went closer and spoke softly. 'You, there, are you hurt? Can I summon assistance for you, help you up?'

There was no reply and no movement from the prostrate form before her and she steeled herself to kneel down and examine further. She was reluctant to reach out a hand, but forced herself to do so. She gave a little shake to the man's shoulder and her fingers came away sticky with blood. This time she could not suppress a sharp cry of fear.

Was he dead? It would seem so, yet, if his blood was still wet and sticky, he could not have been so for long. She whispered to him, aware now that his assailant might still be close and she herself in danger. Again the man did not stir and again she steeled herself to grasp once more at the shoulder and turn him slightly so that she might see his face. He was a soldier, she was sure now, for he wore a leather jack, though she could not discern any recognisable device so that she might tell in whose company he fought. It was still light enough for her to see now that the left side of his body was soaked in blood and it was still seeping. The face was a pale blur and she avoided looking down so that she might not see a distorting grimace, which could have informed her how much pain he had suffered. She was sure now that he was dead, though only recently so, and felt the pulse at his throat to convince herself, as she had seen her father and the grooms do when faced with some terrible injury suffered by one of the pet dogs in the household. There was nothing she could do for him and she must get away from him fast now or she could suffer a similar fate. As she rose she saw that his metal salet was missing and so were his boots. He had been killed and his body robbed while he was still warm. She had heard tales of such ghoulish work on battlefields, whispered by her father when he had believed that she was not close enough to him to hear. She gave a great shudder and turned to run. Before she could move an inch she was suddenly arrested in her tracks by a harsh shout of command.

'Halt there. Do not move. I have an arrow trained upon you.'

Bewildered, she saw piercing the gloomy shadow ahead, the figures of two men, obviously men-at-arms, for, like the dead soldier at her feet, they were clad in leather jacks and still wore their metal salet helmets. One of them had levelled a yew bow at her and she could see the faint gleam of the metal shaft upon the goose-feather arrow.

She opened her mouth to protest or explain but before she could do so, the other man had moved swiftly to her, seized both her hands and imprisoned them in a hard grasp behind her back.

'Well, it seems that we have found yet another looter, Jock, a woman, by God, and a young one by the looks of her.' He gave a braying laugh. 'It seems you learn your craft very young. A pity that, for you can swing for it, my wench.'

She struggled weakly, but he was a strong man, burly of build, older than the archer, possibly, but only two or three years younger than Tom had been. By his authoritative manner he was a sergeant-at-arms, clearly the younger man's superior.

'Please,' she begged, 'let me go. I am no looter. I just happened to find this man and stopped to try to help him. You must believe me.'

Again her captor uttered a contemptuous laugh. 'Oh, aye, my lass, and his blood still wet upon your fingers. If you didn't dispatch him, where are your companions? God's teeth, could you not see he'd a pike wound to the neck and couldn't live long? Surely you could have let him do so in peace or do you think that delivering the *coup de grâce* was more merciful?' His tone was sneering as he looked down at her and beckoned his companion forward, gesturing for him to lower his menacing weapon. 'Run your fingers over her, lad, and see what she's stolen. His boots are gone and there's no sign o' them, but he might have been wearing an amulet or ring given him by his sweetheart.'

'Don't you dare touch me,' Rosamund raged. 'I tell you I am innocent of this man's death. I have no weapon. How could I have killed him?'

A cool voice broke across her protest as a third man loomed out of the gloom and up to the group, startling her further. 'It would seem, sergeant, that the wench has a point there but, just to be sure, search her quickly.'

Rosamund saw that he was taller by a head than either of the men-at-arms and still wore armour. He stood facing them, legs astride, one steel-gauntleted hand resting lightly upon his sword hilt. She saw instantly that the two were under his command and attempted to plead her cause with him. Impotently she thrashed about in her captor's arms, but the sergeant-at-arms held grimly on while, at the armoured man's imperative snap of the fingers, the archer laid down his bow and came to Rosamund to obey his order and search her. Humiliated and furious, she suffered the man's hands upon her body, flinching at his touch upon her breasts and thighs beneath the flimsy linsey-woolsey stuff of her torn gown.

The man stood up and saluted. 'No sign of a weapon of any sort, Sir Simon,' he said, 'not even a metal eating spoon or cutting knife like some of these women carry.'

The knight regarded her coolly, his free hand upon his hip. He glanced round, peering into the distance. 'Indeed? And you heard no one else about? These women rarely go about their murderous work alone. She'll be from one of the baggage trains, I'll warrant, and one of her men will be somewhere about, so keep a close watch.'

'I tried to tell your men I am not from the battlefield,' Rosamund panted out defiantly. 'I was just crossing the meadow when I fell over this dead man. I was looking to see if I could help him when your men grabbed me.'

He did not answer for a moment, but stood looking at her up and down, then down at the dead man. She could not distinguish his features clearly in the gloom, but caught the sheen of metal oil upon his armour as he still wore his mailed coif, though not his helmet. Clearly he had come upon the field expecting to encounter enemies and was on his guard.

'I think you can release her, sergeant,' he said at last, crisply. 'I am inclined to believe her tale but, for the moment, we will keep her under close arrest until one of her menfolk can vouch for her in the morning. She has some explaining to do—why she is so far from the baggage train, for instance? It would seem that she came out here looking for pickings, though, from dead men. Take her to my tent. I'll question her there. Tie her to one of the ridge poles and I'll deal with her when I've completed my patrol.'

Rosamund opened her mouth to make yet one final protest, but he said coldly, 'Think yourself lucky, wench, that my archer didn't let fly immediately he found you kneeling by your victim. My men have fought hard and suffered. They do not take kindly to those who steal from the dead and dying.'

Before she could object further he turned and strode off. The sergeant jerked her forward, though he had slightly released his crippling grasp of her captive hands. 'You heard what Sir Simon says. He'll deal with you later, and pray he be in a merciful mood or else you'll be for the rope in the morning.'

Rosamund stumbled along while the sergeant held her by the arm. The archer, it seemed, had run hastily after the knight. The sergeant was walking fast and she felt she had no breath to argue further and that it would be useless to do so. The man had received his orders and must obey.

Soon they had crossed the water meadow and she saw the light of many cooking fires ahead of her and realised they were now in reach of the Yorkist camp. As they passed, men roasting pigs and fowls on spits turned to gaze at her curiously. One or two shouted ribald comments, which the sergeant ignored. Most of the men would sleep out of doors, but Rosamund saw also the tents of the battle commanders, the lords and knights who had followed King Edward from London and were now celebrating their victory.

In front of one of the tents the sergeant paused and called. A young soldier came out quickly and he, too, gazed at Rosamund with avid interest.

'Sir Simon has ordered me to confine this young woman in the tent until he returns,' the sergeant said, looking over the boy deliberately as if to impress obedience and respect in him. 'Did you finish making preparations for the night, as I instructed you?'

'Yes, sergeant,' the lad returned almost cheekily.

'Then find me a strong coil of rope and bring it to the tent.' The sergeant impelled Rosamund forcibly inside and, for a moment, her eyes were dazzled by the light from a pitch torch which had been set up in the ground. She shielded her eyes with her free hand and moved uncertainly. The young boy soldier had come back quickly and the sergeant urged her towards one of the tent's ridge poles and, taking the rope from the lad, secured her wrists behind the pole, but not so tightly that she would suffer pain. He stood back and nodded slightly. 'You'll do until Sir Simon returns. When he does I counsel you to behave circumspectly. Answer his questions honestly and without impudence. He's a fair man and he'll judge you so, but he'll take no nonsense from anybody. You, boy, stay outside and await instructions from him. He'll be tired and hungry when he gets back after his patrol. And make sure this wench does not leave the tent. She's tied securely enough, but let's make double sure.'

The lad grinned and nodded. As if annoyed by his insolent expression, the sergeant reached out to cuff his ear, but the lad danced nimbly out of reach. The man swore, then grinned himself and shoved the lad from the tent before him. Rosamund heard him speak to one of the men near the campfire.

'I'm going to finish the patrol of the field down by Swilgate Brook. There's a dead man who'll need burial in the morning. We found three more on the field, but that one should be the last of them for the burial pit. Tell Sir Simon where I am if he enquires.'

She could not catch the man's reply, but judged that this Sir Simon was well served. She sank back against the ridge pole, utterly exhausted and frightened. She was almost at the end of her tether. Her fears for the welfare of her father and Arthur had been emotionally draining; then had come the terrifying attack that had probably cost the life of Tom, for whom she had deep affection. And now this had happened. She could not believe that she could actually have been accused of a crime so foul as stealing from the dead! At least the search of her person had revealed no weapon, so she could not be found guilty of murder—or could she be under suspicion of conspiracy with a person unknown? She fumed at the very suggestion. Yet, glancing down ruefully at her torn gown and state of dishevelment, she was forced to accept that such a misunderstanding on the part of the men was possible, considering the circumstances in which they had discovered her, kneeling by the side of the victim.

She struggled ineffectively to free herself, but the sergeant had been very thorough. She must wait until the knight returned and then she must try and explain to him how she had come to be in the water meadows so late. Somehow she thought it would be very difficult indeed to convince him. Outside she could hear the murmur of

voices and occasional laughter. She could discern no signs
of unruly behaviour. The men were eating their supper,
probably stolen from some unlucky peasant farmer, but all
soldiers lived off the land and that must be expected. They
would be settling down for the night soon. If some had
their women with them Rosamund could hear no bawdy
comments, and judged that those who had had joined them
nearer to the baggage train.

She had fallen into an uneasy stupor when she was startled by the imperative voice she recognised as that of the
knight, Sir Simon, outside the tent.

'Here, boy, come and help me disarm.'

The tent flap was thrown back and the tall knight entered, followed by the lad the sergeant had ordered to await
instructions earlier.

The knight cast Rosamund one dismissive glance and
stood in the centre of the tent while the boy undid his
breastplate, gorget and vanbraces, then sat on a camp stool
while the greaves, cuisses and poleyns were removed. Last
of all he kicked off his steel sabatons and gestured to the
boy to bring his leather shoes. He sat for a moment in hose
and padded gambeson, stretching and rubbing his arms and
moving his legs to free the tension after the armour's constraints. Still he did not deign to address his prisoner.

'Pour me some wine, lad, I'm parched.'

Rosamund watched, her anger rising, cancelling out her
former fear as the boy brought a leather tankard and the
knight drained it. While he did so the boy took the pieces
of armour and hung them on a clothing pole.

'Thank you, lad, you can bring me some bread and
meats, aye, and some ale, then you can look to your own
sleeping arrangements.'

As the boy moved to the tent flap the knight said softly,
'You have done well today. Since my squire was killed I

have needed someone sensible to attend my needs. I thought you would fit the bill and I was right.'

Rosamund could see by the flickering torch light that the lad was flushing with pleasure, then he ducked beneath the flap and disappeared into the darkness outside.

The knight rose, went to the camp table which Rosamund saw was littered with maps and rolls of parchment beside the wine jug and tankard. He poured himself more wine and stood, sipping appreciatively then, deliberately, he turned and regarded her.

For the first time she could see his features clearly now that he was bereft of his mailed coif. He was a young man, not much over twenty years of age, she was sure, though his tall, lithe body was well muscled beneath the linen shirt and padded gambeson, the jacket all knights wore beneath their armour, to cushion the deadly blows on metal from sword and mace taken in battle and during jousting at tournaments. She had seen, more than once, the bruises her father had received in sport and knew that this knight must still be feeling the effects from the recent battle. He showed no sign of severe injury but, again, he moved restlessly, as if he were wearied after a long day spent on duty.

The torchlight touched his dark hair, which was cut short and swept back from his high forehead. The features were strong. He had heavy, black brows that almost met across his nose, which was beak-like, dominating the face. His jaw was square, and featured a marked cleft over a mouth that was held in tightly as if, Rosamund thought, he was forcibly keeping in marks of stress or pain. She had heard him say his squire had been killed and she wondered if he had affection for the man. Likely he had lost other companions in this engagement. The eyes beneath the winged, dark brows were startlingly blue for such a dark-haired and dark-complexioned man and were now fixed upon her sternly.

She thought to speak, to demand her freedom, but those eyes held her spellbound. She thought better of the thought, and stared back at him challengingly.

The stern gaze relaxed slightly as she met stare for stare fearlessly and the long lips smiled, but she felt no reassurance from that smile. She struggled to prevent her own lips from trembling.

'Well, well,' he said pleasantly, 'here we have a very young thief. Do you not think it stupid to risk your life for so little a reward? We haven't found your companion, so he must have escaped with the spoils. I hope he had thought to share them with you later, though, unfortunately, that will not be possible now.'

She said tonelessly, 'I did not steal nor was I with any companion, certainly no man. As for risking my life young, would you not say the same for you? Is it not just as foolish to risk a life fighting in some pointless battle against your anointed sovereign, since I think you are a Yorkist?'

'Oh?' One winged eyebrow flew upwards in amusement. 'So you are from the queen's baggage train. You are even more foolish to confess that. I have known of battles where women of the defeated baggage train were slaughtered. Considering your situation, do you not think it wiser to be more accommodating to your captor?'

'I have tried to tell you that I am not from the battlefield and I demand that you release me immediately.'

He laughed out loud then, shaking his head in real merriment for her effrontery.

'Well, you have spirit, I'll grant you that and I do admire wenches with spirit. Sir Simon Cauldwell, at your command.' And he gave her a little mocking bow.

Suddenly he stepped, catlike, towards her. His right

hand snaked out and light flashed on metal. She gave a little startled gasp as she realised that he had drawn a dagger from the small leather sheath he wore suspended from his shoulder. She felt a coldness along her hand, the rope fell to the floor and she was free. She stood for a second or two, confused by the suddenness of the movement, and then gingerly rubbed one hand against the other to ease the soreness caused by the friction of the rope against her delicate skin. Before she could move from the supporting tent pole he had suddenly swept her into his arms, imprisoning her wrists and thrusting them up around his neck.

She struggled in terror and fury, but was borne effortlessly to a camp bed and thrown down upon it, where he bent over her, holding her firmly down with one hand.

'Now, wench, you will pay for your insolence, though I am bound to admit that I am beginning to believe in your plea of innocence.'

'You have no knightly honour,' she stormed. 'Let me go instantly.'

His amusement grew still further. 'Better and better. I have said I admire true spirit. Do you find it gains respect and better pickings from your clients? What in the name of all the saints would you know about knightly honour? In truth, I can tell you now, wench, that it does not exist.'

He was peering down at her in the wavering torchlight. He had not been able to see her very clearly out on the water meadow. Now he saw a pale, oval-shaped face, a high forehead on to which brown hair was falling in heavy waves and a small, slightly tip-tilted nose. The generous, full-lipped mouth was stretched in a silent cry of terror and he checked for a moment and drew back. He could feel her body trembling violently and the rapid beat of her heart. He sensed that she was very young, much younger than he had first supposed. Her voice puzzled him. It was unaccented, haughty, as commanding as his own, but he had known hoydens who had learned to speak so. Her clothing was torn and muddied and she wore no cap, which a sensible, decent country maid would wear, but it was possible that she might have lost that in some struggle across difficult ground or in the nearby copse close to where he had found her. She smelt clean; her gown was fragranced with some herb, rosemary, perhaps, and he sensed a touch of lavender. Certainly she was no ordinary follower attached to the baggage train. It might be that she had been brought to the field by some young knight whose leman she was. He felt a keen longing to hold her close and forget, for a few sweet moments, the terrible sights he had witnessed and sounds he had heard over the last days. In this young girl's arms he might find, temporarily, the solace he sought, a panacea of true forgetfulness.

She had ceased to struggle for seconds and was gazing up at him as if she sought to read his very soul. He made a low, guttural noise in his throat and bent to nuzzle the soft flesh of her throat, where her gown was torn. She fought then, pushing her legs hard against his as he knelt above her. She twisted her face from him, trying with all her might to avoid the hardness of his demanding lips as, despite all her efforts, they found her own mouth and pressed down relentlessly.

Rosamund was strangely excited by the hard pressure of his tongue against her lips as he attempted to force entry. She had never been kissed by any man save her father and he, recently, had not shown her demonstrative affection, not since he had brought his new wife to the manor. She had thought that if any man not her husband made such an assault upon her she would resist to the death or even swoon, but she found this overwhelming excitement terrifying and a great heat suffused her body, even in places she would not have dared to think on. Then she drew upon all her strength of will and fought wildly as he made to lower that hard-muscled body upon her own. She knew it would be hopeless, as she made such ineffective struggles. He was so much bigger and stronger than she was. He would take her, here in this tent, with so many men outside, near and within hearing distance, but if she cried out, screamed, no one would come to her assistance.

Then, suddenly, he drew himself up again and crouched above her, supported on his two arms, staring intently down at her.

'By the Virgin,' he swore softly, 'I have indeed misread this situation. You are no whore, no camp follower. You really do not welcome my attentions.'

She gave a great, strangled gasp and again attempted to avoid that vivid blue stare, tears coming readily now and running unheeded down her cheeks.

'Who are you?' he demanded hoarsely, and she dared not look at him as she felt him withdrawing from her until he was standing upright by the folding camp bed. She turned over, burying her face in the canvas stretched over the rope supports of the bed. She sobbed for a while and he left her and went to the table, filled the tankard with wine again and returned to her side.

She felt his hand gently touch her shoulder and she tried weakly to cast it off, but he persisted and at last she half-sat up. He thrust the tankard into her outstretched hand, guiding it firmly towards her lips.

'Drink.'

She shook her head mutely but he forced the leather rim of the tankard against her mouth. 'Drink, I say. Obey me.'

She made a sound, half-laugh, half-cry, and did as he commanded. The sweet malmsey trickled into her mouth and down her throat, giving her strength. Finally, she swallowed of her own will and he waited until she had drained the tankard. Then he took it from her and sank down beside her upon the bed. 'Now, tell me who are you? No, there is no need to fear me. I never take what is not offered freely. I thought you were trying to—nay, no matter. That is over. It is immaterial now what I thought. Tell me your name and why you are here.'

'My name is Rosamund Kinnersley. My father owns a manor near Winchcome, some twelve miles from Tewkesbury.' Her voice was so low that he had to lean still closer to catch her words.

'*Rosamund?*' He spoke the name in the Latin fashion and smiled. 'Rose of the world. He named you well. I pray that you are a white rose, though I fear not, from what you said to me earlier.'

She shook her head and said a little stiffly, 'My father was in the service of the Earl of Warwick and he...' She hesitated, then pressed on. 'He left home several days ago to—to join the Queen's army. I—I do not know what has happened to him.'

He was silent for a moment, considering, then he nodded. 'As you are now aware, the Queen's army was defeated two days ago.'

'So my father is dead or else a prisoner?'

'What was his full name, mistress?'

'Sir Humphrey Kinnersley.'

He shook his head. 'I cannot tell you if he is numbered amongst the dead. Certainly he is not now a prisoner. Only the queen's principal commanders were taken prisoner after they emerged from sanctuary.' He paused, then added sombrely, 'They were executed in Tewkesbury marketplace today. Your father was not one of them.'

She gave a little sigh of relief.

He frowned. 'I take it you came looking for news of him, but, mistress, did you not realise how foolish that was to come on foot, unescorted, to a town so close to a battlefield? Surely you are aware that men are undisciplined

after a victory and the defeated men have little to lose.'
His lips twisted cynically.

Her voice was stronger now, defiance returning now that
she was no longer so afraid of him. 'Of course I did not
come without escort. I was accompanied by our chief
groom. We were attacked—' her voice trembled again at
the memory '—just outside the town and our horses stolen.
Tom was—I believe he was killed. I had to run to escape
the men. I—I do not know how I can ever forgive myself
for leaving him there, lying on the ground, but it would
not have helped him for me to be captured too.'

'It certainly would not have,' he said grimly. 'I understand now, but it would still have been wiser for you to
have remained safely at home. Did not your mother try to
prevent you from leaving?'

'My mother is dead,' she said woodenly. 'I left without
informing my stepmother, but it was imperative I went to
search for my brother.'

'He was fighting with your father?'

'No, no,' she snapped impatiently, 'Arthur is but twelve
years old. He demanded to go with the company. Naturally
my father refused his permission, but he was determined
to go and left the house secretly yesterday. I was frantic
to find him when I heard the rumours about the battle.'

'I see.' He sat, thoughtful for a moment, then nodded.
'I can understand your concern. We must make enquiries
tomorrow in the town.'

She looked quickly towards the tent flap. 'Now that you
know that I had nothing to do with that poor man's death,
you will allow me to go?'

He shook his head decisively and put a detaining hand
upon her arm as she sought to rise. 'That would be quite
impossible. It is much too late for you to be wandering
about on this field or in the town. You would not be safe.
You have seen for yourself earlier how matters stand.'

There was a movement outside near the tent entrance and he snapped irritably, turning his head in that direction. 'What is it? I am not to be disturbed.'

The voice of the young soldier carried to them, sounding doubtful at the impatient tone of the knight. 'It is me, Rolf Taylor, Sir Simon. You ordered me to find you food and ale.'

'Ah, yes.' Sir Simon rose and held open the flap for the young man to enter carrying a wooden tray. 'Come in, lad, and put the tray down here, on the table.'

The youngster advanced, eyeing Rosamund nervously as she sat on the camp bed and she avoided his gaze, embarrassed by his curious stare.

'Right, that will be all. You can go now. Attend me early tomorrow. I shall need you to go with me into Tewkesbury. I shall escort Mistress Kinnersley here.'

Rosamund started up, horrified. 'I cannot stay here through the night. I—'

'I have already told you,' he retorted curtly, 'it would be dangerous for you to do otherwise.'

He scowled at the youngster, who gave an awkward little bow and exited the tent hurriedly. Rosamund watched him in some panic. While it appeared that her earlier fears had abated, she was still anxious at being alone in the tent with this imperious stranger.

He held out a hand to her to help her rise. 'Come and eat. I doubt if you have touched food since early this morning. What time did you leave the manor?'

She realised suddenly that she was hungry, but to tamely accept this man's hospitality was to admit that she had surrendered to his decision that she should stay. She hesitated but, looking up, she saw the cool determination on his face and, reluctantly, rose. He led her to the camp table, pulling out a folding camp stool for her to seat herself. Her mouth watered at the sight of fresh bread, fowl and a jug of ale. Sir Simon seated himself opposite and pulled out his knife. He cut off large slices of bread to form trenchers for the two of them, carved breast of chicken for her and pulled off a leg for himself. She watched, a trifle bemused, as he poured ale into the tankard for her.

'Now, eat and drink,' he commanded. 'I will not allow my honoured guest to go hungry and, by your own confession, you will have much to do in the morning. Did those men who attacked you take all your money or was your groom carrying it?'

She shook her head, blushing furiously, as she thought of the secret little bag beneath her gown, where her small hoard of coin was hidden. 'No, sir, I have some coin, which I must use if there is sufficient to hire a horse, especially if I find that my brother has lost his pony.'

He watched with some amusement as she delicately picked up the portions of fowl with her fingers and nibbled cautiously, her eyes downcast, then, as her hunger sharpened, ate more hurriedly. She found the ale more satisfying than the sweeter, more potent malmsey and it quenched her thirst more readily. Sir Simon made shift to drink from the jug.

She looked up to find him smiling broadly. 'There, what did I say? You were hungry.' Then, as she made to speak, he said shortly, 'You must not be afraid. I will not molest you. My earlier assault was totally misplaced. I believed that you were willing enough to please me. Now I know that I was wrong and your earlier accusation that I lacked knightly honour stings me to the heart.' He glanced back towards the tent entrance from which could be heard the final hum of chat and the stamping down of cooking fires as the men made shift to retire for the night. 'I urge you to think carefully. If you try to leave this tent without my protection, you could get your throat cut. I do not wish to alarm you unduly, but that is a grim warning. My men will not dare to touch you so long as you remain in my care. Do I make myself clear?'

She nodded, blushing hotly again.

He rose and moved to the tent flap. 'You will find a leather bucket back there and a jug of water and a napkin. Make yourself comfortable for the night. You must sleep on my bed. I shall be comfortable enough on the ground. I will leave you for a while.'

She watched as he left the tent and gazed round quickly to ascertain that the articles he had spoken of were there in place. Hastily she did as he advised, but gave a little shudder as she glanced down at the bed. She could not rest easily there where he had almost—she swallowed hard as she thought what might have happened. He was some time gone, and she moved around the tent restlessly, starting at every sound from outside. Finally she curled herself up as best she could in the corner farthest from the entrance. It would be impossible to sleep, she felt sure, but, in spite of all that had happened, she had come to believe that this man would keep her safe through the night.

When he entered some time later, he glanced down at her with that now-familiar smile curving his lips. 'I assure you that you would be more comfortable on the bed.'

'I shall be quite comfortable here, sir, and thank you.'

He stood gazing down at her, hands on his hips. 'As you wish, but you will likely be chilled in the night. It is still very early for the nights to remain warm.' He moved to the clothing pole where his spare garments and pieces of armour hung and, taking down his cloak, came to her side once more and dropped it over her. 'There, now get some rest and try to still your anxieties. I know how you long to hear news, but you can do nothing tonight and it is best to gather strength for what tomorrow will bring.'

'Thank you.' She gathered the woollen cloak around

her, grateful for its warmth, for she was again feeling chilled. As he moved away she said softly. 'Did—did you witness those executions you spoke of?'

'Yes.' His reply was curt.

'Did—did those men suffer traitors' deaths?'

'No, they were beheaded.' He had seated himself at the table and was surveying a parchment map. 'Give your heart peace. The Duke of Gloucester is Lord High Constable. I told you that he sentenced to death only those great lords who had previously sworn loyalty to King Edward and who recently changed their coats and swore allegiance to the queen. If your father has survived, he will be allowed to go free.' She saw him give a light shrug of his shoulders. 'It is possible and likely that he will be fined or...' a slight hesitation '...your manor could be sequestered, but his life will be spared. And certainly no knight would harm a boy, even if he had found his way to the field.'

She was not so sure. Anything could have happened to Arthur in a town and surrounding countryside where all men lived off the land and swept aside all who would try to prevent them or attempt to protect their own property. Arthur's pony would be a prize indeed for some soldier wishing to escape the district hurriedly and she knew that Arthur would not surrender it easily. She burrowed into the warmth of the cloak and tried to settle. Although he did not come near her she was constantly aware of Sir Simon's presence and tried to keep all movement to the minimum. Despite her determination to remain wakeful and to stay on her guard, she eventually fell into an uneasy sleep, worn out by the terrors and hardships of the day.

Sir Simon sat for a while, busy at the table, then he rose and went over to the sleeping girl. Smiling, he stooped and lifted her, carried her to the bed, placed a linen shirt beneath her head and, once more, settled his cloak around her.

At last he unbuckled his sword belt and laid down the weapon, kicked off his boots, found himself another cloak from a saddle-bag and stretched himself out near the tent flap, after first assuring himself that the pitch torch had burnt low and was no longer a danger.

Chapter Three

Rosamund woke with a start as loud voices outside the tent penetrated her consciousness and appeared to be coming nearer. She sat up abruptly and gazed around her. Sunlight was piercing through the semi-opaque canvas of the tent wall and she saw immediately that she was alone. Suddenly she became aware that she had been sleeping on the camp bed. She thrust back the soft woollen cloak that had been placed around her and felt the roped support of the canvas beneath her.

Frowning, she sat with her hands clasped around her raised knees as she considered what she remembered of the previous night. She had rejected the bed and curled herself up upon the ground as far away from the tent flap as she could manage. She was quite sure of that. She had not wanted to repeat the feeling that she had experienced when—when Sir Simon Cauldwell had started to—she put a hand to her mouth as if to keep back a startled cry. She had certainly not laid herself down on this bed. Then how—who? He had come into the tent and seen her lying there then he had gone over to the table and—— She must have fallen asleep and he had carried her here…

Warmth flooded through her as she thought again about

the feel of those strong, muscular arms about her body. Could he have slept beside her? She rejected the idea instantly. No, the bed was not wide enough and he would not— She bit down hard upon her nether lip. No, he had simply believed that she would sleep more comfortably upon his bed and had decided to carry her there. Her mouth twisted in a wry little smile. The man was an enigma. He had had her arrested, thought ill of her, determined to take advantage of her, and then he had discovered that she was, after all, an innocent victim of events and a virgin to boot, and he had protected her, seen to her comfort. Yet he was her father's enemy—and so hers too.

She must be grateful for his consideration, but cautious too. She must not let down her guard and give him any information concerning her father's motives or his property in case Sir Humphrey had managed to escape the field and might well be in further danger. And if he had not, and the worst of her fears had come to pass and he had been killed, then Arthur must be her first consideration. Arthur would be the heir and most vulnerable. His rights to the manor must be protected. She thought desperately of what she had told Sir Simon. He knew her name and that her home was near. Her heart thudded uncomfortably. If her father was alive, he might be hiding at Kinnersley. Sir Simon Cauldwell knew far too much about them all. She looked round anxiously before scrambling to her feet. How long would it be before he returned? The camp table had been covered with maps last night. Now it was clear. The stools were folded and the clothing pole had been removed. Preparations had already been made for departure. The increasing noise outside made her aware that the men-at-arms were going about the business of packing up camp. The king's army would soon be on the move. The Yorkists would evacuate Tewkesbury, but that did not mean that pursuit of escaping rebels would cease. She had to get to

Tewkesbury soon now and resume her search for her
brother.

There was a jug of water on the small travelling chest
and a clean napkin. She made her toilet hurriedly and was
drying her face when the tent flap was thrust aside and Sir
Simon Cauldwell entered.

'Ah, I see you are awake at last. I left waking you to
the very last moment. Obviously you were totally worn
out by your unfortunate adventures yesterday.' He held out
towards her a folded garment topped by a small white linen
cap. 'I have managed to purchase a clean gown for you. I
regret that it is not of very good quality, nor is it in the
least fashionable, but I assure you it is clean.'

She took it from him somewhat unwillingly. It was, as
he had said, a rather worn brown gown, but her nose told
her that it had been only recently laundered. 'You should
not have…' she stammered awkwardly. 'I do not know if
I have sufficient coin with me to repay you…'

He shook his head dismissively, looking down at her
own ruined gown. 'Come, now, you cannot go into
Tewkesbury in such a state. You would shock the good
townsfolk and worry your brother when we find him. I
will leave you for another few moments while you
change.' His lips curved in a smile. 'Then, when I return,
I shall be forced to act as tiring woman for I see this gown
has back lacing.'

Rosamund's lip trembled. She did not know if she
should cry or castigate him for his insolence, but thought
silence was the best response. As he turned his back to
leave she said softly, 'Once more I must thank you, sir,
for all of your care of me.'

'Think of it only as my attempt at reparation for the
slight I put upon you last night.'

Then he was gone and she tore impatiently at her own

gown and struggled to put on the fresh one, anxious to be ready for him when he returned and not to keep him waiting.

She was glad that she had been quick, for he returned very soon; she wondered if he had hoped to find her still dressing. The lacing was giving her problems, however, and she was glad of his efficient management of it. Glancing at him sharply, she again wondered if he had had quite a lot of practice at the art of dressing and undressing females.

His expression was perfectly composed when she swung round to face him and, red-faced, gave him a hurried murmur of gratitude.

'It is not far to walk into the town. I will escort you to some respectable inn. From there you can make enquiries about your brother and hire a horse to carry you home. Do not concern yourself about the cost. I will see to it personally that you are not cheated.'

'I need not give you so much trouble, sir. Once I am clear of the field I shall manage alone and be safe enough in the town, I am sure.'

'I would not be so sure of that,' he said gravely. 'At all events I am bound for Tewkesbury town. I need to report to his Grace of Gloucester concerning my patrol of the field last night, a task he laid upon me.'

'Oh,' she said, alarmed, 'will you need to advise him about—?'

'No, Mistress Kinnersley, there will be no need for me to mention your presence there.' He glanced round and, hearing the gentle cough of the attentive young soldier outside, called him in.

'See to it that everything is packed and be ready to leave. You will find me at the king's lodging. Come to me there and bring my destrier.'

'Sir.'

Sir Simon smiled. 'I have informed your sergeant that I am in need of your service. He has released you. Will it please you to accompany me when I leave Tewkesbury and to remain in my service?'

Rosamund saw that the youngster's face was wreathed in smiles. 'Oh, yes, Sir Simon. I shall be honoured to take service with you.'

'Good. Then see that everything is ready for our departure by noon.'

The youth held up the tent flap for them to leave and stood respectfully back. Before taking Rosamund's hand and leading her forward, Sir Simon placed round her his cloak.

'No, sir, please,' she said, 'you have done too much for me already.'

'You will find it cooler today than it has been over the last few days. In fact, it has been unseasonably hot recently. This is nothing. I have other cloaks. Come now.'

She drew in the fresh air. As he had said, it was much pleasanter today. All around her the men were stamping out cooking fires they had used to prepare their morning gruel, packing up the tents of the commanders and gathering weapons and supplies for the saddle-bags of the waiting sumpter mules. One or two looked up briefly as she and Sir Simon passed, but there was no lustful curiosity in their glances, merely respectful interest. She gave a little shiver as she realised how safe she was with him and how difficult it would have been for her to walk this field alone.

It was a brief journey into the town and soon they fetched up near the abbey gate. Here, as on the field, there were signs of preparation for departure.

'The king has been lodged with the Abbot,' Sir Simon informed her. 'He hopes to leave at noon for Coventry. His two brothers, the Dukes of Clarence and Gloucester, will be with him.'

'And you will ride in the king's train?'

'I am in the personal service of Richard of Gloucester. I shall go wherever he commands me.' He drew her aside from some hurrying cleric, who was scrambling by, laden with scrolls of parchment, and they picked their way through the ordure that lined the roadway, dropped by the many horses and destriers of the mounted knights, which were, even now, being led from stables and barns by stable boys and grooms. All was bustle and confusion, yet Rosamund noted that many of the shops and houses remained boarded up, as if the townsfolk of Tewkesbury were still thinking it wiser to stay out of sight until the king's train had departed. Then, and then only, would they believe that their womenfolk would be able to walk the streets in safety once more.

Sir Simon escorted her to an inn, the Black Lion near the abbey gate. The innkeeper came into the taproom, red-faced and anxious, when the knight imperiously sent a serving girl in search of him.

'Forgive me, sir,' he said, nervously wiping sweaty palms on his apron, 'I have been busied arranging for the departure of two of my knightly guests and am only now at your service.' He eyed Rosamund doubtfully.

'Mistress Kinnersley is in need of a private bedchamber where she can rest and await her brother who is abroad in the town. Also I will come down to your stables with you and find a suitable mount for her when she is ready to return home to her own manor.'

The innkeeper was clearly in awe of the visitor. He cleared his throat nervously. 'Aye, sir, I'll get the girl to take her above stair to one of my rooms—that is, after we have cleaned out the chamber. The two gentlemen who lodged there have only this moment left and—'

'Yes, yes, I understand that. Meanwhile, see that Mistress Kinnersley is brought refreshment. I shall see to the reckoning,' he said curtly as, again, the innkeeper's gaze passed over Rosamund's poor-quality gown and simple cap and judged her standing to be probably of the servant class. He swallowed, astounded however, as Sir Simon guided the lady to a chair near the fire and, bowing, bent to kiss her hand.

'I will leave you, lady, while I see to your horse and send a man to enquire in the town about your brother. Is he like you in appearance?'

'Many have remarked on the likeness. Arthur is twelve years old, as I told you, tall for his age and brown-haired like me. I think he might well have been riding a piebald pony. It was his favourite.'

'Good, that will certainly be a help. I will also see if I can find any information about the man in your employ, who was attacked and injured. Tell me exactly, if you can, where the incident took place.'

Rosamund explained that the inn was on the outskirts of the town. Unfortunately she had not noted the inn sign. 'I can not delay you further, sir,' she said, 'since you will need to attend the duke and leave Tewkesbury very soon now. Now that I have lodging I can go out and search for Arthur. Then I can send someone later to enquire about Tom.'

'No,' he said firmly, 'you have seen how reluctant the townsfolk are to open up their houses and shops. You must wait until the armies have left or until you have a suitable escort.' He frowned thoughtfully. 'I would be happier to see you on your way myself; if your brother cannot be found quickly, then I will send Rolf Taylor with you. He is young, but reliable and capable of protecting you. I would not have chosen him to serve me if I had not been sure of his qualities.'

'But you need him to accompany you on the journey. I heard you tell him so.' Rosamund was alarmed. She had no wish for any servant of Sir Simon to visit Kinnersley in case her father had taken refuge there.

'Rolf can join me later. You have become my responsibility, Mistress Kinnersley. I will not leave you open to further insult or molestation.' His blue stare was very intense as he gazed at her directly. 'I am only too aware of how close you came to disaster in my tent, for which I cannot expect forgiveness. You yourself reminded me of my knightly honour and duty.'

She felt that he was teasing her although his words were formal and respectful. She blushed hotly. 'You have done much to make amends, sir, more than I could expect, especially from the hand of an enemy.'

His brows drew together again. 'I hope and pray that the realm will soon be in peace once more and that if we were to meet again you would not continue to regard me as such, lady.'

She bowed her head and nodded. 'Circumstances make friends and enemies, sir. It is regrettable but true.'

'Aye. Excuse me. I will see to your needs, then present myself at the king's lodging; I hope that I will be able to see you once more before my departure and assure myself that all is well with you.'

Again she nodded and forced a smile. She bit down on her nether lip as she saw him stride from the taproom. Over these last hours she had come to rely upon his strength and his power. Her feelings were confused. She had been very afraid of him and yet now she was grateful to him for his consideration to a stranger, and someone of little account, for all he knew. Yet she must still remind herself that he was her father's enemy and she must never allow herself to trust him completely.

Sir Simon strode down into the stables where he was informed that nags could usually be hired here at the Black

Lion, but all their horses had been commandeered by the soldiers.

'And without due payment,' the landlord complained angrily. 'As you see, sir, there is nothing here that would suit your purpose. It may be that the Abbot could lend you a mount for the lady if you were to enquire there but—'

'There is a pony there. To whom does that belong?' Sir Simon cut across his diatribe.

'That, sir, that is my daughter's pony. We—well, we hid it until we thought it safe to bring it back to the stable. She is very attached to it and—'

'I am quite sure it will come to no harm under Mistress Kinnersley's care and that she will make arrangements for its return in due course. Now, let us come to an understanding about the hire charge.'

The innkeeper was about to argue further but, looking into those stern blue eyes, changed his mind, sighed and mentioned a reasonable sum.

'Very well. See that the animal is saddled and ready to leave later after noon when the lady is ready to depart. I will send a man with payment. You need not fear that you will be cheated, as I am sure you have been over the last days. Just see to it that the lady is well served and refreshment brought to her shortly. Also see that the bedchamber is clean. Toilet articles should be provided and jugs of hot water and towels. I think it unlikely that she will wish to spend the night here, but, if that becomes necessary, I trust I can rely on you to see that she is not disturbed.'

The stare was coldly penetrating and the innkeeper gave a little awkward bow. He was elderly, bald-headed and overweight and had been bullied mercilessly during the occupation of the town, but he was a shrewd man and judged that this knight, who was not fancifully dressed as other lords from one or other of the opposing armies who had occupied his inn recently, was not a man to be trifled with. There was an authoritative air about him, which told the innkeeper he would disobey instructions at his peril. He sighed again and watched, with a speculative expression, the knight stride from the inn courtyard. He considered that he would be fairly paid for his services and that was enough even if the young woman in his taproom was no lady, but merely the knight's mistress. That was no business of his.

Sir Simon emerged into the crowded street. The noise was deafening. Sergeant-at-arms and grooms and stable boys yelling orders, horses neighing and rearing in their handlers' grasps, impatient to be off on their journey. Wagons were being trundled, laden with armour, weapons and supplies. One or two were bearing injured men towards the designated positions in the army train. Round the Abbot's lodging door were collected a group of Simon's companions and stolidly patient men-at-arms in attendance. All was nearly ready now. King Edward had only to emerge from the lodging with his royal brothers and the exodus from the town would begin.

Simon acknowledged the greetings of his friends and made to enter. Clearly Duke Richard was still within and he needed to make his report and then await the arrival of Rolf Taylor with the horses. There was a little stir amongst the men-at-arms near the gate and one shouted an oath and impatiently shouldered aside a youth who was attempting to badger him.

'I've told you, lad, I've no information about important prisoners. Yes, some were executed, but that was yesterday. As far as I know none are being held now. The monks at the abbey could give you information about some of the dead, them as can be identified, like, but that'll take time. There's no more in the abbey itself, taking sanctuary, as you must 'ave seen for yourself. They all came out early yesterday morning. Go back home, lad, and await news.

That'll be the best thing to do.' His tone softened slightly as he looked down at the slim, brown-haired boy standing before him, who was clearly desperate and anxious to detain anyone in sight in the hope of obtaining the information he desired.

'I was in the abbey myself with the Lancastrian prisoners and I saw no sign of my father then, nor of his squire. There must be someone who can tell me… I must find out one way or another.' Simon heard the shrillness of tone and judged that the boy was close to tears. He glanced back to the abbey wall and saw a piebald pony tethered there.

He moved through the group and caught the youth by one shoulder and swung him round. 'Are you Master Arthur Kinnersley?'

The lad was obviously startled and almost fell, then he recovered his footing and looked up doubtfully into the discerning stare of the man who was holding him. 'Yes,' he stammered, 'I am Arthur Kinnersley. I seek news of my father. Who are you? Can you tell me of him? Please, I must know even if—' he swallowed pitifully '—even if it is bad.'

Simon pushed him clear of the group and drew him towards the pony. 'I am Sir Simon Cauldwell, but my name does not matter. Unfortunately I have no news of your father to give you, but I do know that your sister is frantic for news of you both. I have lodged her, only an hour ago, at the Black Lion where you will present yourself to her immediately.' He gave the lad's shoulder a shake. 'What impelled you to be so stupid? Do you think this foolishness of yours has helped your sister? You have placed her in great danger by her need to find you. Do you think coming here will help your sire, if he lives, or your family, and certainly it will not if he is numbered among the dead! Your stepmother and your sister have need of you at home to help deal with events as they happen. Have you no sense?'

The boy angrily wrenched himself free. His hazel-brown eyes, so like those of his sister, blazed defiance. 'What do you know of my sister? What business is any of this of yours?'

'I was forced to make it my business when I found your sister last night heading for the battlefield, which was thronged with camping soldiers. Do you dare to tell me you have no idea what that could mean?'

Colour drained from the boy's face and he put a shaking hand up to his cheek. 'Is she—is she safe?' he blurted out.

'Yes. I kept her under my protection and she is now lodged, as I said, at the Black Lion Inn where you must go to her at once.'

'I will, sir.' Arthur Kinnersley glanced round the packed street with a hunted expression. 'My father—he— Are you a Yorkist knight?'

'I am.'

'Then—'

'That has nothing to do with my concern for your sister.'

'No.' Arthur swallowed hard. 'I left home to follow my father. It was on impulse. I had no thought that she would come after me.'

'Well, who else was there to do so? I rather got the impression that your stepmother was hardly likely to organise a search party to find you. In any case, I imagine your home is short of able-bodied men. Your father would have taken most of those members of the household with him.'

Arthur looked down at the dirt of the road and awkwardly stubbed the toe of his boot. 'I should not have gone,' he murmured huskily. 'My first thought should have been to guard Rosa, but—'

'But you did not think. Well,' Simon shrugged. 'At your

age I probably would not have done so either. Now you must do your best to put matters right. Your sister needs to be escorted home. On the way here her horse was stolen and your head groom was injured when they were attacked. Your sister was forced to run from the soldiers for her own safety and, naturally, she is very alarmed about the fate of your servant. When you reach home it will be your task to organise an enquiry as to his fate. Someone must know where he is and…' he hesitated '…if he was killed I imagine your sister will wish to have his body conveyed to his home.'

'Yes,' the boy said miserably. 'Poor Tom. We must do all we can to find and help him.'

'Yes,' Simon said grimly, 'but first things first. Get back to your sister. I have arranged for hire of a pony for her. The innkeeper's daughter has affection for it, so it must be returned to the Black Lion. See to it.'

'I will, sir. I will take charge and thank you for your care of my sister, Sir Simon—'

'Cauldwell. I must leave with the king's party or I would see your sister home myself.'

Arthur nodded and held out his hand, which Simon grasped. He knew that it was the boy's way of saying that he regretted his earlier angry response, yet he was also aware that the boy would find it hard to acknowledge and accept the assistance of a man he regarded as an enemy of his father.

'I will go now at once, sir. It is just that—' again he gazed around him frantically '—I had hoped to gain news of my father's fate.'

'I know,' Simon said gravely, 'but, as that soldier told you, it were best now for you to await such tidings at home and, when they come, to deal with them as will be best for your womenfolk. Do you understand me?'

'Aye, sir.'

Simon gave a brief nod, then turned as he saw Rolf Taylor approaching on foot, for the road was too packed with men, wagons and horses for him to ride, leading Simon's destrier and another hack, as well as a sumpter mule laden with Simon's armour and necessities.

'Then I will bid you farewell, young Arthur. I had told your sister that I would try to see her again before leaving Tewkesbury but—' He broke off as the boy gave a sudden despairing cry and rushed across the street, pushing aside several angry men, who were obstructing him. Simon muttered an oath beneath his breath, then swore again roundly as he became aware of what had alarmed the boy. Coming slowly towards them was a war horse, led by a young man. Simon could not fail to note what had distressed the boy. The destrier had slung across its back the body of a man still clad in armour, whose arms hung limply down towards the ground and whose head lurched with each movement of the horse's stately, wearied pacing.

'God in Heaven,' Simon mouthed hoarsely, 'Rosamund's father!' He stopped for one moment to bellow at Rolf Taylor, who stood, open-mouthed, still holding the leading reins of his master's mounts.

'Rolf, find Sir Richard Ratcliffe if you can and inform him that I would have him apologise to Duke Richard and beg him to excuse me from not attending him immediately. I will follow on to Coventry within the hour, but there is a service I must do for a lady in distress. The duke will understand, I am sure.'

'Aye, sir. Will you want me to wait for you here?'

'Yes. That would be best. If I am some time, walk the horses and see that they are watered and ready for departure later this evening.'

He hastened towards the little stricken group. The man leading the corpse laden horse was, apparently, Sir Humphrey Kinnersley's squire and he had stopped some distance from the abbey gate, seeing the concourse gathered there. Arthur had launched himself upon the body of his father and was leaning against the destrier's side, weeping bitterly. It was clear that the boy was known to the war horse, for it stood docilely, without the usual rearing, plunging and aggressive behaviour such mounts showed towards strangers. Simon approached cautiously and the squire turned to face him deferentially.

Simon gestured to the man to stay quiet while the boy exhausted his first storm of grief. 'I take it you are Sir Humphrey Kinnersley's squire.'

'Yes, sir, Andrew Murton. As you see, my master was killed near the horse lines before the retreat. I have only now been allowed to retrieve his body and—'

'Yes.' Simon put a gentling hand upon Arthur's shoulder. It was shaken off furiously.

'Leave me,' he stormed, 'leave me be.'

'I understand your grief, Arthur,' Simon said quietly. He turned once more to the squire. 'I have some slight acquaintance with your mistress, who is lodged at the Black Lion.'

The man's amazement was revealed in the widening of his green eyes. He was, Simon judged, about twenty years of age, sturdily built, not tall, but well muscled like his master, a fighting man who had probably fought by Sir Humphrey's side at Barnet. His face was round, ingenuous, with youthful, well-marked features and a straight short nose, topped by reddish-fair brows. He was still wearing his mailed coif, but Simon saw strands of that same reddish hair falling damply upon his forehead. Rosamund, Simon thought, somewhat dourly, would probably find this young man presentable, even handsome.

He looked towards the boy. 'He is naturally very distressed. Why have you only now come into the town? I understand the boy has been searching for you for two days.'

'Yes.' The squire looked defensive. 'I was wary of showing myself. I took refuge in the wood near the water meadows and kept the horse quiet till I considered that it was safe for me to come out of hiding. My own was killed under me on the field. Many of the Lancastrians were slaughtered even after surrender. I saw some of that. There would have been no point in endangering myself even to carry the ill tidings to Lady Kinnersley. I considered that she, Mistress Rosamund and young Arthur would need me—afterwards. I heard that the king's army was leaving the town and thought it safe to emerge from cover.' He glanced round. 'I see that I was precipitous.'

'I see.' Simon conceded his point. Certainly Rosamund and her brother, to say nothing of the grieving widow, would need support and, most likely, this young man was the most suitable person to give it.

Andrew Murton cleared his throat nervously. 'You say that Mistress Rosamund is at the Black Lion Inn. I should present myself to her immediately now and inform her of her father's fate.'

Simon considered for a moment, watching the evacuating army continue to form up ready for departure. 'I think it necessary for someone to remain with the boy and keep an eye on the horse and—on Sir Humphrey's body. I see that he is still clad in valuable armour. The boy might have need of that in the future and possession of it will bring him some comfort. Arthur is in no state to speak with his sister yet. I suggest that you follow me into the inn yard. Mistress Rosamund knows me and, strange as it may seem, bad news is often received more easily from someone who is not too closely involved with the family.'

For seconds it seemed that the squire would protest, and Arthur stood up from leaning over his father's body to stare antagonistically at Simon. The squire, recognising Simon's authority, obviously thought it best to accept his suggestion without argument. Silently he gestured to Arthur to agree. The boy looked from the squire's face to that of Sir Simon and inclined his chin. His eyes were blurred with tears and he gave a little sob.

Simon said quietly, 'Arthur, I think you should recover your pony from where you have left it near the abbey gate. You will need it for your ride home.'

He watched sombrely as the boy did as he was bidden. 'I think,' he said to the squire, 'caring for the beast will give him something to do.'

The two followed Simon back to the inn. Several of the people in the waiting crowd gave way to the sad little group and one or two townsmen doffed their caps out of respect to the dead man. Simon left boy and squire near the stable and hastened into the inn. The landlord looked up anxiously at his approach as if expecting more demands that he would find difficult to provide, but Sir Simon said brusquely, 'Where is Mistress Kinnersley? I see she is not in the taproom.'

'No, sir, she is upstairs in the chamber I allotted her.'

'I suppose it would be impossible for you to provide a covered cart for our use?'

The man looked up at him curiously. 'Completely out of the question, sir. As I said before, the armies commandeered everything of that nature in the town.'

Simon nodded curtly and left the man and mounted to the upstairs chamber. He paused at the landing, his hand on the door knob of the chamber fronting the building, which the innkeeper had informed him had been allotted to Mistress Kinnersley.

He knew that he was at a loss. He had seen so much bloodshed over the last days and yet he dreaded imparting to Rosamund Kinnersley the news of her father's death.

She had made a great impression upon him over these last hours and he was not entirely sure why. She was not truly beautiful in the accepted standard of the Burgundian and Westminster courts. He had known and courted women whose physical lineaments had stirred his senses momentarily, but Rosamund Kinnersley's spirit and courage had touched his heart. In spite of her fear of him, she had faced him defiantly and had fought fiercely when she believed that he intended to rape her. His lips curled in a little tender smile. She was so very young—he judged that she could not be more than sixteen summers. And yet, despite her determination to defend her honour, he had felt her respond to him, only for moments, but he had known she had been stirred by his nearness, as he had been impatient to slake his lust. The events of that terrible day had taken their toll of him. He had needed to hold a woman in his arms, to reassure him that he was alive and capable of feeling and for deadly minutes he had forgotten his honour. They had both drawn back at the crucial moment, yet both had recognised a need in the other.

He was aware that she had prepared herself for these dread tidings. She had questioned him concerning the executions he had attended, faced the fact that her father might well have trodden on that scaffold. He had sensed also a deeper unhappiness brooding behind those golden brown eyes. Rosamund Kinnersley had been unhappy for months, possibly from the moment that her father had remarried. She had spoken of a stepmother and indicated that the woman would not have been disturbed by the sudden disappearance of her stepson. Very rarely did step-parents meet with the approval of their spouse's children. He wondered about Lady Kinnersley. Was she very young—and beautiful?

He had lost his own father on the battlefield of Wakefield. He had been then only a year older than young Ar-

thur Kinnersley was now. His mother had never taken a
new husband. He had been spared that, but not the un-
bearable pain of bereavement. They had loved his father
devotedly, yet Simon's mother had deliberately deprived
herself of the consolation of her son's presence at that
dreadful time. She had unselfishly sent him to Middleham
Castle so that he might be fittingly trained to arms and
able to defend himself when hard times came once more.
What would happen now to the vulnerable young heir to
the Kinnersley lands? Would the king deprive the boy of
them or, if not, could Arthur be the prey of other mercenary forces from which Rosamund Kinnersley would find
it almost impossible to protect him? Indeed, she would
need protection herself. Simon's fierce blue eyes softened
and he frowned as he considered how best to break the ill
news to her.

Her low voice gave permission for him to enter following his knock. She faced the door, obviously expecting the
landlord or a serving wench, for her eyes widened in surprise at the sight of her visitor. She stood quite still, looking towards him intently and he knew that she had immediately gauged the importance of what he had to say.
She deliberately straightened her spine, her hands clenched
at her sides, as she said evenly, 'What is it, Sir Simon?
You have found my brother? Is he—' her voice trembled
only slightly '—is he hurt?'

'No,' he said gently, 'Arthur is quite unharmed. He is
waiting with your father's squire in the courtyard below.'

She waited, avoiding impatient questioning, but he
could see her swallow nervously.

He knew that to keep her in dread was worse for her
than what she was to hear. He cleared his throat and said
quietly, 'I regret, Mistress Kinnersley, to have to inform
you that your squire has brought your father's body from
the field. He tells me that he was killed fighting bravely

near the horse lines before the Lancastrian retreat. I am
sure he will tell you more of the circumstances when time
permits.'

Her voice was a husky whisper as she murmured, 'Then
Arthur knows?'

'Yes. The boy is much distressed. I thought it best for
your father's corpse to remain attended and so it was left
to me to—come to you.'

She inclined her chin slightly. 'You have been very
kind, sir, and I thank you. This—this cannot have been
easy for you, though you have experienced worse things
recently, I know.' Her voice broke a little on the last
words.

'I assure you, Mistress Kinnersley, there are few expe-
riences worse than having to bring someone you respect
ill tidings.'

She was very calm, too calm, he thought. She was keeping herself strong for her brother, yet he saw that her dark
lashes now were misting with tears, though she did not
sob, as Arthur had done.

'I would that I could provide you with a decent covered
cart, but there are none to be had in the town. Your
brother's pony is safe and I have hired one for you, as I
told you, but your squire's mount was killed under him,
he tells me.' He hesitated. 'He was forced to hide for long
hours with the corpse from pursuing soldiers. As you know
the weather has been uncommonly sultry and you will
wish to return home as soon as possible now for the burial.
Perhaps you could manage to change ponies during the
journey and the boys could carry a double load for the first
miles…'

She forced a smile. 'You have done much for us, strangers and—enemies though we are. I cannot expect more of
you. Andrew will protect us on the journey. It will be a
slow and sad one, but we shall arrive, with luck, before

nightfall. Please, I should not delay you further. I understand that Duke Richard of Gloucester has need of your service and you will be in disfavour if you linger longer.'

'I sent a message to the duke to excuse my absence as I needed to do a service for a lady. He will understand. I have sworn to join his train at Coventry.'

'Will he be so understanding?' she enquired wonderingly.

His lips curved in a smile. 'Oh, yes, I promise you that he will.'

The strain of standing so still and taut was beginning to take its toll on her and he saw that she was about to stumble. Gently he came to her and helped her into a chair.

'I must go to Arthur at once,' she murmured piteously.

'Give yourself a moment,' he said firmly, then he moved to a chest where she had left her cloak and put it round her shoulders.

She half-turned in the chair and gave him a wan little smile. 'I am ready now.'

He helped her up and, firmly, she took his hand from her arm. 'Please do not concern yourself about me. I—I have been half-expecting this. It is Arthur who will be most bereft.'

He stood back from the door for her to precede him, then followed her down the stair. He had already paid the innkeeper earlier and he nodded to the man as they passed down the short little corridor into the sunlight of the courtyard. She halted abruptly at sight of the horse with its burden and the two who stood by it waiting for her. Arthur gave an inarticulate little cry and ran to his sister. He buried his head in the soft cloth of her gown and began to sob again. She bent to stroke his brown hair and looked over his head towards the patiently waiting squire. At last she gently drew Arthur forward and bent over her father's corpse. She made no attempt to look at his features, but put out a hand to touch his side.

'Thank you for bringing him back to us, Andrew,' she said.

'I dared not venture out before,' he explained huskily, 'but I drew him under the shade of the trees and kept close guard. He has not been alone, not for a moment.'

She nodded, then turned to Simon. 'We are ready to leave now, if you will ask a stable boy to bring out my hired pony.'

The boy was waiting with the animal saddled just within the stable and he led it out towards the mounting block. Simon made no effort to intervene as Andrew Murton left his charge and assisted his mistress into the saddle. She took the reins within her hands and smiled at Simon. 'Thank you again, sir, for all your pains on our behalf. I— I think I shall not forget you.'

He walked through the arch and into the still-crowded street as Arthur mounted his piebald pony and Andrew Murton led forward his master's destrier.

As the sad little cortège was about to enter the street a trumpet sounded. Simon saw Duke Richard of Gloucester, preceded by his standard bearer, with his device of the White Boar, about to ride by and join his royal brother, the king, in the van of the departing army.

He reined in for a moment at sight of Simon. His horse reared restlessly and he held it in skilfully. His eyes went to the lead horse with its sad burden, then to the boy and his sister about to follow.

'Well, Simon,' he said, 'I see now your reason for excusing yourself from the company.'

'My friends are about to leave, your Grace, and I shall mount up shortly and follow you.' Simon cast a frowning glance at Arthur who was staring rudely at the duke and his escort of men-at-arms clad in the Yorkist colours of murrey and blue. He seemed about to say something. Rosamund rode close to her brother and put a warning hand on his arm.

The duke's eyes passed over the body of the stricken knight and he frowned. Like all the members of the noble company he was in full armour but unhelmeted, his mailed coif pushed back. 'It would be more seemly for the lady's father, is it, to be conveyed to his home by a covered cart.'

'Certainly, sir, but there are none to be found in the town,' Simon explained.

The duke nodded grimly. He called imperiously to a sergeant-at-arms riding close by. 'Will, Will Scroggins, will you see to it that one of our covered carts is unloaded and placed at the disposal of the lady here?'

Rosamund was clearly startled and moved by his consideration as the sergeant instantly dismounted, signalled for the accompanying men-at-arms to rein in and await the duke's further orders, and hastened back to the rear of the procession to deal with the emergency as commanded.

The duke leaned down to speak to Rosamund. 'I am deeply sorry for your loss, lady. Offer your mother my condolences. All shall be arranged for you to convey your father's corpse decently.'

She bowed her head. 'I thank you, your Grace, from the bottom of my heart.'

The duke glanced at Arthur. 'Is this your brother? Have you an older sibling?'

'No, your Grace, Arthur is my father's only son and heir.'

'Ah, then you will have to be appointed a guardian.'

Again Arthur appeared to be about to expostulate and Simon's eyes snapped out an angry warning.

The sergeant returned and saluted. 'All will be ready for you soon, mistress. If you will ride some paces down the street, I will arrange for assistance in getting your father's remains into the cart. Your squire will be able then to drive you home.'

Rosamund turned finally to Simon and there was a world of gratitude in her eyes, now blurred with tears. She said nothing, but bent down from the saddle to grasp his hand. He bowed and kissed her palm. She allowed the sergeant to take her leading reins and draw her to the rear of the royal procession.

Simon shaded his eyes against the pale sun as he watched her go from him. He felt an unaccountable sense of loss. The duke said curtly, 'I will consult with his Grace the king concerning the welfare of that child there.'

Simon looked up and smiled. 'I will be grateful, your Grace.'

'The lady appears to have made an impression on you, Simon,' the duke said mischievously. 'When we have leisure in Coventry, you must tell me the tale of how you came to meet her.'

Simon sighed. He would have preferred to wait and follow Rosamund with his eyes until the cart was laden and she and her two menfolk departed the town, but his work was done and now he must retrieve his mount from Rolf Taylor and follow in the duke's train.

He gave a sad little smile, saluted and stood back as the duke and his attendants rode by.

Chapter Four

Simon waited in the antechamber of the king's lodging in Coventry. He lounged on a window seat with two more friends of Duke Richard of Gloucester with whom he had served as squires in training at Middleham, Richard Ratcliffe and Robert Percy.

Dick Ratcliffe stood up and stretched, his eyes on the door of the inner chamber, where Duke Richard was closeted with his brothers the king and the Duke of Clarence.

'That messenger who arrived in such a lather this morning is rumoured to have brought news of Queen Margaret's capture.'

'Well, that is about time,' rumbled Rob Percy. 'Surely she will have young Lady Anne with her and that should take some anxiety from Richard's shoulders.'

The three looked thoughtful. They were all aware that Duke Richard of Gloucester was deeply in love with Lady Anne Neville, the widow of Prince Edward of Lancaster who had been slain on the field at Tewkesbury. They had witnessed his suffering when her father, the Earl of Warwick, had broken from his allegiance to King Edward, turned to Queen Margaret and allied himself with her by marrying his daughter to Prince Edward, her son. They had all known the daughters of the earl well from their youths at Middleham and all three shared the duke's anxiety about the welfare of Lady Anne, who was now a hunted fugitive.

'If the queen is taken, she will surely be brought here a prisoner soon,' Simon said, 'and Lady Anne with her. The queen is likely to be placed with King Henry in the Tower of London, but what of Anne? She is the king's cousin and sister by marriage. Surely he is most likely to place her with her sister, the Duchess of Clarence, for safe keeping.'

Dick Ratcliffe sniffed audibly. 'That would be no problem but for the fact that George of Clarence may not be the most trustworthy guardian of such a wealthy heiress.'

Simon glanced round the antechamber packed with attendants and clerics waiting on the king and gave his friend a warning glance. George of Clarence was the king's brother and such remarks could be deemed treasonable.

His own thoughts were concerned with the welfare of the girl he had encountered on the field at Tewkesbury. Had Rosamund Kinnersley reached home safely? She had been escorted by her father's squire, who had seemed capable enough, and had been restrained in her grief. It would be her responsibility to break the news to her father's widow.

She was of marriageable age, Simon reflected. Would pressure be placed upon her now to take a husband, and what decision would his Grace the king make about the Kinnersley lands, since her father would be deemed a traitor? There could be no dower. Simon scowled as he thought that she might well be forced to enter a nunnery. Rosamund Kinnersley had a fierce independent spirit and the life of a religeuse would not suit her, he thought. And the boy—he himself had faced a future without the protection of a father and he hoped that the king would make suitable provision for the boy's safety and welfare.

He found his two friends staring at him and he forced a wry smile.

'Someone else whose thoughts centre on a lady in distress,' drawled Rob Percy and Simon scowled at him in mock fury.

He had been forced to tell the tale of his meeting with Rosamund Kinnersley when the three had been closeted alone with the duke the previous evening. Richard had commanded him to explain his need to put himself at the lady's disposal in Tewkesbury. Simon had been embarrassed by their teasing, but Duke Richard, realising his sensitivity, had abruptly put an end to it by changing the subject. Now Simon wondered if pressure of events had forced the duke to forget his promise to speak to the king on Mistress Kinnersley's behalf.

Any remark either of the friends might make was cut off abruptly as the door to the king's private chamber was opened and Duke Richard emerged. By his serious expression all three surmised that he had received news of the queen's and Lady Anne's whereabouts.

Dick Ratcliffe queried, as they all rose to their feet respectfully, 'The rumour is true then, my lord, Queen Margaret is taken?'

The duke nodded wearily. 'She will be brought here later today.' He gave a little sigh. 'I do not really wish to be present at that audience. She must be devastated to hear the news of her son's death.'

The three remained silent, then the duke said, 'Frank Lovell will be joining my household later today. I know you will all make him feel welcome.'

Simon knew that this was good news indeed. Francis Lovell had also been a squire at Middleham Castle and was known to be one of Richard's closest friends. He would be glad to have his company.

He found the duke surveying him thoughtfully. 'Walk with me, Simon. I have another task for you.'

The other two men bowed as Simon accompanied Duke Richard through the chamber and into the garden at the rear of the lodging. The air smelt heavy with the scent of honeysuckle, lavender and rosemary. Soon, he thought, the roses would bloom and, again, his thoughts went to Rosamund Kinnersley, aptly named Rose of the World.

As if he guessed at Simon's thoughts, the duke stopped and turned to face him. 'I understand that you were anxious about the Kinnersley lands we spoke of last night, Simon.'

Simon felt his cheeks reddening and gave a little wry smile. 'Your Grace, the lady I spoke of is very young, scarce seventeen, I estimate, perhaps even younger, and I sensed that the full burden of responsibility for the manor and her younger brother's welfare would be placed upon her shoulders.'

The duke gave an answering smile, which lit up his narrow face. Only his intimates knew that smile for Richard of Gloucester was restrained in bearing and manners so that many would deem him cold, reserved, unfeeling. Simon knew that to be far from the case.

'Simon, I sensed last night that your feelings for the lady came deeper than you were prepared to admit. That is why I moved to put an end to the badinage. Are you falling in love, Simon?'

Simon gave a little blustering laugh. 'My lord I scarcely know how I feel…'

'But you do feel a strong attraction to the lady. Is she beautiful?'

'Not perhaps in the accepted courtly sense. She is lovely, brown-haired, truly English—a nut-brown maid, like the ballad. An English rose.' He grinned. 'Her father

named her Rosamund. When she told me I informed her
that I hoped it was a white rose.'

Richard laughed. 'A Yorkist rose, but I understood that
her father was a Lancastrian.'

'Apparently he had been in the service of the Earl of
Warwick as we all were formerly, before he forswore his
allegiance.'

Richard nodded soberly. 'The lady cannot be considered
responsible for the disloyalty of her sire. I have spoken
with the king, explained that the young heir has no guardian, and he has consented to declare him a ward of the
crown under my jurisdiction.'

Simon gave a great sigh of relief.

The duke said sardonically, 'I thought that you would
be pleased.'

'I know you will deal with the lad's claims sympathetically.'

'Yes, well, I had the clerks find out something of the
Kinnersley holdings. The manor is fortified and lies some
distance between Warwick and Tewkesbury. The realm is
not entirely at peace yet and I fear that nobles in the vicinity could see it as a ripe plum for the picking and move
upon it. The manor needs a strong seneschal, temporarily,
at least, and I judged that you would prove the man for
the job. Will you ride there with a small company of men
and take charge until later arrangements can be made?'

The suggestion came as a bolt from the blue and Simon
opened his lips to speak then, just as suddenly, closed them
again.

The duke was again regarding him, a glint of mischief
in his grey-green eyes. 'I considered that it would give you
an opportunity for further acquaintance with Mistress Kinnersley,' he said softly. As Simon did not answer immediately he added, 'You hinted that you had mistaken Mis-

tress Kinnersley for a—member of the baggage following?'

'I did, but only for moments, your Grace. She was plainly dressed and had been running over difficult ground. Her gown was torn. I explained that at first I took her to be one of the looters on the battlefield.'

'You did not overpress your attentions?'

Again Simon reddened. Though there were three years between them and he the elder, Duke Richard could make him feel very naïve on occasions and he was helpless to object or defend himself. Duke Richard was the greatest man in the kingdom beneath the king and his authority was supreme yet, despite that, he had held out a hand of friendship to those young men who had formerly served with him and that bond of comradeship would never be broken.

Simon said, 'I—came very close to blotting my knightly honour, but I restrained myself well in time. The lady was unharmed. I realised very soon that she was a virgin and a woman to be highly respected.'

'Good.' The duke nodded sagely. 'And you have not yet ordered your own feelings in regard to this lady.'

'She is young, comely and very brave and high-spirited. The man who weds her will be fortunate indeed, my lord, I am sure of that. I am also sure that she would certainly not find me an acceptable suitor should I even consider such a proposition as offering for her hand. At any rate, since she is under age she is a ward of the crown, like her brother, and her marriage will be decided on by his Grace the king.'

'Or by me,' the duke agreed, smiling. 'Your mother, that redoubtable lady, will not require you to travel home to the north too soon, I trust?'

'As you say, your Grace, my mother is a formidable lady indeed and more than a match for any who might try to muscle in upon my lands. Also no reeve or steward would dare to try to defraud her. I will send her a messenger and put myself entirely at your disposal.'

'Then you will ride to Kinnersley Manor shortly?'

'After noon, if your Grace wills it.'

'Then we are both satisfied.'

Simon bowed low. He knew he was being dismissed and stood watching the young duke move away from him, back into the lodging. He noted that his steps were slow, as if reluctant to once more take upon himself the duties of the Constable of England, which his brother the king had placed upon him.

Rosamund sat in the oriel window of the hall, some distance apart from her stepmother and Andrew Murton who were still sitting at the high table in consultation. There had been no necessity to serve a funerary feast since no one outside the family and members of the household had attended her father's burial. It had had to be hurried and the unsettled situation in the district had made it impossible for those barons and nobles who had been friendly to her father to come to Kinnersley Manor. Yet everything had been conducted in a seemly manner. The little parish priest had attended the moment he had been informed of her father's death and he, with Rosamund, Arthur and Lady Sibyl, had kept vigil near the body until its burial in the chancel of the village church this morning.

Arthur had retired to his own chamber, overcome with grief, but he had conducted himself courageously throughout the ceremony and Rosamund was proud of him. She had told Sir Simon Cauldwell in an unguarded moment that she could not feel the complete grief that she owed her father. She still felt oddly numbed, as she had at the time he had told her of her father's death on the field. Sibyl had sobbed loudly from the moment she had come down from her chamber to view the body being respectfully conveyed from the covered cart in the courtyard, to the arrival of the priest, and throughout the ceremony today. She looked, Rosamund thought dispassionately, exceedingly beautiful in her mourning black. Was she being unkind when she wondered if Lady Sibyl's show of grief was entirely genuine? Certainly Lady Sibyl had declared herself too overcome to assist Martha, Rosamund and two of the servant wenches when, with Andrew Murton's assistance to remove her father's armour, they had washed and laid out the body. But then, Lady Sibyl had never shown the least interest in the usual duties of the lady of the manor. Now in an emergency it could hardly be expected of her.

Rosamund watched as Andrew Murton respectfully laid a gentling hand on her stepmother's arm in comfort as, once again, she burst into sobbing and hid her face in her kerchief. He rose, then turned and crossed to Rosamund before leaving the hall.

'Is there anything at all I can do for you before I go to the stables and assure myself that Sir Humphrey's destrier is being cared for properly?' he enquired. 'You have been so very brave and composed, Mistress Kinnersley. We all admire your forethought. Everything has been conducted as your father would have wished. I saw to it that the priest was repaid for his services and gave him money to say further masses for the repose of Sir Humphrey's soul.'

She inclined her head. 'Thank you for all you have done, Andrew, and in particular for your care of Arthur. I think it best if he is left to himself for a while. Either I or Martha will go to him later.'

Andrew nodded. 'He is overyoung for all these troubles, as you are, Mistress Rosamund.' He glanced back at Lady Kinnersley. 'My lady is also young and so recently married. I am deeply grieved for her. If I could only have reached your father earlier, I might well have been able to save his life. We were separated during the latter part of the engagement and, when all was over for us, and flight came to be an urgent necessity, I made for the horse lines, hoping to find him there and see him safely from the field.' He sighed. 'Alas, I was to discover him badly injured. His armour, as you saw, was badly dented by what appeared to have been a battleaxe or a mace, and there were head wounds... He had lost his helmet by then.' He looked away sadly. 'He—died in my arms.'

'Andrew, you have nothing with which to reproach yourself. You were with him at the last and you bravely carried his corpse to a place of safety and brought him back to us.' Rosamund gave a little shudder. 'I do not how we would have felt if he had been thrust into some pit near the field. You could have left him there and seen to your own safety. After all, Andrew, you might well have been taken prisoner or—slaughtered, as so many were on the field and in the meadow near the river during the pursuit.' Her face clouded as she added, 'One of the grooms was telling the others that he had heard that the river ran red with blood. No, Andrew, you did everything that could have been expected of you. I, for one, am glad to have you back with us. Arthur would have been totally devastated if you had not returned.' She caught at his doublet sleeve. 'It will not be necessary for you to leave us yet, will it? I do not know yet what is likely to happen to the manor lands. We could receive a visit from the king's men at any time, ordering us to vacate the manor house. If you are found here, could you be in further danger?' Her voice rose slightly in alarm. 'If there is any possibility of that, you must leave Kinnersley at once.'

He shook his head decisively. 'I shall stay with you all here as long as you need me. You can depend on that, Mistress Rosa. As for the fear of sequestration, I doubt the king would vent his spleen on an heir so young as Master Arthur.' His brows drew together. 'Our main concern is that the boy has no near relative to act as his guardian and petition the king for him. It might be that a heavy fine is levied and that could put financial constraints upon the household.'

'At the moment that is the least of our worries,' Rosamund said fervently, looking towards her stepmother, who had stopped her weeping for a while and was lifting a wine goblet to her lips. 'Lady Kinnersley must receive her dower rights, so we must look to that. In good time I must summon our man of business in Warwick and discover what, if any, provision has been made for us.' A fleeting thought touched her mind. What of her dowry? Her father had spoken of his proposed marriage plans for her, though he had never mentioned a favoured bridegroom. If the king were to seize their property in reprisal for her father's treason, she and Sibyl, as well as Arthur, could be left homeless and virtually penniless. Seeing Andrew Murton's eyes fixed upon her intently, she wondered if this young man had been in her father's thoughts as an eligible suitor. She felt a blush spreading from her throat to her cheeks at the idea. Certainly she liked Andrew Murton well enough. He was a competent squire, eminently reliable, but, strangely enough, she knew little about him. He had always been markedly reticent about his background. He had entered her father's service shortly before Sir Humphrey's marriage to Sibyl. Vaguely she had thought his family came from Warwickshire, but he had never spoken about his kin, not to her, at any rate. She was aware that he was not wealthy. His clothes were serviceable but, even on festive occasions, he was never clad in finery nor did she see him ever wear jewellery. If Andrew Murton were to seek a bride, he would require her to have a respectable dowry so that he could advance his fortunes. These recent battles had put paid to his hopes of preferment, as they had done for so many. It was unlikely now that he would ever be knighted.

She gave a faint sigh. She liked the man and felt sorry for his lost hopes.

He bent and, turning her hand, kissed her palm. 'Give your heart peace, Mistress Rosa. All will go well for us. I have prayed for that and am convinced that you will all be able to continue to live in this manor in peace.'

She flashed him a grateful smile as he went from her through the screen doors, out to the courtyard to see to the horses as he had promised.

Rosamund rose and went to her stepmother. 'Andrew is a good man. I do not know what we would have done without him over these last terrible hours,' she said. 'My dear, don't you think you would be best now to go and rest in your chamber? I know all this has been too dreadful for you to bear. I can see to it that preparations are made for supper.'

Sibyl looked up at her sadly. Rosamund thought how strange it was that, despite all her weeping, Sibyl Kinnersley's eyes were not reddened and her face not swollen as so many women's were when ravaged by grief. Indeed, she looked lovelier than ever and very vulnerable.

Sibyl dabbed at her eyes with a lace-edged kerchief. 'You are very patient with me, Rosamund, and so capable! What you say of Andrew is true of you. I could not have managed all the—' she broke off tearfully '—all those dreadful funerary rites without you and you must be grieving dreadfully too. I should not be inconsiderate. It is for me to order the household and I should set about it at once.'

Rosamund smiled gently. 'Tomorrow will be soon enough, Lady Kinnersley.'

'Can you not bring yourself to call me Sibyl?' She

smiled shyly. 'After all, we are almost of an age, you and I, and should be firm friends now.'

'Of course,' Rosamund said formally. She considered that never before had Sibyl Kinnersley offered her the hand of friendship—nor, to be fair to her, had her stepmother ever demanded the dutiful attitude often expected from such a relationship. From the beginning, when she had first arrived at the manor, Sibyl had drawn apart from her husband's children and left them to their own devices. At least she had not sought to dominate them and Rosamund had been grateful for that. Possibly, being so very young herself, she had felt inadequate when dealing with her two stepchildren, particularly Arthur.

As Rosamund had suggested, she went slowly from the hall to her chamber. Rosamund called to Martha, who was overseeing the removal of soiled dishes from some of the trestle tables, to accompany her mistress and see to her comfort.

She rose briskly to go to the kitchens herself and set preparations for supper in motion. She reached the top of the steps and was about to cross to the kitchen quarters when she saw that a small covered cart had driven into the courtyard, and frowned slightly. She did not recognise the vehicle and, these days, it was customary for the gate guard to be sure that only friends and well-known merchants and tradesman were admitted.

She hastened down as a groom emerged from the stables to enquire as to the driver's business. Rosamund froze as she saw that the man who stepped from the driving seat was a soldier wearing the blue-and-murrey livery of the House of York, which she had seen often, both on the battlefield and in Tewkesbury town. What was a Yorkist man-at-arms doing here at Kinnersley? Were her worst fears to be realised? Had the man brought a message ordering the family to vacate the manor? Yet, even as she dreaded to hear the man's message, she thought that, surely, the soldier would not arrive alone and he would be on horseback, not driving a small cart.

The young groom stood back at her approach. They were all sorely missing Tom's control in the stables and he was unsure about what to do.

The soldier saluted Rosamund and signalled to her respectfully to approach the cart.

'Mistress Kinnersley?'

'Yes, though I am not true mistress here. If you are seeking the lady of the household, she is resting in her chamber. I could send to her and—'

'Sir Simon Cauldwell dispatched me to make enquiries and institute a search for an injured man of your household, Mistress Kinnersley. He instructed me to report to you the moment I had news.'

'Tom?' Rosamund breathed the name hesitantly and put a hand to her mouth in dire alarm. Then Tom's body had been found and this was the reason for the cart here in her courtyard.

Seeing her distress, the man grinned cheerfully. 'Do not be too concerned, Mistress. We found your man at the inn. He's taken a bad blow to the head and one of his legs is broken, but he'll mend. I've brought him home to you.'

Rosamund dashed to the cart and gave a glad cry as Tom's head appeared from behind the front of the canvas covering. He wore a linen bandage round his forehead and she could see, as he made a move to scramble down, that he was still shaky from the ordeal, but he was back, and, seemingly, on the way to recovery.

The groom ran forward to help his master. Tom groggily turned to Rosamund as the youngster led him to a wooden seat near the stable door.

'Mistress, you can't believe how much I've been worrying about you and so glad to hear that you were safe

back at Kinnersley. This fellow informed me that all was
well and offered to bring me home.'

'Oh, Tom, I've been just as much worried about you.
Welcome back. We must see to your hurts and get you
back to your quarters.'

She turned to the soldier, who was preparing to mount
to the driving seat of the cart. 'Thank you and please convey my gratitude to your master. Will you not take refreshment here before you leave?'

The man touched his cap in a rakish salute. 'Thank you
kindly, Mistress, but I'm commanded to make all haste
and to rejoin my company in Coventry. I hope all goes
well with your man.'

He whipped up his nag and the cart clattered out of the
courtyard and over the drawbridge.

Rosamund turned back to Tom, who was already questioning his young stable lad about whether matters had
been progressing properly in his absence. The boy was
looking flustered and was glad when Rosamund dismissed
him and told him to find Martha who would be needed to
tend Tom.

Tom shook his head dismissively. 'I am tolerably well,
Mistress Rosa, apart from this danged leg of mine. They
cared for me at the inn after those rogue soldiers had left
and that soldier who brought me paid my score. He it was
who helped the landlord to set my leg and find splints for
me. Said he'd been told to settle all debts and offer any
assistance needed by his master.' He cleared his throat
awkwardly. 'He told me about Sir Humphrey as well, Mistress. I'm right sorry to hear that.'

'Yes.' Rosamund turned from him to dab at the tears
forming on her lashes. 'We buried him earlier today, Tom.
Andrew Murton brought him home and Arthur is safe,
you'll be glad to know.'

Tom waved the boy back to his duties in the stable. He

looked at Rosamund searchingly. 'And you, Mistress Rosa? You are safe? You weren't attacked again?'

'No, Tom. I—I managed to get clean away from the inn, though I was frantic about you— I knew I couldn't help by remaining there. Eventually I was found in the meadow near the river by some men-at-arms looking for looters.' She lowered her head to avoid his keen glance. 'It was difficult for a while. I was arrested by order of the man who sent your rescuer, Sir Simon Cauldwell. He—he protected me from harm and took me into Tewkesbury next day, where we found Arthur and—' tearfully '—discovered that my father had been killed. He was a Yorkist knight, but he took pity on my plight and did all he could to see me safe home. His lord, Duke Richard of Gloucester, even went so far as to provide us with a cart so that we could convey my father's body home in some semblance of dignity.'

Tom gave an explosive sigh of relief. 'I feared that you would be molested—or worse, killed. God bless that knight, whatever his sympathies.' He lowered his voice and glanced meaningfully towards the house. 'And how has my lady taken the bad news?'

'She is distraught, as one would expect. She has retired to her chamber with Martha to tend her. Arthur, too, is very upset and left us soon after the burial. I think he is in his own chamber giving rein to his grief in private.'

'And you left to bear the brunt of it, as always,' Tom grumbled.

Rosamund forced a smile. 'Oh, I shall be just as useless after I have made sure that the servants have their instructions. You must be helped to your own quarters now. I'll call the boy back to help you. You must not attempt to put weight on that leg until it is properly mended. You know how dangerous bone breaks can be if there is internal bleeding or infection. Mind me, now, Tom.'

The old man pulled a face. 'You know how important it is to see that the stable work is being overseen. I can get one of the lads to fetch me each day and—'

'You will not,' she said firmly. 'I absolutely forbid it. Young Jed can come and report to you daily in your room and that will have to suffice.'

Tom was about to argue further, but she did not wait to hear him. She went to the stable door to call to Jed and, when he appeared, looking anxious, she gave him careful instructions about helping Tom to his room and the need for servants to be instructed to wait upon him each day with food and the provision of all his requirements. She stood back and watched fondly as Tom, still protesting to the lad, was helped away by Jed and another stable boy.

She made her way slowly to the kitchens. She was so relieved that her adventure had not had the dire results she had feared. She had felt sure that Tom was lost to them and here he was safe, if not entirely sound, and she was sure that he would soon recover fully and be able to recommence his duties. She had great affection for Tom, who had taught her to ride and overseen her equestrian progress over the years. Indeed, the old man had been like an affectionate uncle to her. He was one stalwart soul she would be able to rely upon. She recalled the fact that, so far, none of the men-at-arms who had accompanied her father to war had returned and the manor garrison was depleted. In these unhappy and unsettled times and with the heir so young, they could be open to attack. She wondered how many of their men had died at Tewkesbury or if many of them feared to return in case they might be arrested and held as traitorous felons. She would be glad of Tom's sound advice, even though he was not well enough yet to stand on his feet and fight if need be. Andrew had sworn to remain with them for the present and he was experienced enough to be able to take command of their small garrison. That at least was a godsend.

She thought about Tom's return and how his score at the inn had been paid. Sir Simon Cauldwell had made great efforts on her behalf and she would never be able to repay him. Indeed, she would probably never set eyes upon him again.

She stopped abruptly in the deserted courtyard and thought about that. Surely she must be pleased by that knowledge. He was a Yorkist knight and any further contact they might have could only be detrimental to the welfare of all who lived at the manor. She was also aware that his presence, his touch, aroused feelings she could not explain. Simon Cauldwell was a disturbing personality and she wished him well away from Kinnersley.

For the next hour she was busy in tasks about the house, ensuring that everything went smoothly until her stepmother was able to assume control next day. Martha came down from the lady's chamber to inform Rosamund that she would not come to hall for supper and that she had requested that food be taken to her chamber. Arthur did not appear in hall either, nor did he send to excuse himself. Rosamund thought he might well have fallen asleep after an excess of grieving and she ordered Martha to see that he was not disturbed and that a tray of refreshments be placed outside his chamber door. Andrew came to the hall to report that he had patrolled the manor and ordered the lifting of the drawbridge and that everything was secure for the night. She invited him to join her at high table, but neither of them seemed disposed to talk or to eat very much and, after only a short time, she excused herself to the squire and rose to go to her own chamber. She stumbled as she moved towards the spiral stair leading to the upper chambers and realised that all this long terrible day she had forced herself to carry on as normal for all their sakes and that now she was completely exhausted, both physically and mentally. She doubted that she would be able to sleep, but now she must find some private place where she could give way to her own sense of loss and the fears for the future she was unable to dismiss from her mind.

She was halfway up the stairs when a shout from one of the serving lads busy in the kitchen gathering up the dishes alerted her to some problem. Wearily she descended again.

'What is it?' She looked round anxiously. 'Where is Master Murton?'

Then she saw that one of the gate guards was standing by the screen doors. One glance at his face warned her that something was very wrong.

'Mistress, there is a company of men outside the gate-house and their commander is demanding that we lower the drawbridge and allow them entrance,' he informed her curtly.

'What?' She stared back at him stupefied. 'What do you mean? Are they our men, those who went with my father? If so, lower the bridge at once and—'

'No, no, Mistress, they are strangers and wear the York-ist livery. We could see that by the light of the gatehouse lanterns. Master Murton has gone to investigate. We could not recognise the standard borne by one of the men. It is certainly not that of one of our neighbours.'

'Take me to the gate.'

The man complied hastily. Rosamund soon saw that a little gaggle of household servants had gathered near the gatehouse. She elbowed her way through and joined Andrew Murton, who was standing, feet astride, near the lifting gear. He had obviously just been engaging in parley with the man-at-arms, who bore the standard. He turned abruptly as Rosamund came to his side.

'They demand entry in the king's name,' he snapped.

She stared back at him wordlessly. The little group behind her, too, remained silent, though she could feel and hear their restless shuffling and knew that they were deeply afraid. She leaned forward, peering into the darkness ahead by the dim light of the gatehouse lantern. The standard stirred in the evening breeze and she distinguished the heraldic device, what appeared to be a miniature wall, sable, on a field of vert, topped by wavy lines in blanc and azure. Certainly the device was totally unknown to her.

She said dully, 'If the commander demands entry in the king's name, we dare not refuse, even at this hour of the night.'

Andrew's expression was as grave as hers and his brows drew together in an angry scowl. 'Where is my lady?'

'Still in her chamber. I imagine she has taken to her bed and could well be asleep by now.'

He gave a little angry grunt.

'Even if we had a mind to disobey, we have not the garrison to withstand an assault,' she said quietly.

'There are about twenty of them and, with the drawbridge still in place, we could keep them at bay until we knew more about the situation.'

'Andrew, they wear the king's livery. To try to hold out now would only invite further violence. Reinforcements could be brought up quickly enough and our few men could not man the gatehouse or the walls for long. In any case, what use would that be? King Edward has resumed the throne again. We must submit or be arrested as traitors. We could doom many of our people.'

'Shall I send a man to rouse my lady?'

Rosamund shook her head. 'She will know soon enough.

Let her rest for the present. Give the order to lower the drawbridge and admit the company.'

He opened his mouth as if he would argue with her, but, seeing her determined expression, he turned to the two men near the lifting wheel. 'Do as Mistress Rosa says. Lower the bridge.'

She stood quietly as the machinery wheezed into gear and, very slowly, it seemed, the bridge over the moat was lowered into place. The moment it settled the first horses of the invading company clattered on to its planks. As the man bearing the standard drew abreast, she gave a little gasp of recognition. He was the sergeant who had arrested her on the field near Tewkesbury. At the same moment she realised that what she had taken to be a wall on the heraldic device was, in fact, a well and the wavy blue and white lines denoted water. A cold well! The colour drained from her cheeks and her legs trembled under her as the knight in command rode up to the gatehouse and its lantern glow fell full across his features. The light flickered over his short, dark hair, for he had pushed his mail coif well back and those startlingly blue eyes she knew so well re-garded her smilingly.

'Greeting, Rose of the World,' Simon Cauldwell said, as Rolf Taylor scrambled from his own mount and ran forward to take his master's leading rein so that he might dismount.

Chapter Five

Feeling that her legs were still unsteady, Rosamund led Sir Simon Cauldwell across the courtyard towards the hall steps. Andrew had stepped forward angrily as if he were about to challenge the newcomer, but she shook her head at him imperatively.

Turning her head slightly, she said, somewhat brusquely, 'Will you see to it, Andrew, that Sir Simon's men's horses are accommodated in the stables, watered, fed and settled down for the night? I will arrange for the men to be bedded down in the hall and that arrangements are made for refreshments to be served to all.' She turned to Sir Simon. 'If you will follow me into the house, sir, I will see that your needs are attended to.'

He bowed low. 'Thank you, Mistress Kinnersley.'

He followed her across the courtyard, glancing round once or twice at the courtyard buildings and the gatehouse, on the roof of which two men of her household had mounted guard. Already Rosamund could hear the winding gear engaging, which would, once more, lift the drawbridge and leave Kinnersley safe for the coming night. She led her visitor to the high table in the hall and called to

Martha, who stood awaiting instructions near to the stair door.

'Will you bring bread, meats, wine, ale, if you prefer?' Rosamund looked enquiringly at Sir Simon, who shook his head as if acknowledging a willingness to accept anything offered.

Martha hastened out without questions, her expression grim. Sir Simon had stripped off his riding gauntlets and his cloak, which he threw across the back of his chair, then he moved hastily to draw out the armchair for Rosamund to seat herself opposite to him. Apart from greeting her so jocularly, he had not offered her any explanation of his presence at the head of an armed company.

She said abruptly, 'I cannot think why you are here, Sir Simon, but, as you demand entrance in the king's name, I must offer you hospitality. My stepmother has already retired for the night so I must take charge in her absence. We have buried my father today and are all feeling distressed, as I am sure you will understand.' She hesitated, her colour high. 'I presume that you have orders to sequester the manor. I hope that you will do us the courtesy of allowing us to remain under this roof at least until tomorrow.'

He leaned back in his chair, regarding her thoughtfully. 'Mistress Kinnersley, you do me a disservice to believe that I would come on such an errand. Please allow me to explain. Since your brother is so young, it is the king's wish that the manor lands be placed within the control of an experienced commander until more suitable arrangements can be made for his wardship. He is, of course, now a ward of the crown as, indeed, you are also.'

She gave a sudden start and he smiled. 'You must not be alarmed. No harm will come to you or to any member of your household. I note that the manor is crenellated and fortified. You must understand that the realm is still unruly and that you might come under attack from an unscrupulous neighbour or from marauding soldiers discharged suddenly from one or other of the armies. You experienced such a threat yourself very recently from which you had a fortunate escape.' He observed that the rosy colour, which had come to her cheeks earlier, now swept to her throat, as she recalled the occasion shortly before their disastrous first meeting. He continued. 'My men will swell your diminished household garrison. The king placed your wardship and that of your brother into the hands of the Duke of Gloucester and, since I am in his personal service, he entrusted this mission to me.'

'I see,' she murmured stiltedly.

There was a disturbance at the rear of the hall as Sir Simon's men filed in and settled themselves at the lower trestles. She noticed that they appeared to be under the strong control of their sergeant-at-arms, for there was no unruly nor rowdy behaviour. Of course, that could be explained by the fact that they had ridden from Coventry, she supposed, and were wearied, though she thought a more definite explanation was that they had received strict orders to behave well. Having observed Sir Simon's rigid control of his men at Tewkesbury, she knew they would obey him or risk severe punishment. That, at least, was in his favour. If the duke had thought it necessary to send an enemy commander, it was as well that this man's rule would allow no undue molestation of their womenfolk.

Martha, accompanied by several serving wenches bearing laden trays, appeared from the screen doorway, which led to the courtyard and kitchens. She approached the high table and placed flagons of ale and wine, platters of freshly baked bread, baked pies left over from the funeral meal, and cold meat and fowl before Sir Simon. He thanked her pleasantly and she curtsied and withdrew after Rosamund had enquired about Lady Sibyl and received the answer that she had remained within her chamber undisturbed and was, as yet, unaware of the arrival of their unexpected and unwelcome visitors. Rosamund could see that Andrew had seated himself with the newcomers and she observed, even from this distance, with the length of the hall between them, the grim expression of his countenance.

Before she could make any reply to Sir Simon, the stair door behind the dais was jerked open and Arthur stormed into the hall. He stamped up to the high table and stood glaring down at their visitor.

'What is he doing here?' he demanded furiously. 'How dare he intrude on our grief!'

Rosamund reached out a hand to stem further abuse, but Sir Simon forestalled her by rising and saying mildly, 'I hope that you will offer me a suitable chamber for the night, Master Kinnersley, as I am aware that the manor is yours now.'

Arthur opened his mouth to protest and Rosamund said hurriedly, 'I think it best if we accommodate you in the gatehouse chamber, Sir Simon. The room is comfortable and I believe you will find it acceptable for all your needs throughout your stay. I take it you are attended by the young man I met in your tent.'

'Yes, Rolf Taylor is with me and will see to my needs. You will have no need to put your household servants out unduly.'

Again Rosamund saw that Arthur was about to explode into speech and said quickly, 'Sir Simon comes as the Duke of Gloucester's representative, Arthur, and it behoves us to ensure his comfort and that of his men. I will explain to you later.'

She rose to signify that, as far as she was concerned, their talk was over.

Sir Simon rose also, somewhat reluctantly, she thought. 'If someone could show me to my chamber, I will take

myself from your presence. I'm sure that you still have
many matters on your mind, Mistress Kinnersley. I see that
my men are being adequately cared for and for that I thank
you. I trust that I will be able to make my respects to Lady
Kinnersley in the morning.'

Rosamund was still at a loss as to how to handle this
situation correctly. She could see that Arthur was barely
concealing his fury and that Andrew, too, was angry at this
intrusion. She said quietly, 'I hope you will sleep well, sir.
My stepmother will be better prepared to meet with you
in the morning.'

He nodded and Andrew Murton stepped forward to escort him back to the gatehouse. They had got halfway to
the screen doors when the door behind the dais was opened
and Sibyl Kinnersley stood framed in the entrance. The
light from a flaming torch behind her fell full on to her
flowing fair hair and the splendour of her blue brocaded
bedgown, which complemented the blue of her eyes. Her
mouth was slightly open in a little gasp of surprise.

'What is this, Rosa?' she demanded in her light, girlish
voice. 'I woke suddenly and thought that I heard the clash
of arms outside my window, the trampling of horses and
voices of men and dreaded to think that we had been invaded by a company of marauders. Martha was nowhere
near to answer my questions or to subdue my fears. Who
is this stranger?'

Immediately Sir Simon stepped gallantly forward and
bowed to her.

'I apologise for my late arrival, Lady Kinnersley, and
trust that you have not been unduly alarmed. I have been
sent by the Duke of Gloucester to ensure that what you
fear will not happen. I realise that you are feeling insecure
here and have come with a company of men to help protect
you and your family in your time of need.'

It was a smooth speech and Rosamund inwardly congratulated him on the ease of its presentation. Lady Kinnersley's beautiful blue eyes rounded in surprise as she looked him over, noting his broad shoulders, authoritative manner and presentable appearance. Apparently he had reassured her and she offered him a tentative hand in greeting, which he bent to kiss. The bedgown fell slightly open and Rosamund saw his gaze move to the voluptuous splendour of her lovely form accentuated by the fine cambric of her nightrail. She presented a picture of a vulnerable and grieving widow as tears formed on her lashes and she gave him a little wistful smile. Rosamund could see that he was totally dazzled by Sibyl's beauty and, for the moment, uncertain how to proceed with his explanation.

She cut in hastily. 'This is Sir Simon Cauldwell, my lady. I think that I referred to him briefly when I told you how considerate he was to Arthur and me in Tewkesbury. He it was, with the Duke of Gloucester's permission, who felicitated the conveyance of Father's body to Kinnersley. He is charged by the duke to protect the manor from the possibility of attack from—from any enemy of the king.'

Sibyl's lucent eyes shone in the torchlight and her mouth trembled. 'I hope,' she said brokenly, 'that his Grace the king does not consider us here as enemies. I am a simple woman, Sir Simon, and know nothing of court intrigues. My husband, it is true, went out to fight for the queen, as he considered the Earl of Warwick his liege lord. He considered that it was his duty to do so, even after the earl's death. I dread to think that the king or the duke might find my stepson culpable and hold any of us responsible for my husband's views.'

'I am sure no such thought was in the Duke of Gloucester's mind, Lady Kinnersley, when he dispatched me here; only the need for the interests of so young an heir to be safeguarded.'

She gave a little sigh of relief. 'Then, sir, you are welcome. I trust that your comfort is being assured.'

'Indeed it is, my lady.' He bowed again. 'Mistress Kinnersley has arranged everything.'

She nodded graciously. 'Then, if you will excuse me, I will return to my chamber, sir, and speak with you again in the morning. You must forgive my—seeming distraction. You know that my husband's funeral took place only today.'

'I am well aware of that, Lady Kinnersley, and I assure you that I shall make every effort not to intrude upon your privacy at this sad time.'

She turned and bestowed upon the company a little smile of appreciation and then turned and left them. Sir Simon remained, staring after her, evidently affected by her air of complete vulnerability and his shock at discovering her extreme youth and beauty.

There was a short silence for a moment after her departure, then Andrew, catching Rosamund's eye, moved once more slightly towards the screen doors as a signal that he was now ready to escort Sir Simon to his chamber in the gatehouse. She inclined her head a little as he murmured, once more, his gratitude for her hospitality, then went with their squire. Rosamund kept a firm hand upon Arthur's arm to prevent him uttering any other protest.

Once they were alone he burst out, 'Why should we have to put up with this man's presence? It is an insult, so soon after Father's death. He is an agent of the Yorkist king and—'

'And the Yorkist king is firmly seated upon the throne and we dare not object to whatever he decides to do,' she said quietly. 'Arthur, I know how upset you are, but you must be circumspect. As yet there has been no threat to our occupation of Kinnersley as there might well have

been. Our stepmother saw the need to be welcoming to
our visitor and so must we.'

'She would!' he declared bitterly.

'Arthur, she is as upset as the rest of us at the loss of
our father. We must be patient and leave her to her grief.'

He turned away, biting his lip, and she saw that he was
struggling with what he considered unmanly tears. 'What
are we to do, Rosa? Shall we lose Kinnersley, do you
think?'

'I do not know, Arthur,' she said, 'but the Duke of
Gloucester is now in charge of our wardship and he has
not shown himself as a vindictive man.'

'There are tales amongst the servants that he deliberately
sought out the Prince of Wales and killed him on the battlefield.'

Rosamund blinked, shocked. 'But there can be no con-
firmation of such a charge. Battles are so violent and con-
fusing it would be impossible to know who killed whom.'
She added shakily, 'We shall never know who dealt the
fatal blow which killed our father and I pray God that we
never shall. That knowledge, and the feeling of hatred towards that person which accompanies such knowledge,
would be too terrible to bear.'

'It could have been him, Sir Simon,' Arthur muttered
mutinously.

Rosamund passed no comment. Tears were pricking at
her lashes again and, as Arthur stamped off moodily once
more towards his own chamber, she reflected on the accusation he had made against Duke Richard. She had heard
her father say that the duke had wished to marry his
cousin, the Lady Anne, as his brother had her sister, the
Lady Isabel Neville, but then the earl, her father, had re-
voked his allegiance to the House of York. She had been
married to the Prince of Wales in an effort to bind the
queen to the earl's cause. Had Duke Richard then made it

his business to personally see that she was widowed at Tewkesbury? Battles were opportunities for men to seek revenge for past ills and it was possible that the duke had been tempted to further his own interests—for both the Lady Anne and her sister, Isabel, were joint heiresses to the great Warwick lands and riches. Rosamund turned towards the screen doors where Sir Simon had exited the hall and wondered about his allegiance to such a duke. Somehow she did not think that he would harbour such dishonourable beliefs concerning the man in whose service he was.

She sighed heavily. These last few days had drained her emotions totally, and today most particularly. Lady Sibyl had appeared to be utterly incapable of assuming responsibility for the household and it had fallen upon Rosamund to make the final arrangements for the funeral rites. Now had come this final blow, the arrival of the man who had occupied her thoughts so completely since their encounter at Tewkesbury. Had they anything to fear from his sudden arrival? She prayed that they had not. Should the duke decide to sequester the manor, which was his right to do, she hoped with all her soul that the disagreeable duty to inform her and see to its acquisition to the Crown was not left in the hands of Sir Simon Cauldwell.

She went wearily to her own chamber to find Martha waiting for her.

'Martha, you have had enough to do today. I can manage to undress myself. You get to your own bed.'

Martha clucked disparagingly. 'You are still my nurseling and you need a deal of cossetting tonight, I'm thinking.'

Rosamund was too tired to argue and, indeed, she felt the need of a confidante, so she stood docilely while her former nurse divested her of her mourning gown, her hennin and black veil, and helped her don her linen nightshift.

She sank thankfully down upon her bed as Martha folded the garments carefully and laid them ready for the morning upon her dressing chest. Rosamund thought, ruefully, that Simon Cauldwell had never once laid eyes upon her when she was looking her best. Black, she felt, was not a colour that suited her. Unlike Sibyl, she did not possess that delicate pink-and-white complexion or that shining mass of silky fair hair. She was a very plain little brown mouse. Conversely she was annoyed with herself that such a thought had crossed her mind at this time of tragedy. What in the world did it matter how she appeared to Simon Cauldwell? He was here to fulfil his mission for the duke, not to become reacquainted with her. Indeed, he had probably not given her a second thought while he had been waiting on his duke at Coventry and the sight of her, here, had come as much a shock to him as this new encounter had come to her.

Martha glanced at her shrewdly and came to stand before her, brawny arms folded.

'This knight is the man you met in Tewkesbury?'

'Yes.'

'I could see that he made quite an impression upon you.'

'And upon Lady Sibyl,' Rosamund commented drily.

'Aye.'

Martha considered for a moment. 'He is the last man you were expecting and, probably, the last man you would want to see at this time.'

'What makes you think that? He was very helpful to me in Tewkesbury, especially in the arrangements concerning the conveyance of Father's body home.'

'But he is a Yorkist knight. Arthur is very well aware of that fact and his hostility is going to makes things hard for all of us.'

'Arthur will have to be made to hold his tongue,' Rosamund exclaimed sharply. 'He will put us all in danger if he does not.'

'The lad is in a vulnerable state of mind. He has lost most of all he holds dear,' Martha reminded her mildly.

'I know that.' Rosamund sighed. 'So have we all, yet this man is not one to stand for any nonsense, even from one so young as Arthur.'

'Oh?' Martha's eyebrows rose in concern. 'You have experienced his anger?'

'Yes—no, well, not exactly,' Rosamund floundered. Feeling Martha's steely gaze upon her, she stumbled out her story, finishing, her own eyes averted, with the tale of how she had been mistaken for a follower in the baggage train and a possible looter of the dead.

Martha came closer, seated herself upon the bed beside her nurseling and gathered her into her arms. 'My heart's darling,' she choked, 'how terrified you must have been.' She tilted up Rosamund's chin and looked deep into her eyes, now wet with tears of remembrance. 'Did he—did he harm you? Do not be afraid to tell me the truth.'

Rosamund shook her head vehemently. 'No, he realised—just in time, but—oh, Martha, it was not his behaviour which alarms me but—but my own response...'

'Ah.' Martha hugged her still closer. 'Hush now, child. Give your heart peace. You are coming to full womanhood and this was the first time you knew—dreamed of how strong an emotion this can be. You have nothing to be ashamed of. All maids are confused at such a time and you were in deep distress and afraid. No wonder that you did not know how to deal with all this.'

'I—I fought him with all my strength and...'

'And, praise the Virgin, he realised just how innocent you are.'

'I slept within his tent,' Rosamund whispered.

Martha's eyes narrowed thoughtfully. 'Then we are

dealing with a truly honourable man who wishes you naught but well. Now you must rest and try to sleep. Too much has happened today, so that all of us will find it hard to face this new threat with fortitude. In the morning things will seem clearer. And, meanwhile, leave young Master Arthur to me. I'll do my best to make him see sense.'

She waited until Rosamund had climbed into bed and tucked her in, as she had when Rosamund was a child, then, clucking consolingly, she slipped from the room after extinguishing the bedside rush light.

Simon examined his gatehouse quarters with a wry smile. Certainly they were adequate and had obviously been used by Sir Humphrey's captain-at-arms. There was a cot beside the wall, which appeared to be reasonably comfortable, and the linen was clean and smelled fresh. Beside it was a chest to contain the occupant's personal belongings and a joint stool. The limewashed walls were somewhat spartan and the hooks hammered into them bare of clothing. Apparently the captain had taken all his belongings with him on the march to Tewkesbury and had not returned to the manor house or all trace of his occupation had been removed recently. Rolf Taylor, who had followed his master into the room, placed the saddle-bag containing Sir Simon's baggage upon the chest and eyed the chamber's stark appearance doubtfully.

Simon sank on to the bed and nodded to the gatehouse room opposite. 'Well, it seems that Mistress Kinnersley is anxious to place us as far from the rest of the family and household as possible. That is to be expected.' He grinned. 'You can occupy the room opposite, so the squire informs me.'

'Would it not be wiser for me to sleep here upon the floor with you or outside the door, sir?'

'Heavens, lad, I'm not expecting an attack upon my life;

even if I were, I am perfectly capable of dealing with it.' His expression was comical. 'I'll not be welcomed, especially by the boy, but Mistress Kinnersley will not allow him or any member of the household to behave disrespectfully. The men are settled?'

'Yes, sir. The sergeant saw to that and the horses have been cared for.'

'Good, then I suggest we both retire for the night and inspect the manor lands in the morning. I could see the garrison is sadly depleted. Let us hope that the remaining company is not undisciplined. Off you go, lad.'

The boy hesitated in the doorway. 'Do you wish me to unpack, sir, and help you undress?'

'No, the morning will do and I am not fully armed. Get some rest.'

Rolf saluted and withdrew. Simon divested himself of his sword belt and weapons and drew off his padded brigandine. He noted that someone had placed a jug of wine upon the chest and a tankard. He poured and swallowed gratefully.

This was a pretty task the duke had set him. The household was an odd one, although the attitude of the residents could be understood, being in mourning as they were. The widow was unexpectedly beautiful and so young, scarcely older than her stepdaughter, and the boy clearly resented her presence in the house. He could feel that, along with his hostility to Simon's arrival with his Yorkist company. How had Rosamund received him? She had been surprised, even shocked, but did she, too, regard him as an enemy? It was clear to him that, for the moment at least, Rosamund was in charge of the household. The stepmother had either given up her authority under the stress of grief temporarily or had never taken the reins of the government of the manor completely into her hands. It would be interesting to find out what the relationships between stepmother and children were. He sipped his wine appreciatively. The young squire was held in respect, obviously. The boy hero-worshipped him. Did Rosamund Kinnersley have a special regard for him, too? Simon sighed. He would have to exert his authority and that could be resented. Only time would tell. The situation could be grave. The boy was vulnerable. The stepmother might not be satisfied with her dower rights. She had expected to reign here longer, but the boy would want her to move out of the manor. That was obvious. The duke had seen the difficulties here and the situation was made much harder by the fact that the realm was still unsettled and the boy would continue to need a guardian, one he would not accept willingly, if that man was Yorkist.

Simon completed his undressing and extinguished the rush light. Lying on the narrow cot, which was as comfortable, at least, as the one in his battle tent had been, he thought of Rosamund Kinnersley as he had beheld her in the glow of the gatehouse torches. The light had revealed the severity of her mourning attire and the pallor of her skin. She looked tired and confused and he had longed to reach out and comfort her, but he must wait his time. Rosamund was concerned for the boy and the future of the manor. It would be for him to convince her that she had no need to fear him or the designs of Duke Richard.

Chapter Six

When Rosamund entered the hall for breakfast early next morning she found that it was almost deserted. There was no sign of Sir Simon Cauldwell or of his young attendant, and the servants were already clearing from the trestles the detritus of the early meals that had been eaten by the men of Sir Simon's company. Arthur entered briskly behind her and gazed around in astonishment.

'Where are they all? I suppose it would be too much to hope that they have ridden out and left us.'

Rosamund laughed. 'I am sure you are right. It is too much to hope.'

She signalled to one of the servants. 'Has Sir Simon breakfasted already?'

'Yes, mistress. He and his attendant came down very early and he ate quickly and rousted out all his men to patrol the manor.'

'I see.' She nodded. 'Carry on with your work and serve us with breakfast as soon as you can.'

Martha came to the dais a few moments later to serve them, with the news that she had taken a breakfast tray to Lady Sibyl in her chamber. Rosamund sighed while Arthur scowled.

'Martha, it is time that she emerged and made it clear who is to run this household. I do not like to give orders in her absence, but I have been forced to do so lately.'

Arthur said, 'Surely she will soon move out and leave us to ourselves.'

'But where would she go, Arthur? It is too soon yet. There are still things to be decided. Our father's man of business should come from Warwick to explain the manor accounts and to read our father's will. We have no dower house to which Lady Sibyl could retire.'

'She could return to her father's house in Warwick.'

'I doubt that she would wish to do that.'

Arthur smeared honey on to white manchet bread fresh from the oven. 'I expect she will marry again soon and surely her father will arrange that for her.'

Rosamund watched him thoughtfully. Arthur could not wait to rid himself of his stepmother's hateful presence, but she did not believe that things would arrange themselves as simply as that. Sibyl would most likely be a wealthy widow and would take her own time about arrangements for her future and they could hardly ask her to leave Kinnersley. Another thought struck her, which she was unwilling to share with Arthur. Sibyl had been closeting herself within her chamber recently, declaring herself unwell. Was it possible that she was carrying Sir Humphrey's child?

She looked up sharply as she heard the ring of spurs on stone and Sir Simon Cauldwell marched into the hall. It was the first time she had seen him divested of armour. He was clad now in a leather jacket over a plain linen shirt and hose of brown homespun wool. The leather, she noted, was rubbed and well worn. Obviously it had seen much service on campaigns. Rosamund hastily signed to Arthur to be prudent and gestured to a seat at the high table.

'I hear that you have been out inspecting the manor, Sir

Simon,' she said quietly. 'I hope you found matters satisfactory.'

Sir Simon nodded to Arthur, hooked forward a joint stool and seated himself. Martha came to his side and served him with ale. He drank deep and wiped his mouth. 'That is good. It is hot out there for early May.' He regarded Rosamund gravely over the rim of his tankard. 'The men are behind with the field work, which is to be expected since many of your work force were away with your father. Your reeve appears to have the matter in hand and seems to be a sensible hard-working man. I have left affairs in his hands. I am concerned about your garrison, which is badly depleted. My men will supplement a guard for the time being, but if your men-at-arms do not return in force you will need to recruit mercenaries.'

Her eyes widened. 'You think that we could still be attacked, now that King Edward has won his victories?'

He shook his head. 'The realm will be unsettled for months, particularly in this area so near to Tewkesbury. There will be men who crawled away wounded who will recover and need to live off the land. They will soon hear the rumours of which manors are at risk. We need to take care.' He glanced briefly at Arthur, who was listening intently. 'Your lord is young and will need help to manage so large a manor, but that will be arranged.'

'I will have help,' Arthur declared frostily. 'Andrew will know how to advise me and—'

'I was coming to the matter of Master Murton,' Sir Simon cut in smoothly. 'He was your father's squire and is now masterless. I expect he will wish to move out shortly and find himself another knight to serve.'

Rosamund stared at him blankly. She had never envisioned the loss of Andrew Murton's company. He had been at the manor some time now, and she relied upon him and looked to him for guidance, as she was sure that Sibyl did.

Before Arthur could expostulate she said hurriedly, 'Master Murton has been invaluable in the service of my father and he has been helping to train my brother to arms. I hope he will not see the need to leave us yet.'

She encountered the startlingly blue, intense gaze of Sir Simon and flushed and looked away. Did he believe that she held tender feelings for Andrew? If so, he was very wrong. The man was her father's doughty companion and she looked upon him as a true friend. She would be totally lost here at Kinnersley without him.

Arthur blustered. 'Andrew cannot leave us. We need him...'

'There will be no need for haste,' Sir Simon said quietly, 'but you must realise, Master Kinnersley, that for his own preferment, Master Murton will need to look for a new household and a master who might, in time, give him the opportunity to win his spurs. Indeed,' he added smilingly, 'soon we shall need to place you, also, within a noble household, where you can perfect your skill at arms, very necessary for your security in these hard times.'

Rosamund felt a sudden clutch of ice around her heart. Must she soon lose Arthur, too? Events were happening far too quickly and all brought about by the interference of this man, who had appeared so suddenly and dramatically in her life. She tilted her chin and gazed back at him defiantly. She would not allow her wishes to be overridden so easily.

'I do not think that Arthur is ready to leave his home at the moment,' she said icily, 'and you are hardly the person to advise him, since you scarcely know him.'

'That is very true. The circumstances are exceptional, but so are conditions within the realm and here on the manor. We must think what is best for your brother.' He rose and pushed back the stool with a grating sound. 'You will want to be equipped to serve in battle and protect what is your own when the time comes, will you not, Master Kinnersley?'

Arthur nodded reluctantly.

'Well, we will keep that matter well in hand. Meanwhile, I will go to your stepmother's chamber where she has asked to see me. I can make my report to her and see what she has to say.'

He had stalked from the hall before Rosamund could find the words to gainsay him further. Arthur scrambled to his feet and made to go after him, but she called him back.

'It is useless to argue. At present Sir Simon is in charge here. We must bide our time.'

He came back to the table and, leaning down, laid his two hands flat. She could see that he was crimson-faced with temper.

'I will be rid of him—soon,' he grated. 'Somehow I will find a way. He will not order me so, or try to get rid of Andrew. He is our one friend here and will guard our interests.' He looked thoughtfully at his sister as he straightened. 'Did Father ever broach the matter of a marriage for you—with Andrew?'

She looked up, startled. 'Certainly not.'

'But would it not be a suitable match? You like Andrew, do you not, and he would be able to continue here...'

'That would not serve,' Rosamund said uneasily. 'Kinnersley is yours and the wife you take one day will not wish for the presence of a sister and her husband here.'

He waved that thought away irritably. 'That will be for me to decide. I will be master here and no one will dictate to me about who lives here and who does not. The man is right. You must marry, and soon, and Andrew is of a suitable age and...'

Hastily Rosamund put her hand over his and drew him

down to his chair again. 'Not so fast, little brother. Like you, I am in no mood to be dictated to, not even by a brother whom I love dearly.'

'But Andrew is handsome and brave and—'

'And needs to make his way in the world. We do not know yet whether Father has made arrangements for a dowry for me.'

'Well, if not, I must see to it,' Arthur retorted grandly. 'You are my responsibility now.'

She shook her head, smiling. 'We will see. Go and enquire after the welfare of Tom for me and, for the present, keep out of Sir Simon's way. Do not antagonise him. He can make life difficult for us and we do not want that, do we?'

He grinned broadly, reached for an apple from a dish on the table, and walked out of the hall whistling loudly.

Rosamund sat back in her chair and sighed. She felt that she was doing that a great deal lately. She wondered how much business sense Sir Simon would gain from Lady Sibyl or if she would understand any that he might impart. Her thoughts went to Andrew Murton and she grimaced slightly. Poor Andrew! Arthur was deciding his future for him without so much as a by your leave.

Marriage for her with Andrew might not prove too disastrous. As Arthur had said, he was young and personable and capable of protecting her interests. He had shown a dutiful respect to her. Once or twice she thought she had seen him gazing at her intently, but never once had he attempted any intimacy, not even so much as a touch in passing. Of course, his duty was to his dead lord and he would have waited for some sign that Sir Humphrey regarded him in any way as a possible suitor for his daughter before making any suggestion that might indicate his feelings for Rosamund. She rose and prepared to go about her own duties in the kitchen, dairy and buttery. She had the uncomfortable feeling that the Duke of Gloucester now held her future happiness within his grasp—and he would be advised by Sir Simon Cauldwell!

She was about to leave the hall when Lady Sibyl entered from behind the dais. It was clear that she was in a decidedly agitated state.

'Rosamund, I must speak with you urgently.'

Rosamund came back to the table. 'Yes, of course. What can I do for you, Lady Sibyl? I was about to go to the kitchen—'

'That can wait. I have just been speaking to that man.'

'Sir Simon Cauldwell?'

'Yes, I had forgotten his name and rank for the moment. Rosamund, he says he wishes to arrange for Andrew Murton to leave Kinnersley.'

'Yes, he mentioned that to me.'

'But he mustn't leave Kinnersley—Andrew, I mean.'

Rosamund stared back at her somewhat astonished. Lady Sibyl Kinnersley rarely was known to show any extreme emotion and now she was obviously deeply distressed.

'I said as much to Sir Simon, but—'

'It is vital that he remain here. He has proved himself our most loyal friend and Arthur is very fond of him.'

'Yes, I know.'

'He has been instrumental in preparing Arthur for his training at arms. He will miss him sorely and, to make matters worse, the man is talking of removing Arthur from Kinnersley very shortly, placing him in some noble household.' Sibyl's blue eyes were drawn wide with distress. Rosamund was puzzled. Sibyl Kinnersley had never expressed any concern for Arthur before. Indeed, the boy had not made any secret of his dislike of his stepmother and Rosamund would have thought that Sibyl would be delighted if he were to be removed from her presence immediately.

She said quietly, 'Naturally I am very alarmed by the prospect of both of them leaving. In time, I suppose, we must accept the fact that Andrew Murton will leave us. He has his way to make in the world and we should not stand in his way but, as you observe, Arthur is by no means ready to leave his home. I, for one, would be desolate without him. We must both impress our wishes in this matter on Sir Simon. I imagine that there has been no time to make any definite arrangements. We have time to convince him that it would be the wrong thing for Arthur, for the present, at any rate.'

'Yes, and for Andrew.' Sibyl was clearly distraught. For once she had not taken the usual pains with her appearance. Her widow's wimple was awry and strands of her fair hair poked untidily from beneath her hennin.

Instinctively Rosamund reached out to touch her hand in comfort. 'We are all too upset to face these changes yet awhile but—' she drew a hard breath '—we have to face the unpleasant fact that our futures do not lie in our own hands. We must do nothing to annoy our—appointed *seneschal.*' She emphasised the last word and knew that Sibyl had taken her meaning, that, for her, the word should have been—jailer.

'But you know him better than I. You must speak with him, Rosamund, make him understand our needs.'

'Yes, when the time is convenient I will try—'

'No, no, before more harm is done.'

Rosamund's hazel eyes were widening in surprise. She had never known her stepmother in this guise before. Was the woman more fond of Arthur than Rosamund could have believed? Certainly she was very anxious to have him remain here in his own home. This, too, was her own wish. She could not bear to think of losing Arthur. Everything she loved and valued seemed to be slipping from her grasp. She bit her lip uncertainly. She had no desire to deliberately search out Simon Cauldwell. Indeed, she had every intention of avoiding him as much as possible, but Sibyl had made it plain that to assert herself now was essential. She nodded. 'I will try to find him and do my utmost to impress upon him that he must do nothing in a hurry.'

Sibyl drew a relieved breath and sat down at the table. Glancing at her, Rosamund saw that her stepmother's hands were trembling.

She decided that she should say nothing more. She could not promise to change Simon Cauldwell's mind. Indeed, it was very unlikely that she could influence him in the slightest. She gave a faint sigh and Sibyl looked up at her sharply.

'You will do your best? He did help you once before, over the question of returning your father's body.'

'For that we have to thank his Grace of Gloucester as much as Sir Simon. He it was who provided the bier for Father. Certainly Sir Simon showed me a measure of courtesy when we met in Tewkesbury, but I doubt that he can be brought to change his mind over anything he has once decided.'

Sibyl's lips curved in a wistful smile of regret and Rosamund wondered if she was the best person to plead with Sir Simon. That childlike smile had been known to melt the coldest heart.

She walked slowly from the hall. She would go to the kitchen first and ensure that the men of Sir Simon's company were being comfortably accommodated. It would not do for there to be any complaints from that quarter. Then, reluctantly, she would seek out their commander.

She completed her duties overseeing the kitchen servants, talking with the cook, making sure that the dairy maids had set the milk and newly churned butter to cool within pans of water, and then turned her steps again to the courtyard. It was likely that Sir Simon would either be in his lodging within the gatehouse or in the stables. He proved to be in neither and his sergeant informed her that he did not know where his master was. Rosamund was not sure whether she felt disappointed or relieved by this intelligence. She only knew that she had striven to put off this encounter as long as possible.

The day was again hot and she felt stifled in her mourning gown of black fine worsted and made her way to a shaded arbour in the small pleasance her father had had made for her mother. One or two early roses were budding and she plucked a red one and sank on to a bench, twiddling the stem between her fingers while she plucked up the courage to go in search of Sir Simon once more.

Her mind was troubled and in turmoil. She castigated herself bitterly that she seemed almost unable to grieve for her father as she felt she should. His second marriage had placed an insurmountable barrier between them during the later months of his life and she and Arthur had drawn closer together for comfort. Tears started to her eyes as she thought how soon she could be parted from her brother.

She tried to sort out why she was so reluctant to find Simon Cauldwell. Of course, trying to convince him that he must allow Arthur and Andrew to remain at the manor would not be easy, and she was not at all sure that she was the one to do it. His nearness disturbed her, as she had confided to Martha the previous night, and her own response to it was almost frightening. Certainly she considered him her father's enemy, but that fact she could have handled coolly. No, she could not forget how he had misjudged her, thought her wanton, and her frantic fight with him within his tent. Certainly he had been the soul of courtesy since, but there was no doubt in her mind that she was afraid of him—or was she afraid of herself? Martha had explained that the strange, intense feelings the man aroused in her were not unusual to a girl on the threshold of womanhood confronted by a personable young man for the first time. She was not so sure that was true. She had been close to young men before, Andrew Murton for one, but they had never brought out in her this dual response of anger and fascination.

So intent was she on her own doleful fears that she did not hear someone approach the bench, and started up as she recognised the authoritative voice of the man she had been seeking and who had been occupying her thoughts to the exclusion of everything else.

'Mistress Rosamund, my sergeant tells me you have been looking for me. I hope nothing is wrong, that my men are not causing your household any trouble.'

She shook her head mutely and he saw at once that she had been weeping.

'Rosamund, what ails you? Ah,' he said quickly, 'that was crass of me. I intrude on your grief. Forgive me. I will come to you later when you are more composed.'

'No,' she said, hastily dabbing at her eyes with her bare knuckle, 'please, do not go. I was looking for you. There is no trouble. Your men have been excellently behaved. It is just that I—that is, all of us are deeply distressed by your plans to remove my brother from the manor.' Her voice was choked with tears. 'You must understand he is everything to me. You cannot part us—not now.'

He sank down before her in a crouch and put a hand upon her arm. 'Please, do not cry, Rosamund. Everything can be resolved, for the present at least.'

Instinctively she flinched from his touch and instantly he removed his hand.

'Do not touch me.'

He stood up and stared down at her, his dark brows drawing together in a frown.

'Mistress Rosamund, you are not afraid of me, are you? I have come here to protect you all from possible harm. You must not fear any consequences of your father's past loyalties. I have already explained that to you. Neither Duke Richard nor his brother, the king, would hold your young brother responsible for his father's acts and certainly you must know that you are in no danger from any personal act of mine.'

She was confused and turned from him. 'No, no, that was foolish of me. I did not mean to… Please, do not take offence. I am upset. This has been an unsettling day.'

He distanced himself slightly from her. 'My arrival here has been an added burden.'

She nodded. 'We need time, my brother and I, to take stock of our situation. As you have said, the realm is still at war, or at least will be until all armies have been disbanded. I fear for the manor and for Arthur.'

'Believe me, Mistress Rosamund, I intend no harm to your brother, rather I wish to install him in some noble house where he can be safe until he is old enough to take up the reins here.'

'But what of me?' Her cry was from the heart. 'I have needs. I want Arthur with me, for a while at least. You must see that. And my father's squire is a true friend to him. To separate him from Andrew now and from me would be too much for Arthur to bear. He is only twelve years old.'

He glanced at her sharply. 'This man, your father's squire, you have a fondness for him? There is some understanding between you?'

'Oh no.' Her eyes opened very wide and he could see that she was disturbed by the question. 'Andrew has proved himself our friend, nothing more.'

'Your father had made no marriage contract for you?'

She bridled immediately. These matters were not his concern. 'He did not speak of any such,' she replied stiffly. 'Doubtless he had a suitable match in mind, but he was occupied with more important matters.'

'Indeed, he was,' he commented dryly. 'Then your future is not assured and it will be for his Grace of Gloucester, in his position as Lord Constable of England, to provide for you.'

She said, so very softly that he was forced to bend to catch the words, 'Until my father's man of business arrives here to read his will, I will have no idea whether there is any provision made for a marriage contract, a suitable dowry…'

He gave a little Gallic shrug. 'You are young and personable. Matters can be arranged. Do not concern yourself about that.'

She glanced at him uncertainly and, as if to reassure her, he smiled that wonderfully engaging smile that lit up his stern countenance. His startlingly blue eyes sparkled mischievously.

'As for your brother, leave that matter to me. We will talk later and, be assured, I will do nothing to give you more pain at this time, I promise.'

She felt a sudden warmth of feeling for his consideration and, for the first time since learning of the death of her father, believed that here was someone she could trust.

She was about to thank him when the sound of a trumpet, coming from close to the manor, broke the silence. He turned sharply and she, too, rose to her feet. Both directed their attention to the guard on the gatehouse tower. Taking her hand, he drew her hurriedly from the pleasance towards the gatehouse entrance.

It proved to be one of Sir Simon's own men on guard

and he leaned down cheerily from the battlements at sight of him.

'It's his Grace of Gloucester, sir. I can see his banner of the White Boar clearly from here.'

Simon gave a sigh of relief, but Rosamund's face paled.

Sir Simon called for the drawbridge to be lowered at once and sent one of the household servants to summon Lady Sibyl and Master Arthur. He turned excitedly to Rosamund.

'He honours us greatly. He must be en route for London to join the king and yet he detours to see that the manor is in good hands.'

Rosamund said hesitantly, 'He will have a great force. I doubt if our household can accommodate—'

'Set your heart at rest. The duke will expect no great state, having arrived unexpectedly. Go at once to instruct your cook and your steward and return as quickly as you can in order to greet him when he arrives.' He glanced down hastily at his own work-a-day apparel of leathern jerkin over plain hose. 'I should go at once and make myself presentable.' He gave her a little push towards the keep steps. 'Hasten, mistress. If the van of the company is in sight we shall have little time.'

She turned reluctantly as he hurried to his own lodging in the gatehouse. It was very plain that he was excited by this visitation—no, actually delighted. His loyalty to his lord was great and she could see that it was indeed more than that. There was genuine friendship between Simon and the king's brother. She loitered across the courtyard then, seeing the hurry and bustle in stable, dairy and buttery at the sudden news, broke into a run and headed towards the kitchens. It was vital that this unwelcome and unexpected visitor was well received. Lifting her skirts as she mounted the keep steps towards the hall, she thought, with trepidation, that she was not the only one who wished

Richard of Gloucester elsewhere. How would Arthur take her news?

The cook was in a dither and began instantly berating his assistants but, when she sharply called him to order, he assured her that everything would be ready and acceptable to serve the duke and his companions dinner. She turned back into the hall to find that Martha was instructing the servants to lay fresh damask cloths upon the table and their finest tableware must be produced hastily. While Rosamund was watching the preparations with a critical eye, Lady Sibyl appeared and, behind her, Arthur.

'Is it true?' she demanded, her voice shrill with excitement. 'Is it really the duke who is approaching?'

'Apparently,' Rosamund replied. She looked Arthur over to see if he was presentable and sighed as she perceived that he certainly was not. He looked as if he had but just come from the stable and wore his oldest clothes, which were muddied and torn, and his hair was rumpled and showed signs of contact with the stable straw.

'Arthur, go at once and tidy yourself,' she scolded. 'Put on your mourning black-velvet doublet. Hurry! The duke will arrive at any moment and you, as lord of the manor, should be at the gate to greet him.'

'I do not see why I should be,' he countered sulkily, 'I did not invite him. He is the enemy of my father and not welcome here.'

'You stupid boy,' Rosamund stormed. 'He is the brother of your sovereign. Guard your tongue and go and do what I say.' She caught at his arm and aimed him once more towards the stair and his own chamber. 'Go, now.'

'Really,' Lady Sibyl said disgustedly, 'the boy is impossible. Would he put all of us at risk by his foolish tantrums?'

Arthur, propelled suddenly off balance by his sister's push, recovered himself and turned to stare at his stepmother venomously. Before he could argue further, Rosamund again seized his arm and hurried him towards the stair. At the foot he halted momentarily and was about to snap at her then, noting her grim expression, gave a boyish offhand shrug and mounted, though still unwillingly.

Sibyl Kinnersley had taken a miniature glass mirror from the pocket of her gown and was examining her appearance anxiously, straightening her hennin and adjusting her veil.

'It is a great pity,' she mused, 'that we must all be in this hideous black scarecrow guise at such a time.'

Rosamund could find no answer to this remark. Her whole attention was on how Arthur would greet the duke. He was not in a conciliatory mood. Automatically she brushed down her own gown which she thought must be somewhat rumpled and Sibyl reached over to straighten her stepdaughter's veil. 'You will do,' she said critically. 'You have the composure we all need.'

Rosamund wished that she really felt composed, but, again, she made no answer and the two began to make their way to the hall entrance. They had reached the gatehouse when the first riders of the company were mounting the lowered drawbridge. Sir Simon turned and acknowledged the ladies with a curt nod and with raised eyebrows in Rosamund's direction as he saw that her young brother was not yet accompanying them.

Breathily Rosamund said, 'I sent Arthur to change. He should be here very soon.'

Duke Richard rode into the courtyard flanked by his two companions, Richard Ratcliffe and Robert Percy. He was not in armour, but wore a padded purple doublet and a black velvet hat in which an amethyst smouldered. Simon hastened forward as he dismounted and a Kinnersley groom took the lead rein of his destrier deferentially.

Simon knelt in the dust and Duke Richard put down a strong arm to lift him to his feet, laughing.

'You never knelt to me at Middleham, Simon. If I recall, during those times there were occasions when you ordered me about less than deferentially.'

'I was then an older squire, your Grace, and must request that you try to forget those occasions when I was forced to discipline you.'

Again the merry laugh rang out as the duke turned to survey the courtyard, the drawbridge and portcullis and the surrounding wall with its battlements and watch-tower.

'I was right to think this manor is a prize worth the taking, Simon, and needs careful guarding.'

'The garrison is somewhat depleted and I shall need to send for more men, but for the moment the men of my company are supplementing it and we shall manage. Allow me, my lord, to present Lady Kinnersley and her step-daughter, whom you met briefly in Tewkesbury.'

Sibyl Kinnersley and Rosamund approached and curtsied. The Duke's expression had become grave as he put out a hand to the widow. 'My condolences for your loss, Lady Kinnersley. There have been too many widows and orphaned children made by these recent engagements and I can only express the hope that the realm will soon lie quiet under its sovereign.' He turned his attention to Rosamund, who was rising slowly from her deep curtsy. 'I trust you reached home without incident, Mistress Rosamund, and that your father's obsequies were performed reverently.'

Rosamund was surprised that he remembered her name and stammered, 'Thank you, your Grace, for your assistance. My father's funeral took place yesterday and all went as could be expected.'

He nodded and took Sibyl's arm, indicating that she should lead him into the hall.

'I hope you will forgive this intrusion, Lady Kinnersley, but I decided to detour on my way to London to have speech with Sir Simon here. He has my trust and will hold this manor safe for the king until arrangements can be made for a seneschal appointed by the crown. I wished to see for myself that all was in order, having learned that your stepson is very young, just twelve years old, I understand. He will need a deal of help both in handling his manor and in his own training.' He gave a faint sigh. 'We cannot, any of us, afford to be remiss in preparing ourselves for future combat in these hard times. Is Master Kinnersley away from home?'

The question was mildly put, but Rosamund blushed hotly. It implied gently that the boy was remiss in failing to present himself. How dared Arthur absent himself from this greeting! Before Sibyl could reply crossly, for Rosamund saw a frown deepen on her stepmother's brow, she hastily said, 'We were all unprepared for the honour you do us, your Grace, and my brother had just come in from riding and was in a dishevelled state. He went to change into more suitable clothing in which to greet you.'

Lady Sibyl nodded and added quickly, 'I hope you will honour us by staying for dinner, your Grace.'

'Indeed, I will be pleased to do so, though do not allow your household to be put out. My stay must be very brief. I need some time to talk privately with Sir Simon and then I shall be delighted if you would, both of you, and Master Kinnersley, join me in a simple repast.'

Both women curtsied once more as they entered the hall and stood back to allow Sir Simon to lead the duke to a cushioned armchair upon the dais. His two former companions with Simon took their seats near him. Rosamund and Sibyl withdrew to give the men privacy.

'I had forgotten how young he is,' Sibyl commented. 'Just eighteen, I believe, and already he has proved his valour and skill on the battlefield. He is much handsomer than I had supposed. I had heard that he had some physical defect, one shoulder higher than the other, but I could see no sign of it. Sir Simon appears to be very much in his favour.'

'Indeed,' Rosamund snapped tartly, 'and Arthur must be made to realise how important it is that he does not antagonise either of them.'

They repaired to Lady Sibyl's solar where they gave their attention to the stitching of one of the hall's tapestries, which was in need of some repair. Rosamund had issued instructions to Martha that if she saw Arthur he was to be told that he must not enter the hall unless summoned by one of the duke's attendants. She found it difficult to give her attention to the work in hand for she was worried about Arthur's attitude. He had deliberately absented himself from the courtyard so that he would not be forced to greet the duke. That was very plain. She sighed inwardly. Before the trumpet call that had announced the imminent arrival of the duke's company, she had believed that she and Sir Simon had come to some understanding regarding Arthur's future. Now that appeared to be imperilled by the boy's thoughtless behaviour.

It was Sir Simon's man, Rolf Taylor, who knocked upon the solar door and informed the ladies that dinner was about to be served in the hall and that his Grace of Gloucester had requested that they should attend him.

'Master Taylor, have you seen my brother?' Rosamund enquired as she and Sibyl folded the heavy tapestry and laid aside the hanks of embroidery wool.

'No, mistress. I imagine he is still within his chamber.'

Sibyl frowned and was about to expostulate when Rosamund requested, 'Will you ask one of my servants to take you to his door and insist that he presents himself in the hall? If he objects, tell him that I shall be very angry if he fails to appear for dinner.' She was about to add that Sir Simon would be even more angry, but thought that that intelligence might merely add fuel to the fire of Arthur's stubbornness.

The man gave a little bow and stood aside for the ladies to move from the chamber and down the stair.

The duke rose courteously, as did all the men, as they appeared, and insisted that Lady Kinnersley take her place on his right at table while Sir Simon drew out a chair for Rosamund on the duke's left.

Lady Sibyl gave the signal for dinner to be served and two of the youthful women of the household approached with bowls of scented water and towels to stand near the dais since they had no page in residence. Duke Richard rinsed his hands and set about the food appreciatively. Rosamund was relieved to see that her cook had done them proud, considering the shortness of the notice he had received. There were dishes of roast beef and poultry and the sauces, though not as rich or as varied as she thought the duke would have been served at court, were acceptable.

The duke chatted pleasantly to both women, enquiring about the state of the manor and nearby villages and if they expected reasonable harvest considering the engagement that had taken place so recently, interrupting the men's work. He praised the furnishing and condition of the manor house and the efficiency of the servants. Rosamund picked at the food with which Sir Simon, seated next to her, plied her, her thoughts abstracted. She looked anxiously towards the dais door for sign of Arthur. Had the man, Taylor, managed to find him? If so, it was insupportable of him to fail to appear now. She found Simon Cauldwell's eyes fixed warningly upon her and did not fail to note the stern line of his mouth. There would be a reckoning later. Her confidence ebbed by the moment. Lady

Sibyl, however, did not appear to be in the least concerned and was obviously enjoying this moment of glory with the presence of the royal duke, and having his attention directed at her.

Rosamund's eyes roved over the duke's companions seated at a lower table laughing and talking together, though circumspectly. Here was no drunken carousing or what she thought might be bawdy talk. It would seem that all were aware of the family's recent bereavement and comported themselves accordingly. She was grateful that neither Sir Simon nor any other of the young nobles at the table sought to engage her in talk, as their attention was directed to their lord's conversation with his hostess.

The door behind the dais was abruptly thrust open and Rosamund gave a sharp little cry, hastily repressed, as Arthur appeared in the entrance. As she had instructed, he had changed his apparel and looked elegant in his best mourning doublet of padded black velvet. The duke looked up as the sudden hush within the hall alerted his attention and laid down his goblet of malmsey.

Sir Simon rose to his feet instantly, his chair scraping harshly on the flagged floor and Rosamund half rose also.

'You are late, young sir,' Sir Simon grated. 'Make your humble apologies to his Grace immediately.'

Rosamund saw that her brother was turkey red with fury. As Sir Simon reached his side, for he had gone to the front of the high table, he shrugged off the grip upon his shoulder.

'Why should I?' he shouted, his voice shrill with temper. 'I am master here and I did not invite any of this company.'

There was a buzz of furious response as those of the duke's companions nearest to him jumped to their feet, their expressions revealing their sense of outrage. The duke, however, remained seated, his expression calm, his hand still upon his wine goblet.

'I regret that you should feel that we are unwelcome, Master Kinnersley,' he said mildly. 'We came to visit with our friend, Sir Simon Cauldwell, and to discover for ourselves that all is well at the manor.'

'It is my manor,' Arthur stormed.

'And unlikely to be so for much longer if you continue in this fashion,' Sir Simon snarled, pulling at his arm in an effort to withdraw him from the hall.

Lady Sibyl gave a great snort of disapproval and tugged at Rosamund's sleeve in an effort to persuade her to resume her seat, as the duke lifted one slender hand to indicate that he wished the meal to proceed without further disruption.

'The boy should be whipped,' she said pithily and Rosamund gave a little despairing cry.

'Master Kinnersley,' the duke said quietly, 'what have you against our presence here? No harm is intended to you or to any member of your household, but you must understand that you are under age and both you and your lands are under the protection of the Crown.'

Arthur had succeeded momentarily in freeing himself from Sir Simon's hold and leaned forward threateningly across the table, displacing some of the tableware and jerking at the damask cloth so that wine spilled like blood from one of the goblets.

'Protection?' he mouthed. 'What protection did Prince Edward have when you slaughtered him upon the battlefield, merely because you want his wife and her great possessions?'

Sir Richard Ratcliffe gave a huge shout of fury and reached across the table to seize Arthur, but Sir Simon forestalled him and pinioned the boy's arms behind his back and forced him down on to his knees.

There was consternation within the hall, those seated at the high table on their feet displaying expressions of shock and alarm. Members of the household lower down the hall at the other tables stared in horror at their young master.

Rosamund scrambled to her feet, forcing aside Lady Sibyl's delaying hand and ran to her brother. She knelt beside him, tears streaming down her cheeks. 'What have you done, Arthur?' she cried. 'You have disgraced and doomed us all.'

The duke's voice cut across her sobs. 'No, no, Mistress Kinnersley, the boy is young and has listened to ugly rumours. When we are so young we are liable to blurt out words without thinking, having not yet learned to dissemble. Simon, you are hurting the lad.'

'Not half so much as I will when I have him within his chamber,' snapped Sir Simon. He hauled Arthur to his feet. 'Now, apologise, immediately.'

Arthur was still beside himself and tears were channelling down his cheeks as sulkily and fretfully he avoided the shocked, despairing gaze of his sister. 'I won't,' he said doggedly between gritted teeth, 'and I will not beg for mercy either. These Yorkist lords are the enemies of my father and—'

Sir Simon forced one hard hand across his mouth, cutting off further insults. 'Allow me, your Grace,' he said, his voice dangerously quiet, and, at the duke's nod, forced the struggling boy from the hall.

The shocked silence continued and Rosamund made to follow. She curtsied to the duke. 'My lord, if you would excuse me, I would follow and see—'

He shook his head gently. 'Of course I will if you so wish, Mistress Rosamund, but, frankly, I would not advise you to do so at present.' His lips twitched. 'The proceedings within Master Kinnersley's chamber would only distress you further and, possibly, tend to humiliate him if he is aware, later, when he resumes his senses, that you were present.'

She checked a sob and returned reluctantly to her seat. He leaned over and took her hand. 'Believe me, the boy will learn discretion. I am not offended. I, too, had my difficult moments, as I am sure we all of us have. He is grieving and upset. He will calm down.'

'But can you forgive him, your Grace? He said such terrible things.'

For one moment she discerned a shadow pass over the stern young features and then he smiled again. 'We must all learn to forgive each other, especially for words uttered under the stress of emotion.' He rose to his feet and all fell silent. 'Please let us resume this excellent meal, for which we must thank our hostesses.' He nodded graciously to Lady Sibyl, who was still wide-eyed with dismay. Hastily she recovered her composure and thanked him humbly. He looked meaningfully across at Rosamund. 'Please resume your seat, Mistress Rosamund, and do not distress yourself further. I assure you that Sir Simon is perfectly capable of handling this situation without harming your brother too much, but...' he paused for a moment and his long lips twitched once more '...he must be made to learn manners, as I hope you will understand.'

She nodded uncertainly and sank down once more. As if the ugly incident had not occurred, the duke resumed his gracious conversation with those around him and at length rose to leave.

'Thank you again for your hospitality, ladies,' he said as his gentlemen moved to accompany him. 'I trust that one day we shall receive one or both of you at court. And now I must take my leave. We have some miles to go before our next halt on our journey.'

As if on cue, Sir Simon appeared in the hall and moved immediately to accompany his lord to the door.

The duke placed one gentling hand upon his shoulder. 'Be merciful with the whelp, Simon. He has been allowed too much freedom of late, I think, and will need careful handling.'

Simon nodded grimly. 'I have locked the cub in his chamber to think over his sins,' he said grimly. 'As yet I have not touched him. If I had, at this moment, I might have done him more harm than is good for either of us.'

The duke drew him slightly aside from the attending company. 'Remember the lady,' he said softly. 'She is deeply concerned for her brother.'

'As well she might be.'

A bubble of laughter broke from the duke's lips. 'I would not have you lose your own hopes by too vehemently defending my cause, Simon.'

Simon gave a rueful smile in answer. 'Be that as it may, sir, the boy will have to be dealt with and thoroughly. His accusation was unpardonable—and untrue,' he added fervently.

The duke looked away for a moment, then he patted his friend's shoulder and turned to take his departure.

Though she felt that her legs would betray her and let her down in this august company, Rosamund walked with Sibyl to the gatehouse to see the ducal company ride across the drawbridge. She saw the banner of the White Boar flutter in the wind as the horses and men-at-arms were hidden from her view by a bend in the road and then, and only then, was she free to look anxiously at Sir Simon Cauldwell.

Chapter Seven

Sir Simon Cauldwell curtly ordered the guards on duty to lift the drawbridge and prepared to move towards the hall. Lady Sibyl caught at Rosamund's arm as she made to chase after him.

'What do you think you are doing? Leave this business to him. Only he can extract us from this very difficult and embarrassing situation.'

Impatiently Rosamund jerked herself free. 'Do you think I will stand by idly and allow that man to punish my brother?'

'Of course Arthur must be punished. He insulted the king's brother. He cannot be allowed to get away with it.'

'That man has no right,' Rosamund raged. She could see Sir Simon approaching the hall steps and realised that her opportunity to prevent him now from going to Arthur's chamber was being frustrated as, once again, Sibyl caught her arm in a hard grip. She slapped out at the offending hand. 'Let me go. Do you hear me? I have to go to Arthur, at once.'

Her strength and determination was so great that Sibyl was thrown off balance as she let go her hold and almost fell. Only the presence of Andrew Murton, who had come up suddenly behind the women, prevented her from falling completely to the ground.

Rosamund did not wait to argue further with either of them but lifted her skirts and ran full tilt after her quarry. She managed to catch up with him as he entered the hall, but she was so out of breath that she could not utter a word and could only stand gasping. He turned and put out two hands upon her shoulders to steady her.

'Careful now. Come and sit down. This visit and all the ensuing excitement has been too much for you.' He drew her farther into the hall and seated her upon the nearest bench.

'Do you think I am a fainting girl?' she snapped. 'I am merely winded in a race to catch up with you.'

He stood before her, one hand resting upon his sword belt. 'What can I do for you?'

'You can tell me what you are about to do to Arthur.'

'Now that I have calmed somewhat and am less furious I intend to go to his chamber and discipline him.'

'What do you mean?'

He gave a little impatient shrug. 'Mistress Rosamund, I am sure that you are perfectly aware of what I mean. I intend to deal with Arthur as I would any recalcitrant squire. I intend to whip him.'

She gave a great gasp and put a hand to her mouth.

'I cannot allow you to do that.'

'Really?' His dark brows drew together in a frown. 'And how do you intend to prevent me? I must remind you that, for the present at least, I am master here.'

'You mustn't—cannot—' she begged. 'He is just a child. The duke said as much…'

'He is old enough to know exactly what he was doing and must pay the price.'

'He will hold it against you for the rest of his life.'

His lips curved in a smile. 'I doubt that, not once he

has come to his senses. But, even so, if that should be the case, I will have to accept that.'

'But I will never forgive you.'

'Ah, now, Mistress Rosamund, that is a totally different matter.'

She drew a hard breath. 'Do you dare to make fun of me?'

'Certainly not. Why ever should you think such a thing? You know that your regard is very important to me.' He had stopped smiling now and his eyes were regarding her steadily. 'I would not wound you, Rosamund, but I have to do this. Your father would have seen the necessity. Did he never whip your brother into submission?'

'Yes,' she faltered, 'he did, on occasion, but you, sir, are not his father and he thinks of you as…'

'One of his enemies. Do you, also, Rosamund?'

She tried to avoid his gaze, but felt herself drawn back to it despite herself. She swallowed hard. 'No, I do not believe that you are. I think that you wish us well…'

'Then trust me to deal with this situation as I think fit. Think what he did, Rosamund. He insulted the Lord High Constable of England, who was a guest in this house and before his own men and the whole of this household. Do you think I could allow that to pass without something very drastic being done about it? Your own servants will expect it. Your stepmother has already indicated that she has no objection to Arthur being severely punished.'

She turned her head away. 'As you have observed, Sibyl is his stepmother. She has no love for him—for either of us.'

He was silent for a moment, then he said quietly. 'Yes, that may very well be the case. Nevertheless, she is right on this occasion.'

'He is still grieving,' she whispered. 'Cannot he be excused this one time? To be so humiliated...he will never forget it. It will rankle...'

'For a while,' he admitted. 'I was whipped many times when I was his age and for far less grievous offences, I assure you. When he begins his training as a squire he will be disciplined many times.'

'Which is why I do not wish him to leave home at present. You promised me that you would consider the matter—before the duke arrived. I thought we had reached an agreement.'

'Aye.' He sighed. 'This visit has changed everything.' He looked away as if considering, then he turned abruptly back to her. 'I do not think that you are aware of how grievously his thoughtless words injured the duke. He accused him of murdering the prince and wishing to acquire a share of the Lady Anne's inheritance.'

'And that is not so?' she said bitterly. 'Isn't a good dowry the reason every nobleman embarks on a marriage?'

He looked down at her sharply. 'It can be one of the reasons for a marriage alliance, I grant you, but not the only one. In this instance, I assure you, it is certainly not the only one. The duke has loved the Lady Anne since both of them were children together. His one thought now is for her safety—and he cannot be sure of it.'

Her brown eyes sought his wonderingly. 'You know this—personally?'

'I do. Duke Richard has honoured me with his friendship and I tell you now I am very fond of Lady Anne Neville myself. If I did not believe that her best welfare did not lie in the arms of the duke, I would attempt to see to her safety and happiness myself.'

'Then you know them both?'

'Yes. I was brought up at Middleham Castle. I went there after I, too, had lost my father in battle and I was grieving as deeply as Arthur is now. My mother saw to it that I was exposed to the rigours of training for my own good. Later, Duke Richard arrived at Middleham also. He, too, had recently lost his father.'

She was silent for a moment as she recalled her father's tale of how the vengeful Queen Margaret, following the Duke of York's defeat and death at the battle of Wakefield, had crowned the corpse of the dead duke with a paper crown, after his body had been shamefully exhibited in York. How deeply the young Duke Richard must have suffered then…and now the defeated queen was a prisoner, with the Lady Anne, of the triumphant Yorkist princes.

'How old was he then?'

'About eight years old, if I remember correctly, and very vulnerable. I was three years older and his superior. He, too, knew what it was to feel the lash, delivered by our master-at-arms.'

She swallowed hard. 'I can see that you are personally affected by what happened today in the hall and I am very sorry. I am sure that if Arthur were to realise the truth of it he, too, would express his regret.'

His eyebrows rose sardonically. 'You think so?'

'He is—very angry,' she said softly. 'We must be prepared to understand that, and forgive him.'

'My own father used to say that forgiveness came—after due punishment,' he said succinctly.

'Then he was very harsh with you.'

'No, simply a realist.'

She was beginning to realise that, whatever she said, she was about to lose in this battle of wills. In one sense she knew that what he was doing was right. Arthur was out of control and someone must, soon, bring him to his senses but, perversely, she was angry that it should be this man.

'I can see,' she said coldly, 'that my appeal cannot reach your heart.'

'For your sake, Mistress Rosamund, I would do much but I believe, sincerely, that dealing with your brother now and making sure that there is no repetition of such dangerous behaviour is in the interest of both of you.'

She swallowed hard. He bent and took her hand, and held it firmly as she made to snatch it away. 'Trust me. I shall do only what is necessary.'

'Will you be so severe with your own children when they are old enough to disobey you?' she said quietly. 'And will you not listen to the pleas of your wife?'

His lips twitched. 'I shall expect and demand that she, too, will be obedient.'

'And did she bring you a considerable dower?' It was a cruel shot and she knew she was hoping to wound him.

He surprised her with a loud shout of laughter. 'Whatever makes you think that I am a married man, Mistress Rosamund?'

'I—I—was not sure,' she stammered. 'You spoke of insisting upon obedience…'

He laughed again. 'I was merely speaking of what I shall demand from my future bride and, though I might wish for a suitable settlement, there are other requirements that will decide my choice.'

'A willingness to submit to the master being the first, I imagine,' she said tartly, 'and an acceptance of a rigidity regarding discipline. Do you treat all the members of your household so harshly and unforgivingly?'

'Certainly those virtues are desirable in a wife,' he said, smiling.

She could find no more sallies to direct at him and was aware that she was further angering him towards her hapless young brother. She rose. 'It seems that we have nothing more to say to each other.'

'At this moment, no, and, I think, better I deal with young Arthur without further delay. In my experience swift retribution was preferable to waiting for it to catch up with one.'

He bowed and, as he could see that she was near to tears, he gave a little nod, turned and walked briskly towards the door behind the dais, which would lead him to the family chambers.

She watched him go despairingly. This latest encounter had left her more than ever confused. She had learned a little more about him. He had lost a father young, as she and Arthur had done. He had deep affection for his lord, Duke Richard, not merely an obsequious desire to please in a wish to gain preferment. She had caught a glimpse behind the stern mask of what his life had been during childhood and, she thought, given time, and without this added barrier between them of his harsh punishment of Arthur, they might have come to some understanding and agreement. She had learned, at last, that he was unwed and her heart raced unaccountably at the knowledge. As on their previous encounters, she had been left confused and unsatisfied and she could not have explained even to herself why it was so important and necessary that they should be at peace with each other.

But the happiness of her young brother was the most important thing in her life. Arthur would never forgive this assault on his person. His pride would be deeply wounded. He would never accept a growing friendship between his dearly loved sister and the man he considered his bitterest enemy. She sighed and slowly began to move towards her own chamber. She knew, instinctively, that she would not be allowed access to Arthur for hours yet and she needed solitude to come to terms with her own bitterness of spirit.

It was some hours later that a knock came upon her door and Andrew Murton entered after she called permission for him to do so.

'Mistress, I have tried to go to Master Arthur, but there is one of Sir Simon Cauldwell's men standing guard outside the door of his chamber and he refuses to allow me to enter.'

Rosamund put down her spindle. In actual fact she hated spinning and had made herself take up this work over the last hour in an effort to force herself to face unpleasant facts.

'No, I imagine that Sir Simon will keep Arthur secluded for some time. He would not wish us to fuss over him, would he?'

Andrew's comely face expressed concern. 'I wish I could have done something to prevent this.'

'So do I, Andrew, so do I.'

'But, surely, if he has been punished he will need tending.'

Rosamund gave a wry smile. 'Yes, and I am sure that Martha has already tried to gain entrance.'

'If only I could have saved Sir Humphrey…'

'Perhaps you would only have saved him to face the executioner's block, or worse,' she reminded him quietly. 'Andrew, why is it that a quarrel which concerns people we do not know can affect our lives so tragically?'

'It is the way of the world, Mistress.'

'You men, you accept your warriors' fates so readily, and now I am expected to allow Arthur to train to risk his life also.'

'He has real spirit, young Arthur. He will make a fine warrior.'

'Yes, I am sure that he will and I would accept that if only it did not teach him to hate more readily.'

He could see that there was no way of offering comfort and edged towards the door. 'If you have need of me, Mistress, you only need to send for me and immediately I will be at your service.' He hesitated for a moment then added hurriedly,. 'It has been suggested to me that I should make early preparations to leave Kinnersley. I replied that I now serve Master Arthur and will only accept dismissal from him. He will need my help more than ever now that he is so alone.'

'I have already informed Sir Simon Cauldwell that I have no wish to lose your service yet and I am sure Lady Sibyl will back me in this.'

He gave a little bow and cleared his throat. 'Have you received any indication that the king might wish to take reprisal against this family, Mistress Rosamund?'

'Sir Simon is continually at pains to convince us that we are perfectly safe here but, of course, I cannot be sure. King Edward, I hear, can be capricious.' She gave a little bitter laugh. 'There, I should not be uttering such treasonable words.'

'Mistress Rosamund, you know that you have my total loyalty.'

She looked up at his open, pleasant-featured countenance and judged him sincere. He, at least, she felt that she could trust. She gave a little grateful nod of her head as he took his leave.

She went down to the still room. She found Martha already there gathering salves and a phial of poppy juice in readiness for the moment when she would be allowed to tend her nurseling. She looked up sympathetically as Rosamund entered.

'I see you have the same thoughts as I have,' she said. 'Lady Sibyl has already professed a lack of sympathy for our lad. She says he brought it all on himself and disgrace upon the household.'

'I am afraid that she is right, Martha.' Rosamund sank down dispiritedly upon a stool. 'Loving Arthur as we do, we cannot deny that he has been outrageously foolish. Father, were he alive, would have said as much. But I fear for the mind scars this will leave rather than the physical ones. He is so proud and stubborn. If he were to have companions of his own age and station he would perhaps, more readily, be able to laugh this off, but I fear it will rankle, and we shall have to guard against the possibility of his attempting to take his revenge on Sir Simon, which could spell danger for all of us.'

Martha pursed her lips as she wiped greasy fingers upon her apron. 'Aye, Mistress, I fear that is very likely.'

'I have just been speaking to Andrew Murton. He was anxious to go to Arthur, but has been refused permission. He says there is a guard upon the door.' She sighed. 'I shall miss Andrew when he leaves us. He has always been a particular friend to Arthur.'

'You are feeling very lost at the moment. Your feelings are all in turmoil.'

Martha's tone was somewhat odd and Rosamund glanced at her sharply. 'I have no special feelings for Andrew Murton. I regard him as a friend only. I...'

'I was not thinking that your feelings were directed towards Andrew Murton.'

Rosamund's face flamed and she caught convulsively at one of the pestle and mortar sets upon the table near to her. 'You think that I... You cannot mean it, Martha. You believe that I—I am beginning to fall in love with—why, I have only known the man for two or three days.'

'In my experience, Mistress, it doesn't take even two or three days.'

Rosamund stared back at her, stupefied.

Martha gave a grim little smile. 'Probably I should not speak out of turn. I am, when all is said and done, but a servant here, but I believe I know your heart better than anyone else.'

Rosamund whispered hoarsely, 'You know that I love you almost as much as I love Arthur. You have been like a mother to me. But, Martha, it cannot be. There is so much between us and—'

'And you have taken him to task because he has been forced to discipline Arthur. Child, who else, here, has the authority to do so? Certainly not Andrew Murton, and Lady Sibyl could hardly order one of the servants to punish the boy. You said yourself someone must do it, for Arthur's own sake.'

'Yes.' Rosamund looked bleakly across the room. 'He has no tender feelings towards me. He is here only because he was sent here by the Duke of Gloucester.'

'And why do you think the duke chose to send him?' Martha was smiling broadly now. 'I saw the look which passed between them. It was one of friendship, not a look from master to servant. I also have seen the glances that Sir Simon has directed at you. You were in talk earlier. I take it you were able to discover whether or not he is wed.'

Rosamund coloured hotly again. 'He is not.'

'Ah.'

'But even were he to—to become interested in me, why, as you say, he is in favour at court. I do not even know if I have a reasonable dower or not... There must be ladies at court who would make more fitting brides for a friend of the king's brother than I could ever be. And I am the daughter of a dead traitor, to boot,' she added bitterly.

Martha leaned across the table and took Rosamund's hand in her own callused one. 'If I know my man, and I'm a fair judge of men, Sir Simon Cauldwell will choose his own bride and let no man, overlord or not, interfere with that choice, nor do I believe that the consideration of a suitable dower will influence it either.'

'Arthur would never understand...'

'Arthur will be bitter at present, I grant you, but a sore back heals and so will his wounded feelings, in time.'

'Perhaps,' Rosamund mused, 'but I could not give myself to a man who would not understand how much Arthur needs me, no matter how much I would wish to do so and,' she amended hastily, 'I am by no means sure that I would. All this is mere speculation. I cannot be in love. Sir Simon Cauldwell holds sway over my thoughts at present. He is master here and we are all in awe of him. He has given no indication of any special interest in me…'

'No?'

'He—' Rosamund floundered about for explanations. 'He makes gallant comments. He teases me. He—Martha, I am no beauty. I saw how much he admired Lady Sibyl that first night he set eyes upon her. Any man would…'

'She is beautiful, I grant you,' Martha said briskly, 'but you know the old adage, "Handsome is as handsome does," and any shrewd man is aware of it. Do you think that Sir Simon Cauldwell is less shrewd than most men? Anyway,' she commented, her head slightly on one side, as she appraised her former nurseling, 'who informed you that you were no beauty? You are the true nut-brown maid of the ballad, a real English rose. White or no.' This last hit made Rosamund laugh despite her confusion.

'You are prejudiced, Martha. You love me, you see.'

'Aye, I do,' Martha responded pithily, 'and I am not the only one. We shall see.'

Unwilling to discuss this any further, Rosamund rose to her feet. 'I see that you have gathered everything together to tend Arthur when you are allowed to do so. I hope it will be soon. He must be feeling quite abandoned by all of us.'

'He'll be too busy licking his wounds, both bodily and in his mind,' Martha said grimly. 'I doubt if he'll want anyone to see him just yet, but, yes, I'm ready. You leave him to me when the time comes.'

As often, when she was confused or upset, Rosamund sought refuge once more in her mother's pleasance. Here he could feel close to the gentle woman she had so dearly loved and whom she never ceased to miss. She sat on the bench, chin resting on her two hands, supported by her elbows, staring across the grass to the carefully tended rose bushes. Soon they would be in full flower and the scent from the herb garden teased her nostrils. She wondered drearily if she or Arthur would still be here at Kinnersley for her to collect and dry the herbs later this year.

If not, where would the king send her now that she was a ward of the crown? Duke Richard had mentioned the possibility of her attending at court. She shied away from that thought. There she might be haunted by the sight of Simon Cauldwell in the company of some court beauty. She faced the truth squarely for the first time. She was in love with him. She could not deny it to herself any longer. She had thrilled to his touch during their first encounter in Tewkesbury and now she was aware that her eyes were constantly searching hall and courtyard for a single glimpse of him. She had tried to hide herself from his presence, but that was only a pretence. She needed to have him in her sight, to watch, hungrily, every move he made, to discover how he behaved with friends, his lord the duke and his men-at-arms and servants.

She still knew very little about him. He was still unwed and she thought that he must be past twenty, by which time most young noblemen had made profitable marriage alliances. He had told her that he had lost his father in battle, as Arthur had done, when he was still a child. Possibly that was the reason that he had not been pressed into a youthful marriage. She gave a little secret smile, hugging to herself the thought that he would never allow himself to be pressed into anything he did not wish to do.

Yes, that was so, but it was not possible that he might wish to wed her, Rosamund Kinnersley, soon to be homeless and the daughter of a dead traitor.

She swung round guiltily as she heard booted feet upon the gravel path, unwilling that any other might read her secret hopes and desires in her expression. It was as well she had been warned by the sound, for she saw Sir Simon heading purposely towards her. She sprang to her feet instantly, aware that, despite her determination to remain calm in his presence, her cheeks were flushed with rosy colour.

'Good. I have found you. Your maid said you would most probably be here.'

'You need me?' She was immediately alarmed. 'Arthur' Is there any need to fear…?'

'None whatever,' he reassured her. 'I came to inform you that you are at liberty to go to him any time you wish now. I prevented it at first for I believed he would be best left to himself for a while.' His lips twisted wryly. 'Certainly, after punishment, I always wished to stay so, but have allowed your maid to go to him, since she pleaded with me to allow it. I gather that she was his nurse and well used to binding up his hurts and comforting him when he was distressed.'

'Oh, yes,' Rosamund said shakily, 'Martha will be greatly relieved and I will go to him soon now.' Her lip trembled a little. 'Is he—is he very much hurt?'

'His pride is more sore wounded than his back, I think but he will be able to sleep in comfort again tomorrow night.'

'He—he did not express any regret?'

He shook his head. 'I did not expect it, but he will behave more circumspectly another time when he is in the presence of royal personages, I am sure. If nothing else as he matures, he will realise the sense of it.'

'Yes,' she breathed softly. 'I—I am sorry that this unpleasant task was forced upon you. Earlier I—'

'I understand perfectly,' he said easily. 'There was simply no one else and, Rosamund, it had to be done.'

'I know.'

He reached out and took her two hands within his own. 'The very last thing I wanted to do was to hurt you in any way. You must believe that.' Those startlingly blue eyes of his were staring deeply into hers, holding her still, as a stoat does a frightened rabbit. And yet she was aware that she was not afraid. She drew a hard breath and he pulled her close, cupped her chin in one hand, bent and kissed her.

She rejoiced in the sweetness of it, responding gently at first then more passionately. He held her very close, feeling her slender body tremble against his. Suddenly aware that they might be overlooked and that she was behaving in a most unseemly manner, she hastily drew away after minutes.

'We are alone,' he reassured her. 'I saw the gardener leave as I came through the archway.'

'We mustn't,' she whispered weakly.

'Why not? We are both free agents and...' he lifted one gentle hand to her cheek caressingly '...I would not have done it had I thought you would not have wished it.'

'You cannot know that.'

'Then tell me that I thought wrongly, Rosamund. I felt it deep in my being. I have wanted to do that from the first time we met in Tewkesbury. Oh—' his lips twisted ruefully '—I know that I was gravely mistaken then but later, when I saw how your eyes sought and found mine wherever we were, I knew that you wished for it, too. Deny it if you will to me, but not to yourself.'

Her eyes were shining with her new-found happiness and she reached out tentatively to take one of his hands once more.

'I cannot deny it but, as I said, we must not.'

'I do not understand.'

'It is not fitting. I might very well prove to be penniles
and I am ward to the king. He could refuse to grant yo
my hand.'

He brushed aside her objection. 'Do you truly wish t
wed me, Rosamund?'

'If it is your wish.'

'It is my wish. I will send to Duke Richard. He wil
petition the king for me to grant me your hand in marriage
As for the fear that you might be penniless that is probabl
groundless and, even if it were to prove to be so, it woul
make no difference to me. I want you, nothing else
though…' his lips curved into a teasing smile '…it woul
be pleasant to know that I was to wed an heiress.'

'Arthur would not approve,' she whispered anxiously.

'I was not proposing to ask Arthur for his permission,
he said firmly.

'He hates all Yorkists and now that you have physically
punished him he will never accept you as a husband fo
me.'

He frowned. 'Arthur is a twelve-year-old boy. Are w
to allow his whims to prevent us marrying? I think not
my love. I intend to send to my mother in the north thi
very day and inform her that, at last, I intend to fulfil he
most desperate desire, and take a wife. When she sees yo
she will be as delighted as I am that I shall possess m
Rose of the World.'

He was refuting all her qualms, determined to put asid
all opposition, but that was what she expected from him
He would rule her life as he ruled her heart, and her hear
sang with the joy of it. For the present, at least, she allowe
herself to believe that her happiness could be achieve
without opposition from others, that she, the daughter of

professed Lancastrian, could mate with a Yorkist and one who was high in royal favour.

He drew her close to his heart again and she lifted her face to his as a flower lifts its head to the sun.

Chapter Eight

Arthur did not come to the hall for supper and Rosamund was relieved. She had not really expected him. He would have felt deep humiliation to face the members of the family and the household just yet. His mental wounds were too raw as well as his physical ones and, secretly, Rosamund was not yet ready to face him also. She was afraid that her wild happiness would be all too apparent and Arthur must not know of it yet. This must be kept from him, nor could Sibyl or Andrew Murton know either.

When Simon came to table she managed to give him a cool nod of acknowledgement as he took his seat opposite to her and then kept her head studiously lowered. Her heart was pounding wildly so that she thought everyone near her must be aware of it, yet no one appeared to notice her agitation. Once or twice, when she lifted her head, she caught his smile, but it was a calm, reassuring one, devoid of any passion. She was grateful that tonight he had not chosen to sit beside her. Had she been too close to him, temptation would have been too great and she would have been forced to reach out and touch him and that must not be—not yet.

Sibyl leaned forward eagerly. 'Have you managed to

deal with the miscreant, Sir Simon?' she enquired sweetly and Rosamund, flushing hotly with anger, could have struck her.

Sir Simon waited deliberately while Rolf Taylor poured wine for him. He looked levelly across at her. 'I have dealt with the matter as it fell to me as the boy's temporary guardian to do so. I hope that he will have learned from the experience and I think it wiser that none of us refers to the incident or to his punishment again, Lady Kinnersley.'

It was as if she sensed his displeasure at her mentioning the matter and, like Rosamund, she flushed hotly.

'Why, yes, Sir Simon, I am sure you are right,' she countered, somewhat flustered. 'It was just that I felt it necessary to assure myself that the unpleasant incident can now be forgotten. I am grateful for your forbearance. I am sure that this must have caused you some embarrassment. The Duke of Gloucester is your liege lord.'

'He is the Lord High Constable of England and liege lord to us all,' he reminded her quietly, 'yet Lord Richard is also a man, and one young enough to remember his own youthful follies. I am sure that he will not hold any grudge against young Master Kinnersley or, indeed, against any member of this household.'

His manner was coldly formal and definite and it was clear to all present that, as far as he was concerned, the matter was over and that he would not refer to it again.

Rosamund flashed him a glance of supreme gratitude and he lifted his goblet to her in a kindly salute. Lady Sibyl gave her full attention to her plate for the rest of the meal. At its close Rosamund rose and Sir Simon escorted her to the foot of the stair. He glanced round quickly to assure himself that no one was close enough to observe them, then he took her hand and bent to kiss it. It was a formal kiss, but she could feel the heat of his lips upon

her skin and she lifted her eyes to him, her love shining
clear for him to see. As she could hear Sibyl drawing near
and in talk with Andrew Murton, she snatched her hand
free and said very softly, 'You will say nothing of—of
your intentions until Arthur—until Arthur has had time to
recover from this?'

He smiled a trifle grimly. 'I fear that might take longer
than I am prepared to wait, sweetheart, but I can say nothing until I have received an answer from his Grace, the
duke. I will dispatch a messenger tomorrow early.'

She nodded tremulously and hastened to mount the stair
before Sibyl could come up close and question her about
what he had said.

Outside the door of Arthur's chamber Martha was waiting for her. She put a gentle, detaining hand upon Rosamund's arm as she made to enter.

'I should not disturb him, Mistress. He is sleeping. I
gave him a draught of watered wine laced with poppy
cordial.'

Rosamund gave a little sob. 'Have you tended his
hurts?'

'Yes. He has a very sore back, but I think there will be
little scarring, if any. His pride is hurt more than his body.
It is as we said.'

'Was he— I mean, did he cry out at all? Did he say?'

'He was very stoical when I cleansed the wounds, as I
expected. He was very white about the gills, but he made
no sound. I doubt that he did during punishment.'

Very carefully Rosamund pushed open the chamber
door and stole just inside. She could see her brother lying
hunched in his bed. He was lying face down, but did not
move, and she judged that Martha was right and that he
had fallen asleep.

She stole out just as quietly and beckoned Martha to
accompany her to her own chamber. 'Thank you, Martha.

You are the one person he can trust now. He looked to be at peace.'

'He will appear to be his own self in the morning. Do not be alarmed about him.' Martha shook her head, smiling a little. 'You, yourself, have taken as severe a punishment from your father in the old days and so has he. He will mend soon enough.'

'I hope and pray so,' Rosamund murmured as she removed her hennin and veil and began to prepare to undress. She turned back to her old nurse and made sure that her chamber door was securely closed. 'Oh, Martha, I am truly in love. You guessed at it. He loves me. He has made arrangements to send a messenger to the Duke of Gloucester to ask formally for my hand in marriage. It must be a secret until...' she hesitated, her face crumpling oddly '...until Arthur is prepared to accept such news. Tell me he will, Martha, I beg of you. He must. I love Simon so.'

Martha gave a heavy sigh and came forward, turning her mistress so that she might undo the back lacing of her gown. Her expression was hidden from Rosamund and she remained silent for moments until Rosamund impulsively turned back to face her and demanded, 'You do not believe that Arthur will forgive me if I wed Simon Cauldwell? That is it, isn't it?'

'Child, I do not know, but I think you will be wise to keep this from him for a time at least. His fury is directed at this man and no one else. He is mistaken. His own folly has brought this upon his own head. We all know that, but it will be both hard and cruel to make him aware of it just yet.'

'But, Martha, what can I do? The king holds jurisdiction over me and, at any time, could order me to marry some stranger, some old or repulsive man I could not accept.'

'Aye,' Martha said bleakly. 'This is a bad time to ask

you to make such a decision, I know that, and you with no mother to advise you.'

Rosamund's expression became dreamy. 'He came to me in the garden to tell me that you had gone to Arthur. He—he kissed me. I—tried to resist but, Martha, it was intoxicatingly sweet. I have known, I think, from that moment in the tent in Tewkesbury that I loved him. I was frightened then and confused but—but since I have been able to think of no other. Those startlingly blue eyes of his, they fascinate me, take away from me any will of my own. I need to have him near me, within my sight. All the time my eyes are searching for glimpses of him. I watch his every mood, observe his smiles, his frowns, the tightening of his lips. Almost before he does any of those movements. I seem to know in advance, how he will react to others, to news given to him. I know so little about him. I know he is unwed, that his father is dead but that his mother still lives. Martha, how will she receive me?' She gave a little crowing laugh. 'If he is like her then I am bound to like her, aren't I?' She broke off for a second, her hand against her mouth. 'I do not know where his home is, if he is a penniless knight dependent upon his lord. None of this matters. All I want is to be with him— to lie close to him, to—' Her eyes widened at the enormity of what she had just said and Martha gave a little, triumphant laugh.

'Well, well, my nurseling is become true woman at last and, in my opinion, could not have found herself a truer man. There, I have said it. Hush, hush, my darling. You must not fret. There will be time to convince Arthur. He is but a boy and boys' moods change with the weather. Only be circumspect for just a little while. His wounds are too raw yet.'

'I know.' Rosamund sat back upon the bed, hugging her knees. 'If—if he is penniless, as I said, will the king consent to the match? I will not care a fig and I do not know yet whether I will have a suitable dower to take to the marriage bed, but I know noblemen take heed of these matters and discard all else when everyone should know that love is the only true reason to make a match.'

Martha nodded grimly. 'Aye, the king will need to be assured that you are not dependent upon the Crown purse but, since your Simon is so friendly with his brother Gloucester, I think he will allow himself to be persuaded. Leave it all to your man. He will arrange matters for his own satisfaction. I am sure of that.'

She assisted Rosamund to finish undressing and left her to sleep, but Rosamund lay wakeful for some time. She was torn between a desire to dream of her future happiness with Simon Cauldwell and her concern about how long they must delay informing the household and, most of all, her greatest dilemma, the problem of explaining her love to Arthur. At length she fell asleep, remembering the final words of reassurance Martha had given to her. When Martha had been about to leave, Rosamund had posed one question.

'Martha, you will come with me when I am wed to Simon, to my new home, wherever that may be?'

Martha had given her a little crooked smile. 'When I am assured that all is well with Master Arthur,' she replied quietly.

And with that Rosamund had had to be content.

She descended to the hall to break her fast early next morning, anxious to see her brother, but their steward informed her that Master Arthur had already left the manor house to ride out with Master Murton.

As Martha hurried in a few moments later with a laden tray, Rosamund said anxiously, 'Arthur has already gone riding, Martha. Can he be feeling well enough?'

'I imagine he will do,' the former nurse said stoutly. 'I
haven't seen him this morning so he must have risen bright
and early. Now, don't you go worrying about him. Master
Murton will be there to see to his needs. He will bring him
straight home if necessary.'

For all that Rosamund felt little like eating. She was
consumed with concern for Arthur's well-being. Sibyl
came down soon after, but the two women found little to
say to each other. Rosamund felt anger at her stepmother's
lack of sympathy for Arthur and her tactlessness in showing it openly. Sibyl appeared totally immersed in her own
thoughts and only asked one question of the steward:
Where was Master Murton? She seemed to be somewhat
put out to discover that he had left the manor with Arthur,
but did not dwell on the matter. Since Simon did not join
them for the meal Rosamund concluded that he, too, had
breakfasted very early and had either left the manor or
found some important business with which to occupy himself. Rolf Taylor proved to be similarly unavailable for
questioning and Rosamund wondered if he had been sent
south with Simon's urgent request to Gloucester or, at the
very least, had been sent to dispatch some other member
of Simon's company upon that errand.

Rosamund left the hall the moment that she could find
a convenient excuse to leave Sibyl's company and repaired
to the kitchen where she gave instruction about the day's
coming meals to the cook. She wondered, fleetingly, who
would perform this duty in the future, when she left Kinnersley as Simon's bride. Even if Lady Sibyl remained at
the manor for any length of time, and Rosamund did not
think that likely, since she was still young and would most
probably remarry soon, Sibyl had never properly performed the function of the chatelaine of the manor house.

Rosamund was crossing the courtyard later when she
saw Simon ride in. He signalled to her imperatively to wait

while he dismounted and gave his horse into the care of a groom. She did so, though gazing round doubtfully. At any moment Arthur might ride in with Andrew Murton and she did not wish him to see her in talk with Simon, certainly not this morning.

He came to her side and she looked up at him, approving the serviceable cut of his apparel, most suitable for his work of overseeing the manor workers. There was little of the dandified courtier about Simon Cauldwell and she was glad of that.

He tilted up her chin, smiling down into her eyes, regardless of any member of the household who might be passing. Hastily she attempted to draw away.

'Please, we might be seen.'

'I have nothing to be ashamed of, sweetheart. I have dispatched a man to London, for Duke Richard should be there very soon now. It is rumoured that the bastard Fauconbridge is threatening to sack the town and the king will want the most loyal of his brothers close to him. Gloucester will take my request to the king and I am sure he will consent to our marriage. At all events I do not intend to allow anything or anyone to prevent us. If necessary, I shall carry you off and wed you without the king's permission.'

'But that would be treason,' she said uneasily.

'Nay, Edward will understand my need, never fear. He has never been a man to allow difficulties to prevent him from possessing the woman of his choice.' His tone was sardonic and Rosamund was aware that many of the king's most loyal Yorkist supporters had not approved of his marriage to Lady Elizabeth Grey, which had cost him the allegiance of his greatest supporter, his cousin the Earl of Warwick.

She said quietly, 'We must not let Arthur know of this yet. You promised.'

He pulled a wry grimace. 'Well, let that be for the present, but I am an impatient man, Rosamund. Once I have the king's consent to the match I want to make you mine immediately.'

'I am still in mourning,' she said doubtfully.

'Aye, I know, but there will be many young widows after these last engagements who will wish to remarry hurriedly. They will need powerful protectors.'

'But you will wish me to go north with you.'

'Of course. My mother will be anxious to receive you. Incidentally, I have sent another messenger north to inform her of my choice.'

Her lip trembled. One part of her rejoiced at his fierce determination to wed her quickly and remove her from Kinnersley, but she could not envision life for herself apart from her vulnerable young brother, who certainly would not willingly consent to accompany them. She could not imagine that he would ever agree to accept Simon Cauldwell as a suitor for his sister's hand.

She turned, guiltily, as the sound of approaching hoofs told them of riders approaching the courtyard and Arthur rode in, accompanied by Andrew Murton. Even from a distance and while he was still mounted, Rosamund detected the black scowl that disfigured his comely young features when he saw her with Simon. Andrew Murton dismounted and moved close to Arthur's mount as if to assist him from the saddle, but the boy impatiently thrust him away and swung down lightly. Despite his determination to move as if devoid of pain, he could not prevent a little wince of discomfort and, as he landed on his feet, he stumbled awkwardly.

Concerned, Rosamund made to run towards him, but Simon gave her a little warning signal to remain still. Arthur would not thank her for betraying her alarm at his condition. His very decision to ride so early, despite enduring considerable pain and discomfort, had been made to show defiance and Simon was aware of it. He gave the boy a little formal bow as a salute. Arthur remained where he stood, insolently giving no indication that he was even aware of his guardian's presence. Rosamund cast Simon a glance of appeal and he bowed to her and again to Arthur and made his way towards his own quarters in the gatehouse.

Arthur stared after him balefully, then he seized his sister's arm. 'Come, I wish to talk to you privately in my chamber.' He nodded towards Andrew Murton, who was standing near the stable door holding the lead reins of both their horses. 'Thank you, Andrew. I shall do well enough now. I am grateful that you rode out with me so early. Now I am sure that there must be matters you will wish to attend to.'

Andrew Murton gave a little bow directed towards Rosamund, then moved to take their mounts inside the stable. Arthur tugged impatiently at Rosamund's arm and hurried her into the manor house and up the spiral stair.

Once inside his own chamber he flung his riding gloves upon the bed and jumped down upon it himself, then gave a little triumphant jump once more before settling. Rosamund was forced to smile at him. This was the old Arthur, whom she knew and loved, the twelve-year-old boy, not the youth who had aped his elders yesterday in the hall or even the one who had given his orders so imperiously just now in the courtyard. Arthur's moods were changing constantly under the stresses of the recent events and she was sometimes unsure quite how to deal with him.

She said anxiously, 'How are you feeling? Martha and I were quite worried about you. It was foolish to go riding so early this morning when possibly your hurts needed tending.'

He shrugged impatiently once more, dismissing her sisterly concern. 'I am not a baby, Rosamund. Do you think I cannot take whatever that man decides to mete out to me? Martha fussed enough over me last night. It's true my back is sore, but I am well enough now to do whatever I wish to do.'

She smiled and sat down beside him. 'Very well, but you must not be annoyed by my sisterly concern for you. We are all in all to each other now, Arthur. Do not forget that.'

He seized her hand and squeezed it. 'I know, Ros, and am sorry. I am not annoyed with you.'

'I looked in on you last night, but you were sleeping and I thought it best not to wake you.'

'Of course. I know you love me, Ros, as I love you. We must look out for each other now. No one else will care about us.'

'Martha cares about you and so does every member of this household.'

He nodded and she realised by his expression that his heart was full. 'I know that they are all loyal.' His mouth tightened into a hard line. 'We must do everything we can to rid ourselves of the dominance of that man.' He thrust his lip out in an expression of childish petulance. 'How dare he touch me! Oh, he did not hurt me so much that I should notice, but he dared to lay hands upon me and— Did he think that he would get me to cry out, to show fear? Well, if he did so he was greatly mistaken.' He drew a little rasping breath. 'I will pay him back—in time.'

Rosamund's heart went cold within her. Arthur's venom towards the man who had humiliated him was clearly revealed in the chilling quality of his youthful tone. He could never be brought to accept Simon as his mentor. To the boy, Simon Cauldwell was a mortal enemy.

She made a little attempt to reason with him, although, in her heart, she knew that it would be useless.

'Arthur, it was deemed necessary to show the—visitors that you had been punished. You were insolent, speaking words of real treason. You must realise, on reflection, that it was very unwise, even dangerous. Since our father fought for the queen, our very hold on this manor is tenuous. Sir Simon Cauldwell has been given authority from the Crown to rule here.' She hesitated. 'I fear it was considered appropriate that he should take on the task of— punishing you. Oh, Arthur, I am so sorry. I know how humiliated you must feel, but no one blames you, not in their hearts, and everyone knows how bravely you bore it all.'

He fixed her with a cold stare. 'Do you censure me for saying what is the simple truth?'

'But we cannot really know who killed the Prince of Wales, Arthur. In a battle everything must be so confused that it would be impossible to tell anything for certain. I do not think that you should have openly accused the Duke of Gloucester and for so dishonourable a cause.'

'Do you not believe it is true that he will wish to wed the Lady Anne Neville now that she is a widow, and for the obvious reason that she is co-heiress to the Warwick lands and fortunes?'

'Sir Simon believes that Duke Richard truly has affection for the Lady Anne.'

'Does he, indeed? And I suppose he believes that it is honourable to wed some unsuspecting maid because he needs to enhance his own fortunes.'

Again the boy's words sent a lance through her heart. Did she believe that? Could her foolish heart be leading her astray? Was Simon asking for her hand in order to enrich himself? Yet he had no idea how great or small was her dower. Neither had she.

Arthur rushed on, leaning forward eagerly. 'I have been thinking hard about what we can do to resolve some of our problems. As I said, we need to rid ourselves of this Yorkist knight and, incidentally, of Lady Sibyl, who cares nothing for either of us. The king would allow me to remain here on the manor if you were wed to some man who could be responsible for the care of the estates and who could train me in martial skills.'

Rosamund's heart leaped again, then dropped like a stone at his next words.

'Andrew Murton could be that man. If you were to wed Andrew, then it would solve our problems. You know him and like him and he would treat you well. I would see to that.' He pushed out his chest in a boyishly boastful gesture. 'He is young and not unattractive, I suppose, in the way that maids like—' He eyed her doubtfully. 'You do like Andrew, don't you, Ros?'

'Yes-es,' she agreed and he plunged on again.

'If you were wed to Andrew, no one could force you into marriage with some Yorkist knight of the king's choosing and,' he added triumphantly, 'there would no longer be any need for Sibyl to remain here to chaperon you. She could return to her father in Warwick with, I suppose, her dowager's share of my father's fortunes, and find herself a new husband and never trouble us again.'

Months ago, even weeks ago, Rosamund would have seen some sense in Arthur's proposal. She did like Andrew Murton, had even, on occasions, allowed herself to dream that he might have feelings for her, might think of asking her father for her hand in marriage. She would have been agreeable. He was a brave, sensible young man who would likely one day win his spurs and she believed that he would make her a considerate husband. Added to that, she would, probably, have been allowed to remain on the manor for a while with those she loved and even, later, when possibly Andrew obtained land of his own, not moved too far away. But now she could not bear to even consider such a marriage. She had met and fallen totally in love with Simon Cauldwell, a man who would never meet her brother's criteria.

She swallowed hard. 'I see you have thought about this a great deal,' she said cautiously, 'but have you broached the matter, even delicately, with Master Murton?'

'Well, no, of course not, without speaking to you first.'

'I see.'

'Well, do you not agree that it would be the answer to all our difficulties?'

'Arthur, you must realise that, even if I were to agree and Master Murton did find the notion acceptable—'

'Well, why shouldn't he? He likes you—a lot. I have seen him looking at you as if—well, you know what I mean.'

'Yes, well, you didn't allow me to finish, Arthur. Even if we were both agreeable to the match, you must remember that, like you, I am a ward of the Crown. The king, or his representative, and that might well prove to be his brother, the Duke of Gloucester, must give his consent. While Master Murton might be acceptable to you, he is completely unknown to the king. Also, he, like Father, fought in this last engagement at Tewkesbury and on the wrong—that is, the defeated—side.'

Arthur digested this information thoughtfully, chewing the side of his mouth, a habit Rosamund knew well. At last he proffered, 'Could you not marry first and—and inform the king afterwards?'

'That, like your behaviour yesterday, could be deemed treasonable and dangerous—to all of us.'

He looked away from her, his eyes stormy. 'Perhaps if

we wait a while until the matter of this recent rebellion has blown over—'

'Yes,' she agreed hastily, 'but, meanwhile, Arthur, you must promise me that you will not even broach the subject of our discussion with Andrew Murton.'

He nodded his head ruefully.

Rosamund rose to her feet and was about to leave him when a tap came at the chamber door and instantly Arthur stiffened. Rosamund realised that the boy thought it possible that Simon Cauldwell might be on the other side and her heart went out to him in silent sympathy. He might try to appear a seasoned warrior but he was still a boy, and deeply vulnerable. She said quickly, before he could utter a word, 'Yes, who is it?'

'Martha, Mistress.'

Arthur breathed again, clearly relieved. 'Come in, Martha,' he called.

As she entered he said, 'I have been wanting to thank you for your care of me last night. I slept very well.'

'Yes,' she replied briskly, 'and I told you that those wounds would easily break out again if you put undue pressure upon them, Master Arthur. I will have a good look at you again tonight.' She smiled at Rosamund. 'Master Blanschard is here, Mistress, from Warwick. He asks if you will both attend him in the hall. Lady Sibyl is already there, waiting.'

Blanschard was her father's lawyer in Warwick and Rosamund presumed that he had come to explain to them the details of her father's will. She glanced meaningfully at Arthur. 'Yes, of course. We must attend him together. We should not keep Lady Sibyl waiting. You will see him now, Arthur?' Deliberately she deferred to him as the new lord of the manor.

He rose slowly, his expression grave. The presence of their father's lawyer and the importance of his news had brought home to him, once again, the depth of his grief and the understanding of how much they needed to be aware of their situation.

'Yes, certainly. We must go and discover for ourselves just how we stand,' he said quietly.

Martha and Rosamund exchanged telling glances as he moved out before them and preceded them down the spiral stair.

Master Roger Blanschard was a thin, stooped little man of some fifty years. Although his countenance was sharp-featured, his looks belied his appearance. He was, in fact, quite a jolly-natured man whom Rosamund had found both kindly and entertaining on his former frequent visits to Kinnersley. He had always tried to spend some time with and amuse Sir Humphrey's children, and he beamed at the two of them as they entered the hall. He recollected quickly the solemnity of the occasion and bowed gravely as he drew out a chair for Rosamund to seat herself.

'It is good to see you both at last and to offer my sincere condolences for your loss personally,' he said quietly. 'You must understand that, since I have had news of Sir Humphrey's sad death, I have had to spend time assessing the current situation regarding the manor, particularly as you, Master Arthur, are now the sole heir to the property and, due to your extreme youth, have been declared a ward of the Crown. Since that is so, I have been forced to as-certain how matters stood regarding the right of inheri-tance, after taking into consideration the circumstances of your father's demise.' He gave a little delicate cough and his shrewd grey eyes met Rosamund's hazel ones over the trestle as he seated himself. He gave his attention then to the parchments laid out before him and tapped them with one gnarled finger. 'I can inform you all now that I have been informed that the king has no intention of sequestering the manor and its appurtenances and that, I am sure, will relieve you all. I have been informed that a permanent guardian will be appointed to protect Master Kinnersley's interests and, until that is decided, Sir Simon Cauldwell will fill that position.'

Arthur scrambled angrily to his feet, banging the table with his clenched hand. 'I will not accept that, Master Blanschard. You must petition—'

The little lawyer gestured respectfully for the boy to resume his seat. 'We are in the hands of his Grace the king, and no objection of mine or yours, Master Kinnersley, will make the slightest difference,' he observed blandly. 'I have to advise you to accept the situation as it stands and make the best of it.'

Arthur snorted in fury and Rosamund, seated next to him, pulled at his sleeve to compel him to resume his seat. Lady Kinnersley stared at him contemptuously across the width of the trestle. She made no comment but her expression revealed, all too clearly, that she thought him a spoiled brat, who needed to be further disciplined. Rosamund could only be grateful that Simon was not present and could not be made further aware of her brother's intense hatred of him.

Master Blanschard continued. 'There remains only the contents of your father's will, which is a simple enough document. He made it shortly after his second marriage and, in it, he made provision particularly for his daughter, Mistress Rosamund Kinnersley. His son, naturally, he knew would inherit the lordship of the manor subject to royal approval and his new wife, should she become a widow, would inherit what is usual and legal on such occasions, her dower rights—that is, the value of one-third of the manor's worth. I have estimated that and assure you all that the estates stand in good stead and will not be too financially damaged by such a payment at this time. There are one or two small personal bequests for some of the valued members of the household, which I will not trouble you with at this time. Vouchsafe it to say that that, too, will not affect to any extent the value of the property or place in jeopardy the ability to pay the rightful taxes due to the Crown.'

He paused and looked deliberately at Rosamund. 'You will be anxious to know what is to be your portion, Mistress Rosamund. The dowry you take to your future husband will be all-important now. You will have no grounds for complaint or any concern for your welfare. Your father has made you the bequest of the small manor in the north of Leicestershire, in Charnwood actually, which your mother brought to him on her marriage as her portion. I visited the manor some months back and assured myself that all was in good order under the steward there.' He beamed at her across the table. 'Needless to say, your future suitor will be delighted by the generosity of your father's provision. Sir Humphrey also bade me tell you that he loved you well and his first thought on his new marriage was to ensure your welfare, Mistress.'

Tears sprang to Rosamund's eyes as she thought of her father's concern for her. If she had doubted his love when his attention appeared to go solely to his beautiful young wife, she now knew that he had never faltered in his deep affection for her and she was comforted by this assurance.

Since Sibyl remained silent and Arthur was still considering, broodingly, how he might rid himself of his hated guardian, Rosamund thanked the kindly lawyer.

'Master Blanschard, we all thank you for the trouble you have taken tirelessly on our behalf. You will perhaps stay with us at least tonight, possibly for the next few days? You know you are always welcome here. I will make arrangements for your accommodation.'

She half rose to see to it when Arthur said brusquely,

'Now that my stepmother is assured of her future welfare, would it be possible for her to receive some gold quickly? This house is such a sad place now and most likely she would prefer to leave, either to rent property in her home town of Warwick for a while until she can find a suitable house to purchase, or to return to her father.'

Master Blanschard gave a little bow in Lady Sibyl's direction. 'Certainly, funds can be placed at your disposal, Lady Kinnersley. You have only to consult me and I will expedite matters for you.'

Rosamund looked at Arthur reprovingly. This was no time to press the matter. There was a little silence, then Sibyl Kinnersley said coolly, 'I am afraid it would certainly not be suitable for me to travel at this time, nor appropriate. I have waited until I was quite sure, but now I must inform you all that I am with child. Kinnersley will soon have a new heir.'

She remained sitting and she appeared quite grave, but Rosamund thought she could detect a gleam of triumph in those blue eyes. Arthur stared at her, clearly totally stunned by her revelation.

Master Blanschard cleared his throat deliberately, possibly to give himself time to think. He said blandly, 'I am sure your news will bring comfort to this grieving family, Lady Kinnersley.' He glanced hurriedly at Arthur. 'Sir Humphrey's child will be welcome, even at so sad a time. Naturally you will wish to remain here for the present, I take it. Afterwards, when the child is born…' He spread his two hands expansively.

Rosamund saw the muscles in Arthur's throat tighten as he swallowed down his distress. For him these were disastrous tidings. There could be no challenge to his inheritance of Kinnersley—he was Sir Humphrey's heir, even should this child be a son. But custom demanded that the child be brought up in its father's house and be provided for. Rosamund knew that Arthur would have no objection to that, but his dislike of his stepmother would continue to dog him for however long she continued to remain at the manor, which promised now to be for some years.

The lawyer remained for a while in the hall, murmuring his congratulations to Lady Kinnersley. Arthur remained completely silent, then, at length, he rose, pushed back his chair, acknowledged Master Blanschard with a little nod, and strode from the hall. Rosamund uttered some commonplace remark to cover his abrupt departure and then followed him. She saw him talking with Martha beyond the screen doors, presumably acquainting her with Sibyl's momentous tidings, then he hastened out down the steps and into the courtyard. Rosamund caught up with Martha, who grimaced.

'Well, this announcement has shocked our young master.'

'You thought perhaps it might be so.'

'I wondered.'

'She did not confide in you?'

'No. It seems that she did wait, as she said, until she was quite sure.'

Rosamund sighed. 'I must go to Arthur. He'll be in the stable with his favourite pony, I dare say.'

Martha nodded. 'He told me all went well for you in your father's will.'

'Yes, he had arranged a very generous marriage portion for me.'

'Then Sir Simon Cauldwell will be very pleased.'

Rosamund looked away uncomfortably. The remark dealt her a momentary spasm of unease. Had Simon supposed that she would have a considerable dowry? Was he, like many young and impoverished knights, anxious to wed in order to enhance his fortunes? He could not have known of the extent of her dowry right, yet he was aware

of Kinnersley's prosperity and must have been assured that
her father would leave his only daughter well provided for.
He had never spoken much about his own home or his
fortune, but his plain dress and forthright, competent manner spoke to her of a soldier anxious to make his way in
the world. He was loyal to Gloucester through companionship and affection, she felt sure, but also as a possible
means of preferment.

Rosamund closed her eyes momentarily to shut out her
own distress. 'Yes,' she said tonelessly, 'but it is as we
said. Arthur will never be able to accept my marriage to
him, and now this blow makes it doubly difficult for me
to tell him.'

She lifted her skirts and followed Arthur down the hall
steps and across the courtyard. She found him, as she expected, with his beloved horses. Here, in the dimness of
the stable and alone, he had given way to boyish tears and
she pulled him to her and allowed him to sob out his anger
and distress against her bosom while she stroked his hair.

At last he lifted a tear-streaked face to hers. 'It is not
that I am angered about the baby. Father would have been
pleased to know about it and since it will be a brother or
sister we must welcome it, but we shall never be rid of
her now and she will have domination over me while she
remains here.'

'Not necessarily.'

He pulled at her hand. 'If you were to do what I said,
marry Andrew, then you two could remain here and you
would be, in essence, the true mistress until I come of age.
Tell me you will do it, Ros. If you were to leave me I do
not know what I should do.'

Over his bent head Rosamund bit her lip, finding it difficult to hold back her own frustrated tears. How could she
disappoint him and how could she explain matters to
Simon?

She said softly, ruffling his hair, 'We must consider all this very carefully, Arthur. Promise me you will say nothing to Andrew for the present.'

'But—'

'Now is not the time to broach so important a matter and—and you could embarrass him if he is not willing.'

'But why should he not be, especially as now we know you are generously provided for?'

'Promise me.'

He wriggled his shoulders in a boyish gesture of rebellion, then gave a heavy sigh. 'Oh, very well, but we cannot wait too long before the king orders you to wed elsewhere.'

Her lips moved in a silent prayer that, somehow, the Virgin would grant her a way to emerge from all this without hurting Arthur too greatly.

Chapter Nine

From the gatehouse window where he had his apartment Simon watched young Arthur Kinnersley's stumbling progress across the courtyard and into the main stable door. He had gone to his own chamber in order to remove himself from the personal business of the household being enacted in the hall. He had no wish to intrude on the privacy of the family, but now he stroked his chin thoughtfully as he considered what calamitous tidings had caused young Arthur to dash off so suddenly. Surely the lawyer had not brought the family bad news.

Whatever the problem, Arthur would not welcome his questions and certainly not his assistance. He must wait until he could consult with Rosamund and he knew that that meeting, too, must be apart from the young master's eagle gaze, for a while at least, until the dust of the boy's punishment had settled.

He sank down upon his bed and stretched out, arms linked above his head. He had dispatched his messenger to Gloucester and he knew it would be some time yet before he could expect a reply to his request, but he was impatient. Duke Richard, he was sure, would immediately forward his petition to his royal brother but, even then, he could not be sure it would be successful. He bit down savagely upon his nether lip at the merest thought that Rosamund could be given in marriage to another man. She must be his. He would not accept refusal at the king's hands; and yet he knew that, though he was loyal to the core, and Edward was aware of that, he might still have other plans for the disposal of this personable young heiress. Of course, Simon was not fully aware of what her marriage portion was likely to be, but Sir Humphrey Kinnersley had been well endowed with land and he did not believe that he would leave his only daughter without sufficient gold to allow her to make a suitable alliance. And also there was the fact that the boy was a minor in law and that Rosamund Kinnersley's future husband would have the right to order the estate, unless the king appointed another guardian, which was unlikely. He gave a wry grimace at the thought that he would have the unenviable task of dealing with the lad until he came of age. Even that Herculean burden he was prepared to shoulder for Rosamund's sake.

Rosamund. The image of her swam before his eyes. He recalled how he had found her dishevelled and frightened upon the field at Tewkesbury and not even her arrest and threat of dire punishment had caused her to lose that indomitable spirit. His heart beat faster as he remembered how he had held her close in his arms and how, for moments only, he had felt her response. Her lips had clung sweetly to his, her body cleaving to his hard one. Had he been less honourable she could have been his there, in the tent, and he would have had a stronger case to present to his Grace the king. Yet, almost instantly, she had recollected who she was and under what dire threat she lay, and he had recognised her innocence. His lips curved in triumph as he thought how she had confessed her love for him here in the garden, that same rose garden that breathed her very name to the world, Rosamund. That glorious English rose with the soft brown hair and golden eyes was his and he would win her and take her to his home in the north where he knew his mother would welcome her and come to love her as he did. But first they must both endure the contempt that the boy held for him, and obtain the consent of their sovereign to the match.

He frowned. Whatever the outcome, even should Edward withhold his consent, he would wed Rosamund and, if there was need, flee with her to Burgundy or France. And she would go with him, risk all for his sake, he was sure of that. Meanwhile he must be patient, though his heart yearned for her and his body burned to possess her. He must remember that she was still in mourning and that decorum decreed that she must wait a decent interval before marrying. He stiffened as he could hear, faintly, the murmur of feminine voices and he rose and went to the window again, sure that Rosamund's loved voice was one of them.

He was right. He saw Rosamund poised on the topmost step leading from the hall in talk with Martha. He could not hear what was said from this distance but, by their very posture and demeanour, he could detect that his love was as disturbed as her brother. Then he saw her run hastily down the steps and follow the boy into the stable. Clearly Master Blanschard had brought tidings that had alarmed both of them.

Since he was acting seneschal of this manor he should make an effort to discover what the problem was. Surely Sir Humphrey had not been behind with the payment of taxes, or been in debt to some merchant and so placed the family's finances in difficulty? Simon had been assured that Duke Richard would see to it that King Edward took no vengeful action against the youthful pair, so the possession of the manor house could not be in doubt.

He was considering the possibilities of disaster for the family when Rolf Taylor knocked at his door and informed him that his messenger had returned. Curtly Simon ordered him to be admitted.

The man doffed his metal salet and bowed. 'I managed to reach the duke at the Tower of London, Sir Simon, where he had taken temporary residence, and he received me personally and read your letter. He commanded me to assure you that he would send your request immediately to his Grace the king, but that he could not wait to receive an answer or request an audience with the king to press the matter, as he was ordered to advance into the city and confront the army of the bastard Fauconbridge, who was causing such devastation within the town. I could see that he was in a great hurry to leave and had only called to check the Tower arsenal and to take possession of some armaments he required. I could hear the noise of armed clashes from the fortress, sir, and waited only to take my leave of the duke and hasten back to you. I was afraid that if I delayed I might find myself trapped in the city and knew you would be anxious to know that your request had been received. His Grace, though clearly absorbed in his preparations for armed conflict, was fully aware of your need. He promised me that he would do all in his power to see that you received your just reward for your past loyal services to the king's cause.'

Sir Simon nodded brusquely, glancing at the man's dust-stained appearance. 'It would seem that you have half-killed your mount in your haste to come back to me. Get yourself to the kitchen for food, man, and get some rest.'

The messenger saluted and moved to the door when Sir Simon recalled his attention. 'I take it you heard no news of the Lady Anne Neville, the widow of the late Prince of Wales? Is Queen Margaret a prisoner in the Tower with her lord, King Henry, and her daughter-in-law with her?'

'I heard that the Lady Anne Neville was at the Duke of Clarence's town house in the city with her sister, the Duchess Isabel, sir. The former king and his queen were at the Tower, I understand, but I glimpsed no sight of either of them.'

'No, no, of course not. I would not expect that you did. Both would be closely guarded. Thank you. Get you about your own comfort now.'

He sat on for a moment in deep thought. He was as concerned about the happiness of his young lord, Duke Richard, as he was his own. Richard, he knew, would be alarmed at the knowledge that his heart's love, the Lady Anne Neville, was held in the charge of her brother-in-law. George of Clarence had by no means proved either his loyalty or his reliability during these recent engagements. He had married the Lady Anne's older sister, Isabel Neville, against the king's express command and had allied himself with the king's enemy, the Earl of Warwick, their father. Warwick had then forged an alliance with Queen Margaret of Anjou and married his younger daughter, Anne, to the Queen's son, Edward of Lancaster, Prince of Wales, who had recently been killed at the battle of Tewkesbury. It was true that Clarence had again changed his colours and returned his allegiance to his brother, the king, before that final battle, but his actions had not endeared him to his brothers. If greed for the great Warwick holdings and fortunes had caused him to wed Isabel and cleave to his cousin Warwick, what would he be likely to do now that Isabel and Anne were joint heiresses and only Anne stood between him and his ambition to possess the whole of the inheritance? Now that Richard was again involved in conflict in the city against the bastard Fauconbridge and in loyal service to his brother the king, he was helpless to come to her assistance should she need it. He and the duke were both in need of the assistance of the little Greek god of love, Simon mused.

Since he would not be welcome in the stable with Rosamund and her brother, Simon decided he must seek out the lawyer and reassure himself that all was well with the two young Kinnersleys.

He questioned a serving maid as to where the lawyer had been accommodated and took himself to the chamber. The lawyer rose to his feet hastily when he knocked and announced himself, for Simon saw that he had been resting on the bed.

'Please come in, Sir Simon,' Master Blanschard murmured deferentially. 'In what way can I be of service to you?'

'I hope I do not intrude upon your rest, Master Blanschard. I know that you have been forced to do some considerable amount of travelling recently, which must be tiring for a man of your years, but as seneschal of this castle I feel I must be certain that the affairs of the household are in order. Please understand that I need to know no details of Sir Humphrey Kinnersley's will but, as the welfare of his two children are in my charge for the present, I need to be informed as to their situation.'

The little lawyer bowed fussily and saw to it that his guest was comfortably seated upon the one chair the little chamber boasted. 'I have enquired into the standing of the manor.' He cleared his throat awkwardly. 'After, well, you know, sir, after the professed loyalties of its previous lord...I am assured by the king's clerks that he has the interests of the two children at heart as his own wards and that the manor is in no way threatened.'

'Good, that too was my understanding.' Simon pursed his lips. 'I—I happened to see both Master Arthur and Mistress Rosamund rush away from the hall recently and

I judged them to be in a state of distress. I trust that if there is cause it can be remedied.'

The little lawyer peered at him uncertainly through shortsighted eyes. 'Well,' he said doubtfully, 'I imagine that it has come as a great shock to them to learn that the dowager Lady Kinnersley is with child and that there will soon be another heir to Kinnersley.'

Simon stared at him blankly for a moment, his eyes wide with surprise. 'Oh,' he said at last. 'I see.'

Master Blanschard wriggled uncomfortably where he sat perched on the edge of his small cot. 'I do not think that has come as welcome tidings, particularly to young Master Arthur, who seems anxious to have the lady gone from the manor.'

'I see you speak bluntly. Yes. Master Arthur has no wish to have his life governed, especially not by someone he thinks has come only lately into the household. I have seen myself that he tends to resent his father's recent marriage—and to so young a lady.'

Master Blanschard nodded. 'The dowager Lady Kinnersley is very well provided for in her widow's portion but, naturally, she will wish the child to be brought up at the manor, which could make difficulties.'

'Master Arthur should be placed with some noble household as soon as possible so that he can do service as a squire and learn his martial skills. The manor could then be placed in the care of a permanent seneschal chosen by his Grace the king. I am anxious to arrange that but Arthur is unwilling and, of course, his grief and that of Mistress Kinnersley is very recent so we must be careful of his sensibilities.'

The lawyer nodded agreement and Simon moved to the door of the chamber. As he did so Master Blanschard said quietly, 'It may interest you to know, Sir Simon, that Mistress Rosamund's dowry is considerable. It consists of some gold, but mainly of a manor in Leicestershire, which, I understand, her mother originally brought to her marriage. The manor is a prosperous one. I have been to oversee matters there quite recently and found the steward to be a very trustworthy and loyal servant.' He looked at Simon deliberately and the knight gave a little laugh.

'I see you are very shrewd, Master Blanschard. You only saw me glance at Mistress Rosamund briefly before she passed into the hall with her brother but, already, you have drawn the conclusion that I have tender feelings towards her. I also feel that you have her interests at heart as much as I do. I assure you there will be no compulsion on my part. I have already discussed the possibility of a match between us with the lady and, to my joy, I have discovered that my feelings are reciprocated.'

The lawyer's eyes creased in a smile. 'That relieves my mind, sir. I have known Mistress Rosamund most of her life and I have great affection for her.'

'I am about to petition the king for permission to marry her, since, as you know, she is a ward of the Crown, but the difficulty lies again with her brother, who will oppose the match.'

'Ah.' Master Blanschard picked at his nether lip in a gesture of concern. 'I hope, sir, that difficulty can be overcome.'

'For the present I wish the matter to be kept close, you understand?'

'You can trust me, Sir Simon.'

Simon nodded to the man, mentioned his approval of the lawyer's opinion and loyal service, and withdrew. He passed down the spiral stair and made to go towards the screen doors when his attention was caused by the murmur of voices coming from the hall. Servants generally tended to shout to one another when in the hall or, at the very least, to make no effort to lower their voices, particularly when working without supervision, and he was puzzled by what appeared to be a certain secretiveness in the very manner of the conversation. Cautiously he pushed the screen door to the hall partially open to see just who was engaged in such quiet talk there.

Lady Kinnersley stood near to the door leading from the dais to her solar apartment. She was bending her head very close to her companion and Simon recognised the man to be Andrew Murton. As if aware that someone was listening to them, the lady lifted her head briefly and gazed round the hall as if to spy any eavesdropper, but Simon was well hidden behind the door and she failed to detect his presence.

Andrew Murton gave a little dry laugh as she gave him her attention again, presuming that they were quite alone.

'I take it the boy was greatly displeased by your revelation.'

'He was. He is hoping that I shall soon be gone from here. He rushed out of the hall in a temper without stopping to question me or to congratulate me on my condition. His sister remembered her manners and did linger to do so, then she dashed off herself, presumably to comfort her brother.'

'Then he will be sadly disappointed. The child must naturally be brought up in its father's house.'

'Indeed, he will be furious, as, I think, Mistress Rosamund will be also. She resents my position as chatelaine here as much as he does though she is more polite about it.'

'Sir Simon Cauldwell has made pointed suggestions that I should seek for a new master.'

Lady Kinnersley's voice sounded almost shrill with alarm. 'You will not leave here, Andrew. Promise me.'

'Of course I do not intend to go.' Simon saw him give a shrug of his shoulders. 'The boy is as anxious to keep me here as you are, and his recent disagreement with the knight and the punishment that followed has made him even more resentful. My place here is assured for the present.'

Simon saw the squire move to leave her and she reached out a hand to clutch at his sleeve. 'Andrew, you will be very careful?'

'Of course I will, my lady.' He hesitated. 'If there is need, I still retain for my use the lodging near to St Mary's in Warwick.'

'Yes.' She watched him walk away towards the screen door rather wistfully, Simon thought. He removed himself quickly against the possibility of being discovered overhearing their obviously private conversation and ran lightly down the steps into the courtyard before the squire should reach the door. He was in a thoughtful mood as he made his way once more to his own quarters in the gatehouse.

He remained there for some hours, careful not to intrude upon Rosamund and her brother and mulling over what the lawyer, Blanschard, had told him and the somewhat curious nature of the conversation between Sibyl Kinnersley and the squire, Andrew Murton, in the hall. Its very secrecy made him suspicious. It was clear to him that Sibyl Kinnersley was very determined indeed to keep her husband's former squire at the manor. Why? he asked himself. He had not noticed any particular closeness between the pair until this one incident. Indeed, Sibyl Kinnersley appeared to have kept all the family members and the servants of the household at a distance. He could understand that. She was the latecomer, beautiful, young and likely to have very great influence over the master. He had had little opportunity to question Rosamund about her mother, but the first lady Kinnersley had probably been greatly loved by all those at Kinnersley and the arrival of her successor was resented. Yet Lady Sibyl appeared to have a special rapport with Andrew Murton. Simon had discovered that they had both come to Kinnersley from Warwick. There had been that odd reference to a town house in Warwick made by Murton, which both of them appeared to know. Had they known each other well before their arrivals at the manor? It was certainly possible. Sibyl Kinnersley had been the daughter of a wealthy merchant living in the town. So much he had gathered. If they had been acquainted that was natural enough, but Simon suspected that, since the lady had deliberately kept herself secluded, she had had reason to conceal the fact of their acquaintanceship; and, if so, that in itself was suspicious. Now she had suddenly revealed that she was carrying the late Sir Humphrey's child. Had the knight been aware of her condition when he left for Tewkesbury field? If so, why had he not mentioned it to his two other children? Perhaps the lady had only just discovered the fact for herself, or suspected it, and had had to be sure.

His musings were cut off by a light, almost secretive tap upon his chamber door and he sat up on his bed, suddenly alert. Rolf Taylor would certainly have given a bolder request for entrance and Simon was intrigued. His pulses raced. Had Rosamund decided to come to him at last? His eyes yearned to see her.

He was a little disappointed, on giving permission to enter, to find that it was his love's former nurse, Martha, who entered softly.

'Yes, Martha?' he enquired. 'What can I do for you? I hope that neither of your charges are unwell—or perhaps they are in need of my services?'

The maid gave an awkward little bob of a curtsy and stood aside to usher in Rosamund. Simon sprang up immediately to take her hand and draw her farther into the chamber. She was flushing rosily and turned to her nurse.

'Keep watch for us, Martha,' she pleaded. 'I do not want Arthur to discover that we have been talking privately together.'

Again the former nurse bobbed a curtsy, flashed Simon a knowing glance, and withdrew. He chuckled as he visualised her keeping a dragon's watch from the gatehouse door.

Once the door was closed, he pulled Rosamund more tightly to him and lifted her chin with a single finger to gaze into her eyes. 'I was waiting and praying that you would come to me, sweetheart,' he murmured, as he bent to kiss her. This time she made no move to extricate herself but lifted both arms to encircle his neck and her lips opened sweetly beneath his. Very gently his tongue probed for entry, knowing her inexperience, but she allowed him entrance and her passion met his. His senses swam as he felt her heart beating faster and faster close to his own and her body cling to his. Through the thin stuff of her black velvet mourning gown he could feel the heat of her and he could sense the hardening within his groin at the need to possess her, here and now, so that no one could ever deny his right to wed her. Common sense and decency prevailed, however, and he gave a deep groan of frustration and gently put her from him. She opened her pansy-dark eyes wide and stared at him as if, for one moment, she had forgotten where she was and all need for caution.

He put up one hand to touch her lips and drew her down upon the bed, then sat beside her, but keeping a careful distance between them.

'Heart of my heart, you go to my head,' he murmured brokenly. 'We must be very careful when alone together, you and I. If we forget ourselves and I take you now we would regret it for ever and the king might very well see to that by accusing me of treason against the Crown.'

'I did not think—mean for that—' She pulled away from him, clearly frightened by her own response.

'I know it, sweetheart. Only have patience. I must be the one to guard us both from ourselves.'

She said hurriedly, 'Something dreadful has happened. At least it is so for Arthur. Sibyl is with child and—'

'I know,' he said gravely. 'Master Blanschard told me and I saw you both rush into the sanctuary of the stables. A brother or sister now cannot be welcome if it means that Arthur will have to wait a long time to rid himself of the presence of Sibyl and feel that he is his own man here.'

'I should have realised,' Rosamund said shakily, 'at least that it was possible—and she has secluded herself so very much recently.'

He considered, eyes narrowed. 'Rosamund, tell me, did Andrew Murton arrive at Kinnersley Manor at the same time as Lady Sibyl? Did he form part of her escort?'

'Oh, no.' She stared at him, bewildered by the question. 'He came some months later. His brother had informed him that my father was in need of a squire and he presented himself and requested service in our household.'

'Did she appear to know him?'

'I do not think so. She has never said so. Of course, she might have met him in Warwick. They both lived there for a while. Why do you ask, Simon? Do you distrust Andrew Murton?'

She was clearly disturbed by his probing and he reached out and took her hand. 'It is just that I heard them talking.' He shook his head. 'Nothing sinister could be implied from what was said, but she was very anxious to have him remain here. They appeared to be closer, more intimate, than I had imagined.'

'He has been very helpful to all of us since—' her eyes filled with sudden tears '—since Father—and he took such pains to bring us the body when it might have been easier and safer for him to make his escape from the field, as many did. Arthur is very fond of him, trusts him completely.' She broke off abruptly and turned from him. 'Simon, Arthur wishes me to marry Andrew.'

'What?' the single word was harshly jerked out

'It would seem to be the perfect solution for Arthur. He thinks that—that if I do so, I will be safe from any unwelcome suitor the king might provide for me, particularly a Yorkist one. He believes that if he petitions the king for permission to allow the match, it will be granted. Of course, just now, especially not just now, I cannot tell him that we—that I love you and that you have already written to the Duke of Gloucester. To know that now, to even contemplate the possibility that I might leave him, to go with you to your home, would break his heart.'

'Yes,' he said grimly, 'I am aware of that. And what exactly did you say?'

'I—I stalled for time. I was completely taken aback. I have made him promise that he will not speak to Andrew on the subject.'

'And what is your opinion of Andrew?'

'He is a pleasant enough young fellow. As I said before, since taking service with my father, he has always proved himself reliable and trustworthy. I can see why Arthur would think this a suitable solution especially as...' she paused and looked away again '...my father apparently left me very well provided for as a marriage settlement. There is a manor in Charnwood in Leicestershire, which will be mine, at least the revenues from it will be. We can be very comfortable on that, can we not, Simon?' She added in a sudden rush, 'And perhaps we could live there for a while instead of moving north so far from Kinnersley where Arthur will need me.'

'I know about that too,' he assured her. 'Master Blanschard was obliging enough to inform me of it.'

'Oh?'

He grinned broadly. 'He is a very shrewd old gentleman. He could see in one glance what Arthur certainly cannot.'

'Then you are pleased?'

'Why should I not be?'

Her head was lowered and the black veil edging her hennin hid her face from him. His lips curved in a little wry smile as he wondered what was passing though her mind just now. Did she think him mercenary? Likely so. All maids were aware of the need for a suitable dowry to entice a good husband or even a not so good one. He passed no comment and, when at last she lifted her head and looked directly into his startlingly blue eyes, she answered his smile with a little wan one of her own.

'Has Murton ever shown you any indication that he might have eventually asked your father for your hand?'

'Never. He has always been most assiduous in his services to me, but totally dependable and correct, behaving as was to be expected to the daughter of his master.'

He nodded, satisfied.

'Do you doubt his loyalty to Arthur?'

He said curtly, 'I certainly do not doubt his loyalty to his mistress.'

Her brown eyes widened once more, betraying her astonishment and sense of unease. 'You cannot believe that—that he loves her...'

He shrugged. 'She is extremely beautiful.'

'But beyond his reach. Even now she is a rich widow...'

'Exactly,' he said brusquely. 'Whatever is in his mind, he will not succeed in taking his master's daughter as a prize. You belong to me. Don't you forget it, even for a moment.'

She gave a little shaky laugh and reached out to take both his hands. 'Simon, you know that I am not in the least interested in Andrew Murton. I want to be your wife.

I only beg you to be patient and allow me to bring Arthur round to the idea.'

He frowned slightly, squeezing her hands hard. 'I think once I have Gloucester's reply and then the king's permission, and I am reasonably sure of that, we should consider marrying at once.'

'But you promised that you would wait…'

'I know I did, but I am impatient and I would not run the risk of the king changing his mind. I could arrange for a priest to marry us secretly. Would that please you?'

She lowered her head so that, again, he could not read her expression. 'And if we did that,' she whispered shyly, 'would you want—expect—me to become your wife—properly?'

He gave a laugh and drew her to him, once more lifting up her chin so that she was forced to look into his eyes. 'Look at me, Rosamund, look well. Do you trust me?'

'Of course.'

'Are you afraid of me?'

'A little,' she confessed.

'That is good. A maid should be a little afraid…' he chuckled '…else would her husband believe that she was more experienced than he had thought.'

'Simon!' she said sharply and he laughed out loud again.

'Come, my sweet, I am in no doubt concerning your virginal state. I trust you completely.' He shrugged. 'And even if I were to discover that you had had a lover before me—well, even then, I would want you.'

'Really?' she said guilelessly.

He kissed her, his hand fondling her breast beneath the velvet of her gown, 'Yes, really, but I prefer to know, as I do, that I shall be the first to bring you to that state of ecstasy. Yes, my sweet, I shall want you to be my wife, in name and in body. In that way, after we have consummated our marriage, we shall be sure that no one can part

us, at least not without some great gift being offered to the
Curia in Rome to obtain a dissolution and that will not
happen.'

'But if I should conceive?'

'Well, then everyone will know and Arthur must make
the best of it. But I will accept that to keep our love from
him for as long as we can will be the best thing for all of
us—for a while.'

She gave a deep sigh and gently pulled her hands from
his grasp. 'Possibly it would be best for us to wait until
Sibyl's child is born.'

He was about to expostulate that that would be longer
than he intended, or indeed could bear, when their attention was drawn to some small commotion down in the
courtyard and he went to the window and leaned out.

'It seems that a pedlar has arrived,' he said, turning towards her, for she had kept well back from the window,
careful that she should not be seen alone with Simon in
his chamber. 'The grooms and house servants are clearly
delighted to see him.'

'Yes, of course,' she said breathlessly. 'I should go
down and give permission for him to sell his wares to the
housemaids. There are one or two small things I require
myself, a new comb and pins…'

'Go then and buy the gewgaws your woman's heart fan-
cies. I wish that I could openly buy those things for you,
but the next time he arrives I shall do that.'

She skipped from him, blew him a kiss, and opened the
door softly to find Martha still on guard. Together they ran
into the courtyard to find Arthur there already. He had
come from the stable when he had heard the noise. The
pedlar was a jovial, fat little man, who led his equally fat
pony and cart farther into the courtyard and, jumping down
from the driving seat of his little cart, turned eagerly at the
sight of Rosamund and her brother approaching. She rec-

ognised him at once. He had called often at the manor during the years of her childhood and had always been welcomed by her father for, as well as the quality of his wares, he frequently brought long-sought-for news from the neighbourhood and the more distant towns like Warwick and Tewkesbury.

'Good morrow, master and mistress,' he said doffing his cap respectfully. 'I trust I can get permission to sell my wares here.'

Rosamund turned to Arthur and waited for his nod of approval. It was so necessary for the boy's dignity, at this juncture, that he should know that he was master here. She could see that he was as pleased as she was to receive the pedlar.

'Aye, fellow,' he called. 'You are welcome, as always. After you have sold your goods to the servants, take some refreshment in the kitchen and see to it that your pony is fed and watered. Do you stay the night here?'

'I would be very glad to, master, if you will allow it.'

'Certainly. You can bed down in the stable where you will be comfortable enough.' Arthur pointed to the courtyard behind him where, already, servant girls and grooms were gathering excitedly. 'I think you will not want for customers and we have some soldiers here too who should welcome your arrival. But first, what news do you bring from abroad?'

The pedlar came closer. He looked round the courtyard as if expecting to be overheard by some eavesdropper who might wish him harm, then, feeling that he was amongst people he trusted, he said excitedly, 'Well, master, I heard some very interesting news from a chapman in Warwick who'd travelled from the south. It seemed that rumours were trickling through that King Henry has been found dead in the Tower of London. Well, I wasn't prepared to believe it at first. You know how tales about royal person-

ages get bandied about especially after, well, what happened to Prince Edward at Tewkesbury, but it seems it is
true. It were confirmed later by a sergeant-at-arms in the
household of the Duke of Clarence. He was going to the
castle to report and he told us that indeed King Henry had
died and...' the man lowered his voice conspiratorially
'...that the young Duke of Gloucester was present that day
at the Tower.' He paused dramatically, surveying his silent
audience for their reaction. 'Well, it's being said as how
the king wanted poor King Henry dead right enough, as
did all them Yorkist nobles, and that the duke took the
opportunity to put the old man to death personally like.
It's true that King Henry's son was done to death on
Tewkesbury field and it's said Duke Richard did for him
too, 'cos he wanted his wife, the Lady Anne, so it's likely
enough, since he were there, that he did do it.'

There was an uncomfortable silence and one or two of
the soldiers from Sir Simon's company moved away, as if
anxious to disassociate themselves from the accusation.
Rosamund felt very sick. She swallowed the sharp bile
rising in her throat. Surely the amiable young man who
had only recently sat at their table here in the hall and who
had proved himself so helpful to her in Tewkesbury at such
a sad time, the man who was Simon's lord and friend,
could not have perpetrated so foul at deed!

Arthur gave out a yelp of contemptuous laughter.
'There, what did I tell you all? I spoke the very truth and
got abused for my pains. Now it's clear to everyone that
Richard of Gloucester is nothing but the foulest of murderers. King Henry was helpless and sick and done to
death so cruelly just to clear the way for those Yorkist
scum to rule the realm.'

'Have you not learned your lesson yet?' A chillingly
cold voice broke across the embarrassed silence following
this remark and Rosamund turned to find Simon walking

across the courtyard towards the assembled group. To her horror he marched up to Arthur and struck him hard across the mouth.

'How dare you speak treason in my hearing! You accuse my lord and friend of the foulest act without an atom of proof. So, the duke was present at the Tower. He was there to inspect the armaments and, incidentally, to prepare to defend London from attacks from an enemy force. We have no evidence yet to prove that King Henry died on that particular day or that his death was not from natural causes. You are a stupid, insolent boy. Take yourself to your chamber and away from my sight before you make any more wild and dangerous statements. As for you, fellow, you had better watch your tongue before someone cuts it out.' This was directed at the now frightened pedlar who was stumbling backwards away from the naked fury he read in the knight's eyes.

Before Rosamund could move to speak any word in Arthur's defence or intervene, the boy drew himself up to stare back at Simon, one hand moving wonderingly, almost unbelievingly, to his wounded mouth, from which a slow trickle of blood was issuing. Rosamund read in his eyes his disbelief that he could have been so humiliated before his own people. Since Simon continued to stare at him grimly, arms folded across his chest, he moved slightly backwards, then turned and ran towards the hall steps.

Simon snapped. 'All of you, go about your duties. And do not allow any further treasonable talk to come to my ears or the perpetrator will suffer for it. Do you hear me?'

Unwillingly the group began to disperse and, some distance away, one or two turned to stare furtively at the seneschal and then break into surly muttering. Rosamund stood quite still, white to the lips, then, once they were alone, she advanced towards Simon and, in her turn, struck him hard across the face.

'How could you?' she said hoarsely. 'How could you do that to Arthur, here, before all the household?'

'Rosamund, did you hear him? He said—'

'I know what he said,' she snapped, 'and for all I know he was speaking the truth. He doesn't appear to be the only one who thinks it. That doesn't matter. What does is that you could not contain yourself. You had to insult him. You know what he means to me…'

She turned from him, tears streaming down her cheeks, and, before he could reach out and touch her, she had swept by him and run full pelt after her brother into the manor house.

Chapter Ten

Rosamund kept to her chamber for the rest of the day. Several times Martha knocked upon her door and requested that Sir Simon be allowed to enter and talk to her, but she refused. She did not even attempt to leave her chamber to speak with Arthur but, when Martha brought her supper later, she enquired about him.

'How is he, Martha? Have you seen him?'

'Like you, he refuses to leave his chamber. I have taken him some supper, but I do not think that he is in a mood to eat anything. His pride has been hurt once again.'

Rosamund sighed heavily. 'He was always prone to speak exactly what was on his mind without thinking. One day that could cost him his life but, this time, I am inclined to think that this was not his fault.'

'And you will not see Sir Simon? He is growing very insistent.'

'No, Martha, I cannot.' She turned away, tears pricking once again at her eyelids. 'I know he was shocked to hear what was said, as we all were, but he should not have reacted so brutally. Arthur was completely humiliated and how is he ever to receive respect from the servants of his own household now?'

'I do not think they will behave badly, mistress. They know that he is just a boy still, but they are all fiercely loyal. Anyway,' she added darkly, 'they are all inclined to agree with Master Arthur that the rumours were true and they feel, as he does, that, if so, what was done was shameful.'

Rosamund stared gloomily at the food on her tray, unwilling, as Arthur was, to eat. There was still that sharp feeling of bile in her throat which had come when she had first heard the pedlar's calamitous tidings.

Martha appeared to be about to speak, then changed her mind and silently helped her mistress to undress and prepare for bed.

Rosamund spent a miserable night. She knew that it would be impossible for her to sleep and she sat for hours upon her bed crying softly. What could she do? Arthur relied upon her totally and the hostility between him and Simon was now even worse than it had been following Simon's harsh punishment. She could not suddenly announce to him that she loved Simon Cauldwell and wished to marry him. It would break Arthur's heart.

She was also very angry with Simon, not only because of his summary treatment of Arthur, but because of his unshakeable allegiance to the House of York. How could the two of them resolve their differences? She had been prepared to accept the fact that Edward of York was now indubitably king, and that Simon and she and, indeed, Arthur, must offer him allegiance, but this talk of the murder of the hapless King Henry VI sickened her. Her father had talked of the late king's sickness of the mind and, to Rosamund, it had always seemed that he was vulnerable and that his redoubtable queen, Margaret of Anjou, was the true power behind the throne. He had been captured after the Lancastrian defeat at Tewkesbury and taken to the

Tower of London. That he would be held a prisoner there, Rosamund could have accepted, for peace could not have been established while King Henry and his queen were free—but murdered in cold blood! That was a deed too cruel to be contemplated, and that it should have been Simon's lord, Duke Richard, who had perpetrated it! Could she ever forgive Simon for defending the man? Certainly she could not envisage life as Simon's wife if he continued to serve in Gloucester's household. The future looked bleak for both of them, for it did not appear likely that he would renounce his loyalty to his friend and liege lord. Some time she would have to face him and present him with her ultimatum. He must leave Gloucester's service or she could not marry him, now or in the future. That prospect filled her with total despair. She loved him with all her heart and would continue to love him until the end of time, but she could not live amicably with him, knowing that she would have to be present at court and appear to offer the young Duke of Gloucester her loyal obedience and respect. She also knew that Simon would never agree to leave Gloucester's service. She was not sure whether she truly believed his friend to be innocent of that heinous accusation or whether he would continue in his unswerving loyalty and devotion in spite of knowing that Gloucester was indeed guilty.

She did manage to doze fitfully for some time during the night but was still wakeful soon after dawn and glad to see Martha when she arrived with breakfast. Rosamund dressed, fingering her mourning robes sadly. It seemed that there were so many poor souls losing their loved ones these days and that death and its bitter consequences was on everyone's mind to the exclusion of all else.

Martha took her leave and, as she did so, Rosamund

called after her, 'Try to find out if there is any further news from the towns, Martha.'

'You mean about King Henry?'

'Yes, and tell Arthur that I would like to see him. By the way, how is my lady today?'

Martha shrugged. 'As usual. She keeps to her chamber most of the time, but she did emerge for supper last night in the hall. She chattered away quite brightly to Sir Simon, but he remained silent and morose for the most part. Lady Sibyl does not appear to be greatly shocked by the news about the late king, but stated quite openly that she considered it a mercy for all concerned.'

'And how did Sir Simon take that comment?'

'Without any great enthusiasm. He remarked that rumours were flying around too loosely and that it was far too early for us to receive creditable information from the capital.'

'He did not demand to see Arthur? You do not think he will punish him again?'

'He has not mentioned the young master, neither did Lady Sibyl. Indeed, no one appeared to care whether he ate or not. It was a good thing that I was there to see to his needs.'

Rosamund found herself strangely hungry and made a hearty meal of fresh manchet bread, beef and honey, and drank some ale. She looked up anxiously as a loud knock came at her door.

'Who is it?'

'Arthur. Let me in, Ros.'

She rose hurriedly and undid the bolt. Arthur charged in impetuously and seizing one of the remaining small bread rolls, broke it, smeared it with sweet butter and honey and munched hungrily. Rosamund noticed that the small wound at the corner of his mouth, probably made by Sir Simon's seal ring, had not yet healed and that he winced once sharply as he finished his bread.

'So you are staying out of the seneschal's way, as I am,' he announced. 'He's striding about the courtyard issuing orders to his men and ours this morning, and his tone is such that they are all scuttling to obey him as if their very lives were at stake.'

'Perhaps they are,' she said curtly, 'if he hears them listening to scurrilous gossip, as they were yesterday.'

'Do you believe it to be true?'

She hesitated. 'I think it's unlikely that a tale of King Henry's death could be bruited about without some element of truth behind it. We do not know the full facts, of course. He could have died naturally.'

'It has not been given out that he was ill.'

'No.' She regarded Arthur steadily. 'Whatever is true or untrue, it would be unwise for you to comment about it any further, Arthur. Surely you realise that.'

'Yes.' He subsided sulkily on to her bed. 'But if Gloucester was indeed at the Tower on the day the king died…'

'It still would not be proof that he did murder, Arthur. The Tower is a large place. He may not have even seen the king, who was a prisoner.'

'But if he was there, he could have seen to it that King Henry did not survive.'

'Possibly.' Rosamund broke off, lifting her hand in warning as another knock came upon the door and Martha entered once more.

She closed the door behind her carefully so that they would not be overheard.

'One of our grooms came back early this morning. He had been to see his sweetheart in Warwick. He says the town is buzzing with the news of King Henry's death and that the Duke of Clarence is delighted with the outcome. I think we can assume that, undoubtedly, the king is dead.'

'And was anything said as to who was responsible?' Rosamund asked.

Martha's lips twitched. 'Well, the same tale abounds as we heard yesterday. His Grace, the Duke of Gloucester, was visiting the Tower that day but…' and she paused thoughtfully '…Dick says that he was told that the king must have died after the duke left because of some wardrobe accounts being made up later or something, though I don't see as how that can mean anything.'

Rosamund considered. 'The wardrobe and household accounts of royal personages are calculated very carefully, Martha. It could indicate that, indeed, the duke was not at the Tower of London when the king died.'

'And nothing was being said as to the cause of death?' Arthur demanded.

Martha gave a shrill of laughter. 'Oh, well, everyone's sure that whatever is given out, the poor old man was done to death. It stands to reason that the new king would not want to have a living rival, not even as a prisoner.'

'Then, surely, we can assume that King Henry was killed on Gloucester's orders,' Arthur cried triumphantly. 'He was there just before. He was obviously there to see to it that the deed was done. He is a Yorkist prince like his brother, George of Clarence. It's to his advantage.'

'To the king's advantage,' Rosamund said quietly. 'Thank you, Martha, for telling me all that folk seem to know. We should say nothing more about this. Inform the servants that they are not to spread this rumour further.'

'Aye, mistress.'

'Perhaps the Duke of Gloucester will recall Sir Simon south soon now, to his side, since he is such an advocate on his behalf,' Arthur said, rising from the bed. 'I'm going riding again with Andrew, Ros, if anyone asks for me.'

He strode to the door, whistling more cheerfully than she had heard him of late, and took his leave. She and Martha watched him go, both their eyes narrowed in doubt.

'The ride should keep him out of Sir Simon's way, at least for a while,' Rosamund commented and Martha nodded.

They both stood silent for moments listening to Arthur's booted feet descend the stairs, and then Rosamund held her breath as a firmer tread followed the sound, as an older and heavier man ascended.

Sir Simon Cauldwell's voice called peremptorily, 'Open this door at once, Mistress Kinnersley. If you do not, I shall be forced to kick it down or to order my men to break in. I assure you that I mean to enter—now.'

Rosamund gave a great shuddering breath. 'Let him in Martha, please,' she whispered.

'But, Mistress...'

'Do it, please. It would be useless to object.'

Unwillingly Martha went to the door and opened it wide. In actual fact it was not bolted from inside following Arthur's departure, but Sir Simon had not been aware of that. He stood on the threshold, hands upon his hips, his expression grim.

'Leave me with your mistress,' he commanded Martha.

As she was about to argue he said curtly, 'Close the door and wait just outside if you must, where she can call to you in need. Now go, woman.'

Martha cast one backward glance at her charge, but Rosamund made a little gesture signifying that she should do what she was commanded. She remained by the bed, hands by her sides, her cheeks almost as white as the linen sheets.

He stood gazing at her, filling his eyes with her beauty. She was still attired in her brocaded bedgown of softest green and silver and for once free of her mourning. Her brown hair cascaded down her back in lustrous waves, and the sadness reflected in her glorious eyes made him want to rush forward and take her into his arms. He needed to kiss away all care and anxiety, to crush her to him so that she would feel nothing but the strength of his arms around her and the ardency of his lips upon hers. Something prevented him from doing that, as if he knew in his heart that she would be further hurt by such actions. He reached out slowly and deliberately made fast the door before moving, so giving her time to prepare herself to face his anger.

For a moment neither of them spoke, then he said abruptly, 'What is this, Rosamund? I have asked repeatedly to be admitted to you and been refused. How can this tittle-tattle of the gutters touch us?'

'You call it tittle-tattle? So you deny any truth in it?'

He gave an impatient shrug. 'I do not know if there is truth in it or not. I—'

'And you do not care that your lord and friend has been accused of such a vile crime?'

He moved a trifle uncertainly and she sensed his discomfort. 'I cannot see that any of this concerns us. It seems likely that King Henry is truly dead. Deposed monarchs often meet such ends. Do you think that King Richard the Second died quietly in his bed after his defeat by Harry of Lancaster? We are all aware that King Edward the Second was murdered and horribly, so horribly that I would not offend your ears by talking of the details of his death. So poor Harry has now, like as not, joined them. Some would say this was necessary for the peace of the realm. Do you believe that those Lancastrian nobles who survived and fled following the battle at Tewkesbury would remain quietly in exile without attempting to put their figurehead of a king back upon the throne again and so plunge us all into warfare once more? For he was merely a figurehead, Rosamund. You must accept that. Harry the Sixth was unfit to reign. Your own father would have told you that.'

'And you think that excuses his murder, that of a help-less, vulnerable, ageing man? That is your defence of your lord's actions?'

He frowned. 'I did not say that I believed Duke Richard to be guilty. If the deed was done and the king did not die naturally, which is surely possible, it was done by order of Duke Richard's brother, King Edward.'

'So you think the command of a brother excuses the deed?'

He shrugged again, more uncomfortably, it seemed to her this time. 'I cannot say. That brother is a king and Richard dearly loves him and is always anxious to please him. I have no brother.'

'But I have,' she said bitterly, 'and you seem to forget that and my love for him when you castigate and abuse him publicly.'

'Ah,' he said. 'So it is Arthur and my summary treat-ment of him that is the cause of this rift between us.'

She did not answer. He came closer, took her chin in one hand and gazed deeply into her eyes. 'When are you going to allow Arthur to grow up, Rosamund? Yes, I will admit that I was angry and did not think before striking him. I should not have done that. Any reproach I made to him should have been in private, not before members of his household. I belittled him and for that I beg your for-giveness, but you must remember that I am human and reacted under stress. Such scurrilous talk needed to be quashed and immediately before it caused further harm and endangered all of us.'

She shook her head wearily. 'It made me realise that there is too much between us, Simon. You talk of this killing as a political necessity. I cannot contemplate it as such. I know that you saw men brutally killed on the field, may do in the future, and so the death of one ageing man to prevent further bloodshed appears acceptable in your eyes. The thought of his lonely death in the Tower fills me with horror and I could not find it in my heart to approve your allegiance to a man who could sanction it.'

'Then it is my allegiance to Duke Richard that you abhor?'

'I cannot believe that he would do such a thing. I have met him twice and believed him honourable and kind and—'

'And so he is.'

'And you will continue to serve in his household?'

'Certainly. He has my friendship, has had it since we were boys together.'

'And you will be loyal to him whatever he does?'

He hesitated. 'He is my liege lord. Would you have me dishonour myself in betraying him?'

'I cannot marry you, Simon, if you persist in this. Arthur has an unswerving antipathy towards this man. I could not break his heart by allying myself to you.'

'What is this nonsense? Have you ceased to love me, Rosamund?'

Tears sparked at her eyelashes once more and she shook her head almost angrily to clear her vision. 'You know that I cannot deny my love for you.'

His mouth hardened and he scowled. 'Do you not realise that if the king chooses another husband for you his allegiance will be to the house of York as mine is?'

'But Arthur will not be so opposed to the match.'

'Arthur!' He ground out the name in helpless fury and she turned away from him.

In moments he had stepped closer and drawn her into his arms. His lips scorched hers and she felt the hardness of his muscles beneath the wool of his doublet. She gave a little moan of frustration. She longed to surrender herself completely, but dared not do so, and she tried, impotently, to beat at his chest in an effort to free herself. His iron grip held her tightly and again she gave a little cry as she turned her head in an attempt to avoid the pressure of his lips on hers.

'Let me go, Simon, please. I appeal to your knightly honour.'

'My knightly honour!' He gave a harsh, derisive laugh. 'You think I have none. Why should I cleave to what you think non-existent now?'

He was pressing her inexorably towards the bed, as he had done in Tewkesbury, and she began to feel her legs fail beneath her when, suddenly, there was a knock upon the door and Rolf Taylor's voice called, 'Your messenger from London is here, sir. He awaits you in the courtyard below. Shall I take him to your chamber?'

Abruptly Simon straightened and lifted her so that they were both standing, still tightly locked together and panting with the exertion of their struggles. He freed one hand to reach up and caress her bright hair.

'Now we shall see whom the king commands you to wed, madam.' He released her fully so she that she half-stumbled and put out a hand to steady herself against the bedpost. He gave a little mocking bow. 'You must excuse me, madam. I will acquaint you with the king's command in due time.'

She lifted a trembling hand to her lips and watched, helplessly, as he strode determinedly from the chamber.

She sank down again upon the bed, sobbing convulsively as Martha swept in hastily and came to her side.

'My dear, oh, my dear, did he hurt you? He looked so angry…'

'No, no, he wanted to… Oh, Martha, I am so unhappy. I wanted—I can't tell you what I wanted. I am so ashamed…'

'Child, you cannot blame yourself for what has hap-

pened or for the natural womanly feelings you may still
have for him.'

'I love him, Martha. I shall always love him, but I must
not marry him.'

Martha drew her gently to her bosom and rocked her
for moments. 'Men have their own standards of honour,
Rosamund. Love is not all in all to them as it is to us. Is
it that you cannot accept these latest revelations from London? But, Rosamund, Sir Simon is not responsible for what
has happened.'

'He is duty bound to service with Duke Richard and—'
Rosamund drew a gasping breath '—Arthur hates them
both. Now, while my brother is grieving I cannot marry a
man he despises.'

Martha shook her head gently. 'Time is the answer to
all your problems. I am sure of that. If only you could wait
patiently for Master Arthur to grow up a little, I think he
would begin to accept the world as it is and not the way
he would like it to be.'

'And now there is the added problem of Lady Sibyl's
coming child. That is a great blow to Arthur. He wants the
woman gone from here.'

Martha grimaced. 'In that he is joined by most members
of the household.'

'Is she so disliked?' Rosamund looked surprised. 'I had
not realised.'

'She has little consideration, Mistress. Your dear late
mother was so different and you are like her, always wishing to help with household matters, not demanding attention at all hours of the day and night.' Martha's expression
became grim as she compressed her lips. 'And, believe me,
that attitude will not improve now that she is with child.'

She rose and went to the casement window as they heard
the sounds of arrival down in the courtyard. Rosamund
was puzzled. She had certainly not expected Arthur back

from his ride so soon, nor had any other visitors been expected. She hoped that this did not herald some new disaster for them all. 'That is Master Arthur riding in with Andrew Murton. They must have returned for some reason, perhaps a summons from Sir Simon. That will not please the young master if it is so. There is one of Sir Simon's men with them, so it looks as if they have been called back. He must have been sent after them. That personal servant of Sir Simon has waylaid Master Arthur. They appear to be arguing somewhat fiercely. It looks as if Sir Simon has definitely issued some order that Master Arthur resents.'

'Oh, no,' Rosamund groaned. 'Please God, do not let us have another public row. Arthur is bound to come off worse in such an altercation and he does not seem to have realised that yet.'

Martha turned and nodded. 'I think I should help you dress, Mistress Rosamund. You may be needed below to try to make peace between the two of them.'

She was right, for they had only just completed Rosamund's dressing and toilette when an urgent knock came upon her door and Rolf Taylor's voice deferentially requested Mistress Kinnersley's presence in the hall.

'Sir Simon says he has news, which he wishes the members of the household to hear at once, Mistress. Will you come down?'

Somewhat angered and alarmed at the same time, Rosamund descended to the hall, attended by Martha to find Arthur lolling indolently in their father's carved chair, Sibyl, also apparently mystified by the summons, seated at the table and the steward of the household, who was looking distinctly worried. Sir Simon was standing at the end of the top table, arms folded awaiting her arrival. He nodded curtly to the steward to withdraw at her approach.

'Leave us. See to it that none of the servants disturb us until I or a member of the family send for them.' He glanced briefly at Martha and nodded. 'You may stay with your mistress.'

The steward looked to Arthur for guidance as to how he was to proceed. He simply raised his eyebrows in mock surprise then, also, nodded to signify that the man should obey the seneschal. Rosamund was surprised to find that Andrew Murton was not present until she realised that he was not a member of the family although, over the past months, they had all come to look upon him as one.

Sir Simon gestured pointedly to a chair near to her brother. 'Please be seated, Mistress Kinnersley.'

Since he was obviously determined to wait for her to seat herself before declaring the reason for his summons, she advanced to the chair he indicated, but remained standing.

'Sir Simon, I wish to know why I have been summoned so imperiously from my chamber. Is this matter so urgent that it cannot wait until supper time when we are all likely to be assembled, or, at the very least, relayed to us by one of your men?' she demanded icily. Sibyl looked up, suddenly curious, alerted by the coolness of Rosamund's tone to some undercurrent of unrest between her and Sir Simon.

'That is exactly what I was thinking,' Arthur drawled, crossing one leg insolently over the other. 'I suppose it is too much to hope that you have summoned us all to inform us of your imminent departure, perhaps in answer to an urgent summons to London to wait upon your master, the murderous Duke of Gloucester.'

Lady Sibyl gave a horrified gasp at his treasonable utterance. Rosamund moved to silence her brother, but Simon was not to be goaded by this piece of foolish bravado and merely smiled grimly.

'When I am about to leave this manor, Master Kinnersley, you will be informed in good time, for the excellent reason that I shall be taking your sister, Mistress Rosamund, with me.'

Arthur stormed to his feet, his eyes flashing fury. 'What, do you dare to tell me—'

'I have to tell you, Master Kinnersley, when you do me the courtesy of listening to what I say without boorish interruption, I have requested the hand of your sister and have just received from his Grace, King Edward, his gracious approval of the match. That being so, I wish to inform you all now that I intend to arrange for the marriage ceremony to take place within the next few days. I am sure you need to prepare yourselves and I understand that this household is in mourning so that a simple ceremony will be appropriate. Since that is so, we need not delay to invite neighbouring gentry.' He bowed in Rosamund's direction. 'You will appreciate the need for haste since, as Master Kinnersley says, it may be necessary for me to leave Kinnersley without very much warning.'

Rosamund felt that she had been poleaxed. She tried to keep on her feet and was forced to put out a hand to the nearest chair arm to steady herself as her limbs seemed paralysed. Arthur had stormed to her side and stood belligerently facing Sir Simon. As if from a long distance away she heard his youthful, rather high-pitched voice stutter his furious challenge.

'Marry my sister? I will never allow it.' His arm went protectively round Rosamund's waist as he helped to lower her into the chair. 'Do you not see how distraught she is? How dared you make such a request without informing me, as her nearest relative! This is not to be countenanced—'

'I think, Master Kinnersley, we should allow the lady to speak for herself,' Simon reminded him silkily. 'Rosamund, will you tell him that since I love you, and that you return that love, this is not a surprise to you?'

A second astonished gasp came from Lady Sibyl. 'Well…'

Rosamund fought to find her voice. She could not believe that Simon had done this to her. Only an hour ago she had informed him that she could not marry him, that marriage between them was unthinkable; and not only had he refused to accept it but he had announced the king's decision to the family, uncaring that it would wound Arthur to the heart.

She said levelly, 'I have already made my wishes plain to you, sir. To make this public now only adds to the embarrassment of all concerned.' She drew a hard breath and turned in the chair to face him. 'I do not wish to wed with you sir, now or in the future.'

His eyes had become hard sapphires, boring into her, as he stood unblinking. For moments, which appeared to spread out into eternity, no one spoke, then Simon said harshly, 'I have made my wishes plain. I wish to marry you, Mistress, and I will do so, whether it pleases you and other members of the family or no. The king has commanded the match and we shall obey him. See to it that you make suitable preparations.'

He bowed to her, then advanced and taking her hand, which felt like ice in his grasp, he bent and kissed it. So that only she could hear, he said softly, 'Please, Rosamund, do not make this hard for both of us. You know this is truly what you want, what we both want. Arthur will accept it in time as he knows in his heart that he must.'

She tried to pull her hand free, but he held it fast, gazing deep into her eyes, so that she thought that she would drown in the cold glare of his sea blue ones. She gave a little sob and he released her hand, stood back, bowed to the company, which still remained in the bemused silence, then turned and strode from the hall.

Sibyl was the first to break that silence. She looked accusingly at Rosamund. 'What is this that he said, that you have told him that you love him? Surely that is not so.'

'Ros?' Arthur breathed hoarsely. He was staring at her, appealing to her silently to explain herself.

She said tiredly, 'Too much has been said and we should all go our separate ways and try to come to terms with this situation.' She jerked back her chair and rose to her feet.

'Ros, tell me that you will not marry this man.' Arthur's face was a mask of suffering.

'At this moment I do not know how I can avoid this fate, Arthur,' she said dully. It seemed that all emotion had drained from her and she could move and breathe and even speak completely without feeling anything. She was exhausted, as if she had been working at some impossible task all day, yet she had remained in her chamber without even overseeing the usual tasks of the household.

Arthur said through his teeth, 'We must find a way. We cannot sacrifice you to this man. You can surely see his purpose. Your dowry will provide him with a manor, fine clothes on his back and sufficient gold to allow him to flaunt himself at court and win Gloucester's favour. You must not so demean yourself.'

Rosamund smiled wanly and moved slightly from him. She could not bear that anyone should intrude upon her bewilderment at this time and Arthur's furious exclamations merely irritated her inner wounds. 'I will attend to matters in the kitchen,' she said automatically and went to the screen door. Arthur was about to protest, to attempt to detain her, but Sibyl put a hand upon his arm to prevent him.

'Your sister has a great deal to consider,' she said sensibly. 'Nothing can happen for the moment. Let us remain calm and think this through.'

Rosamund was about to pass out of the hall when Andrew Murton came towards her, intent upon entering. 'Is all well?' His pleasant features were creased in a frown of concern. 'I have been told that I should not intrude upon matters which concerned the family only, but I was worried in case…'

Rosamund shook her head. 'Arthur will explain the situation to you.'

He scanned her face worriedly. 'You are very pale, Mistress Rosamund. I hope you have not received more bad tidings.'

Rosamund's lips twitched slightly and she felt an absurd desire to laugh, which was totally at odds with her true feelings of despair. 'I suppose one must decide what exactly is bad news,' she said sardonically. She shook her head again and pushed past him to leave the hall, ran down the hall steps and made towards the kitchens. Considering and conferring with the cook about the mundane decisions of what should be served for dinner then supper might just possibly take her mind, even for a brief respite, from the problem which was troubling her.

Later she returned to the deserted garden, praying that Simon would not seek her out there. She could not bear to be near him at present.

His ultimatum was frightening. She must marry him, he had declared, nay, in actual fact commanded, giving her no option to object or even to wait until a more suitable time to explain matters to Arthur. Perversely, her mind fought against the idea of a forced marriage. It would suit no one. She could not bear the prospect of being unwillingly joined to a man whose allegiance was to the House of York. How could she accompany him to court and feign deference to the king and his courtiers and kin, whose hands she believed to be red with the blood of the hapless late king? Arthur would never accept the match and the two men whose personalities dominated her life would fight for her love and attention. At all events her will was one not prone to give in tamely to the domination of another. Love Simon Cauldwell she did with her whole heart, but she could not bring herself to totally surrender her will to his. She had, at first, been lulled into a belief that, if they were to wait for a while, matters would ease and they would be able to mate without the rancour of a disgruntled young brother. Now Simon was determined to force her hand and she could not accept that. She would thwart him in this—but how? He had the king's permission. She was virtually a prisoner in his hands and could see no way of escape.

She jerked upright on her seat at the approach of another, for she had been sitting despairingly with her head buried in her hands. She must not come face to face with Simon at this moment. If she were to do so, unforgivable things would be said, which could never be forgotten. She gave a great sigh of relief when she saw that it was her brother who was coming determinedly towards her at a run.

'Ros, I have been searching for you everywhere,' he panted and flung himself down beside her.

'I just needed to be alone for a while,' she said, blinking away tears.

'You have been crying,' Arthur accused. 'Ros, you must not give in. This man cannot force you to marry him, despite the king's wish.'

'And how do you propose that we avoid it?'

Arthur glanced round hurriedly to assure himself that they were not in eavesdropping distance from any of the gardeners or stable boys.

'I have spoken to Andrew and—'

'I begged you not to do that,' Rosamund said angrily.

'I did not suggest a match, though if you were indeed to marry Andrew Murton secretly it would solve everything, for you could not be forced into this unholy match which Cauldwell proposes.'

'And if I were to do that, to defy the king, how do you think we should all fare as a result?'

He looked back at her blankly and she explained.

'The king could sequester the manor. He could imprison you for being involved. He could even execute you. He could certainly imprison me, possibly in a nunnery, and what he would do to Andrew I dread to think.'

Arthur chewed his lip while he pondered on this and, not for the first time, Rosamund considered, fondly but with irritation, what a child her brother still was. He looked up then, a triumphant gleam in his eye. 'We could petition the king ourselves.' He hesitated, then looked hastily away as if embarrassed. 'I have heard it said that King Edward is partial to the pleading of pretty young women. If you were to throw yourself upon his mercy, Ros...'

She sighed. 'I do not believe that Sir Simon would allow us to depart from the manor so easily, Arthur.'

He bit his lip again. 'If we could manage to escape and go to London, would you do it?'

Rosamund drew a hard breath. Such a proposal threatened untold danger, but it would allow her a breathing space. She said softly, 'Yes, I would consider it as long as it posed no direct danger to you, Arthur. The king could hardly punish us for appealing against his ruling even if he were to dismiss that appeal out of hand.'

Arthur's lips parted in a smile. 'Andrew will find a way,' he promised. 'I will go with you, of course, and Andrew will be our guard and escort. Leave it to me, Ros.'

She leaned across and put a hand upon his arm. 'You have not spoken of any of this in Lady Sibyl's hearing?'

He opened his eyes wide in puzzlement. 'You think she would try to prevent us from leaving?'

'I would not trust her. She is anxious to at least appear to conciliate Sir Simon.'

He nodded, tapping his teeth with his fingernail. 'Yes, you could be right.'

She rose and held out a hand to get him to come with her. 'Do nothing rash, Arthur. This is a serious business.'

For once his expression mirrored adult concern. 'I know, sis,' he said quietly, 'but I will not allow you to be forced into a life of servitude.'

They walked together in silence until he suddenly blurted out, 'Ros, what he said about you loving him, that wasn't true, was it?'

The breath caught in her throat for moments as she struggled to answer him without prevarication. 'There were moments,' she said, a trifle hoarsely, 'when it seemed politic to give Sir Simon the impression that I would not be averse to such a marriage. But then we heard the news of King Henry's murder and—and I could not contemplate allying myself with a Yorkist knight. He is too involved in his allegiance to the household of the Duke of Gloucester.'

He nodded, satisfied, and they passed from the pleasance into the courtyard. Rosamund prayed, silently, that they would not encounter Simon on the way and her prayers were answered. Thankfully she parted with Arthur in the hall and hastened up to her own chamber. There was hope. She would leave the matter in Andrew Murton's hands now. Even if nothing came of Arthur's escape plan, at least her brother would have the solace of believing that he had tried to assist his sister in her bid to escape the fate of becoming Sir Simon Cauldwell's unwilling bride.

Chapter Eleven

Rosamund refused to go down to the hall for supper that night. She remained fearfully within her chamber, believing that Simon would storm up the spiral stair, threaten to break down her door and drag her downstairs but he did not make an appearance, nor did he send a messenger. Martha brought her supper, but Rosamund had no appetite and pushed away the tray with the food uneaten. When Arthur came to her door before retiring for the night she sent Martha out to tell him she was too exhausted to receive anyone. He went away reluctantly but did not insist upon disturbing her.

After Martha had undressed her and left her, Rosamund sat upon the bed and watched the guttering candle for hours.

It finally went out and grey dawn light began to filter into her bedchamber through a gap in the shutter. As she had told Arthur, she was utterly exhausted physically and mentally and was unable to indulge in more weak tears. She wondered why Simon had left her alone. Had he accepted her rebuff and finally believed that she was determined not to marry him? If so, that was foreign to his

nature. She did not think he was used to being thwarted
and she could not believe that he would give in so easily.
If she remained here, he was capable of forcing her to the
altar before a priest, but she could steadfastly refuse to
take her marriage vows. Yet what would happen to her
then? Could she and Arthur remain here? Would the king
agree to find her another husband? She doubted that. Yet
did she really believe that she could escape Simon's sur-
veillance, go to London and seek the king's permission to
marry another man? Arthur had set his heart on her marriage to Andrew Murton, yet she could not see herself as
his wife. She liked Andrew, believed that she could trust
him to help them both. He had many virtues, but she did
not love him. Dolefully, she accepted the fact that, despite
her misgivings and her anger at his continued allegiance
to the Duke of Gloucester, she would always love Simon
Cauldwell. But Arthur remained her responsibility and she
could not break his heart by marrying the man he considered his bitterest enemy. Somehow she must get to London, obtain an audience with King Edward and beg him
to allow her a breathing space. If all else failed, she considered bitterly, she could always enter a nunnery. Indeed,
that might be the best solution when Arthur was grown
and would bring a young bride to the manor who would
not wish to have a rival chatelaine at her side.

She lay down at last, but did not sleep, and was still
tired and listless when Martha brought her breakfast. Determined not to allow herself to wallow in self-pity, she
decided to descend to the kitchens, oversee preparations
for the day, then spend the rest of the morning in the still
room.

It was there that Andrew Murton found her just before
noon. He pushed open the door hesitantly.

'Martha told me that I might find you here, Mistress

Rosamund,' he said half-apologetically. 'Could I have a private word with you?'

Rosamund was tying up bundles of rosemary for drying and nodded for him to enter and close the door.

'Yes, please come in, Andrew. I confess I was hiding out from most of the household and from Sir Simon. I did not even want Lady Sibyl to question me this morning.' She hesitated as he advanced into the room slowly. 'I presume that Arthur has informed you of what was said in the hall yesterday.'

'Aye, mistress, it is all over the house and desmesne that Sir Simon has announced his intention to marry you.'

'Against my will,' she concluded.

'Your brother is strongly against the match and believes you to be of the same mind.'

'Yes, he is right. I have no wish to be wed to anyone at the moment.'

He looked back at her steadily as if he were in no way shaken by her determination to remain a virgin for the present. Apparently he had not, as yet, heard Arthur's proposal that she should wed him or, at the very least, was in no way anxious to press her into such a hasty decision.

He came close to her and looked anxiously into her eyes. 'Do you trust me, Mistress Rosamund?'

She looked back at his sturdy, familiar figure, dressed as usual in serviceable brown leather jacket and hose. His round, pleasant face was wearing a somewhat troubled expression this morning, but she read no guile in those widespaced grey-green eyes. She knew that Andrew was a relatively penniless squire, as his plain clothes and few possessions indicated, but she did not believe that he was out to enrich himself by a marriage to her, though he must know by now that she would be a worthy prize. Sir Simon Cauldwell was well aware of that, she thought bitterly. Both he and Andrew had much to gain by a marriage with her and Simon Cauldwell was prepared to press her into that against her will. Had he deliberately courted her with preferment in mind from the beginning? She thrust aside that unworthy thought and made up her mind quickly.

'Yes, Andrew, I trust you, as Arthur trusts you.'

'He has spoken to you about his desire to leave the manor and beg the king for an audience at Westminster, I understand.'

'Yes.' Her voice was a mere whisper, but she continued more strongly, 'I wish to do that, but I fear it holds much danger for all of us.' He did not speak for a moment and she plunged on. 'Sir Simon Cauldwell will do everything he can to prevent that. It is in his interest to promote this wedding as soon as possible. For that reason, if we must fly from Kinnersley, it must be soon, and—'

'I have considered that, Mistress Rosamund. I am prepared to take you both to London.'

'If we were caught, you might be the one to suffer the most.'

'I have not overlooked that fact,' he said quietly.

'Then thank you, Andrew.'

He smiled. 'The opportunity to serve you both is all I desire. Your father was a fair master to me and I have a great affection for young Master Arthur and...' He hesitated for a second and blinked, then added, 'And for you too, Mistress Rosamund.'

She made no reply to that and fiddled awkwardly with the hard stems of the rosemary plants she was attempting to tie together.

'I have been working out some plan that I think might work. It would be unwise for you and Arthur to attempt to leave the manor house together, though, in the past, Sir Simon Cauldwell has made no objection to Master Arthur riding out daily with me. I propose that he does that early, as usual, tomorrow morning. Before that, possibly tonight during supper, I will secret a small bundle of necessities in the coppice just down the road where we ride. I will speak to your maid, Martha, with your permission of course, and ask her to provide some simple necessities for you too.'

'Yes; I trust Martha utterly.'

'Good, because we shall need her participation to accomplish your escape from the manor. I propose that tomorrow morning you announce your wish to go to the village church to pray for your father's soul. Martha must accompany you. If she decides to risk herself with you for the journey, all the better, but if not then she must stay hidden for a while after I join you with Arthur and return to the manor house later. I am sure she will be capable of making up some excuse for parting with you and returning alone, possibly a tale that you have insisted upon visiting some sick villager. She may come under suspicion for complicity, but I doubt that Sir Simon would punish her or, if he does, not too severely.'

Rosamund's fingers clenched upon the woody stems of the rosemary so that they made small indentations upon her palm. 'Then you will ride back to the church to meet with us?'

'Yes. It were better if the priest was unaware of your intentions so you must stay for an hour and pray and then leave. Walk into the village as if, indeed, you do intend to visit one of your tenants, then slip out by the path to the water meadow. I shall be waiting in the little wood just beyond the stream. Wear sensible shoes. You know where it is safe to cross in shallow water?'

'Yes, of course. Arthur and I used to play near there and step into the water to catch fish in our hands.' She frowned slightly. 'Then you want me to go to the village on foot. Martha and I can do that easily enough. We have done it often, but it is a long ride to Warwick or a nearby town and...'

'It would excite suspicion if we take other horses. Arthur can take you up behind, pillion, and I will do the same for Martha if she decides to come with you. Arthur will have sufficient coin with him to buy fresh mounts in Warwick.'

She nodded. 'It will be late by the time we arrive in the town.'

'Yes. I believe that enquiries might be made for you and on the road south. I have a small, somewhat paltry house near St Mary's Church in Warwick where you and Arthur can remain hidden until I think it safe for us all to proceed.'

She considered thoughtfully. 'You seem to have thought of everything, Andrew. I can find no fault with the plan though, of course, we could be discovered and there is a risk to you as I said before...'

'That is no great matter, Mistress.' He brushed off her one objection. 'I think Sir Simon's men will be anxious to continue their search on the London road, but we must take the risk that they might search the houses in the town. However, he has no authority to enforce such a search, and I have owned the house for some time so no one will think it odd that I should be there.'

'How long do you think it will be necessary for us to delay our journey?'

'No more than one day or two. We should travel on in some simple disguise, you and Arthur in plain, drab clothing, as my younger brother and sister. I believe that Sir Simon's men will have completed their enquiries for you then and have returned to Kinnersley to report to their master.'

It seemed a good plan, though there were dangers, Rosamund considered. Both she and Arthur could be questioned about their need to leave the manor and now, particularly, since she had declared her intention not to marry him, she thought that Simon would be suspicious and watch her closely, but she could think of nothing else that would fit their need. Andrew Murton appeared determined to take the risk with them and she must carry out his instructions. She nodded.

'I will speak with Martha as soon as possible. Until then it will be better if we do not talk together again openly.'

'Certainly. I have thought of that. Just in case I am seen leaving the still room after being alone with you, it would be wise if you provide me with a small pot of salve or a phial of some herbal brew that would explain my visit here.'

She handed him a little pot of comfrey salve and he grinned at her confidently. 'You are a resourceful lady, Mistress Rosamund. I have no fears, for you and young Master Arthur will be guided by you, and you will be able to curb his too-wild enthusiasm on the journey. Now I wish you farewell until I see you soon at the ford soon after noon tomorrow.'

He saluted her and she watched anxiously as he opened the door into the corridor, turned to assure her with a look that there was no one about and slipped out to go about his business.

She stood for a moment, irresolute, then finished tying up the rosemary and began to prepare to leave the still room. She must send for Martha and put the plan to her. She bit her lip thoughtfully. She hoped that Martha would have the courage to accompany her, for she could not bear to embark on this without a stout ally and confidante by her side.

She was about the leave the room when her way was blocked by a grim-faced Simon. She blanched at the sight of that angry scowl and attempted to push by him.

'Please, sir, let me pass.'

He shook his head, but remained full in her path, feet firmly astride, arms akimbo.

'I think we need to talk, Mistress, and in private. Please go back into the room.'

She tried to find the words to defy him, but her mouth was dry; she swallowed painfully and backed before his steady advance.

'I see that you have been in talk with your father's squire.' He closed the door behind them decisively, leaving her feeling terribly vulnerable, here, with him, enclosed within this small chamber.

She managed to find her voice. 'Andrew came for some comfrey salve. He and Arthur were practising swordplay together yesterday and it has left them both with some severe and painful bruising.'

'Ah.' The single word was uncompromising and she was alarmed by the fact that he did not believe her. What if he sensed, rather than knew, what she and Andrew Murton had been planning? But that was not possible.

'You wanted me? I—I do not think that I have anything to say to you,' she said lamely, her voice tailing off uncertainly.

'But I have much that I wish to say to you.'

'It were better, sir, if you were to say it when others are present or at least in earshot.'

'You are afraid to be alone with me? It was not always so.'

She blinked back angry tears. 'I was not being forced then to accept what you said without question. I believed that I was allowed some voice of my own—that you would listen to me and—and understand.'

'What am I supposed to understand? That you have suddenly fallen out of love with me because of some baseless rumour which, in the fullness of time, I am convinced can be disproved?'

'There is too much between us,' she stammered. 'There always was. You are my father's enemy—'

'Your father is dead, Rosamund,' he said brutally. 'You cannot be governed any longer by what he would think. Knowing the way of the world, I imagine that, by now, were he alive, he would counsel you to accept the inevitable.'

'And that is what you do,' she snapped, wounded to the quick, 'you serve Richard of Gloucester because it is politic for you to do so, because he is powerful and rich and can prefer you at court.'

'No. I serve my Lord Richard because I trust him to do what is right, because he is my friend and because I believe that I know him better than you can do after so short an acquaintance.'

'Then you do not believe that King Henry is dead, that the pedlar lied?'

'I believe that the king is dead, certainly, but as to how he died I am not able to say with authority. I will not comment on this matter without proof of someone's guilt and I would not expect you to do so either. I thought better of you, Rosamund, believed you to be fair-minded.'

'Yesterday you said that the possible murder of a king might well be best for the realm,' she said icily.

He gave a heavy sigh. 'Aye, I said something of the sort and, God forgive me, I believe it to be true if we are to have peace at last, but I also said that none of this should affect us. It cannot touch us. We love each other. No, do not turn away from me. You still love me, I can read it in your eyes, whatever your lips frame. I understand that you feel totally responsible for that headstrong brother of yours and I promise that I will do my best to win him over and make arrangements for his future welfare. I plead with you not to oppose me in this, for I tell you now, Rosamund, that you will marry me. I want you and I will have you. The king has given you to me...'

'As some reward, some spoil of war, a chattel,' she stormed. 'I will not be used so. If I have to commit my life to God in a nunnery, I will not accept the fate you decree for me. You cannot force me to declare my marriage vows, even should you drag me before a priest. You must find some other heiress to enrich your coffers, sir.'

It was a terrible insult. His blue eyes blazed with fury and he reached out as if he would strike her, but kept his temper under control with a supreme effort and drew back.

'The saints know that you try my patience to the limit,' he said through gritted teeth. 'Listen to me, Rosamund, and listen well. I will not lose you to a nunnery, nor to any other man. That will not happen. You will see sense if I have to imprison you until you do so.'

Her face flamed and she gave a great sob. 'Then do your worst, sir. If you should imprison me for months you will find me intractable. I am not some tame creature you can force to your will.'

'God's blood, Rosamund, you tempt me to take extreme measures,' he murmured hoarsely. 'There are limits to my patience. Remember that I am master here by the Lord Protector's will and nothing could save you from my decree if you try me too far. I have already spoken to the priest and, at sundown tomorrow, I shall send for you to take betrothal vows in the hall before witnesses. Until then I will not force my unwelcome presence upon you. After that, if you are still stubborn, we shall see.'

Before she could find words to proclaim her further defiance he turned and swept out. She stood stock still, eyes wide with shock, staring at his unresponsive back, and shivered as the heavy door slammed to with a hollow crash as a prison door would slam against a condemned felon.

She forced her limbs to obey her at last and went to the hall to find a servant to send in search of Martha. There she encountered Lady Sibyl.

'Oh, there you are, Rosamund. I was concerned about you.'

'Really?' For once Rosamund did not attempt to conceal her bitterness and active dislike.

'Sir Simon was storming about looking for you.'

'He found me in the still room.'

'Oh.' Sibyl fiddled awkwardly with the girdle of her gown. 'I wondered—what exactly you intended to do. You were very angry yesterday and—'

'I do not intend to marry Sir Simon Cauldwell, whatever the king or the Duke of Gloucester commands.'

'He told me he has called a priest in order to hold a betrothal ceremony tomorrow…'

'So he informed me.'

'It would not be wise, Rosamund, for you to antagonise this man. He holds us all in his power.'

'And what do you suggest that I do, Lady Sibyl? Sacrifice myself for the good of the manor?'

'I would not go so far. Perhaps you could play for time.'

'Yes, I have thought of that, but it seems that Sir Simon is in haste and will force the issue. Excuse me. I must send this girl to find Martha for me.' She caught the arm of a somewhat frightened-looking young serving wench, who was attempting to pass the two without being noticed, since she was aware of friction between them. 'Tell Martha that I need her within my chamber urgently. Hurry, girl.'

Rosamund turned to Sibyl. 'Do you need me further?'

'No. I simply needed to explain—'

'That I could make matters difficult for you if I refuse to bow to Sir Simon Cauldwell's wishes. I understand that. Now, please allow me to go to my chamber. I do not wish to see the man again today.'

She left a gaping Sibyl abruptly and made for her own room. Martha arrived only a few minutes afterwards, visibly panting in her haste to dash up the stairs. Immediately Rosamund was guiltily aware that her nurse and confidante was growing older and now she was about to ask her to endanger herself or, at the very least, to submit herself to considerable discomfort upon the journey ahead of them. Without preamble she explained Andrew Murton's plan. Martha listened, her lips tight with concern.

'This could be very dangerous, you realise that,' she said at last, 'particularly for Arthur.'

'He knows that. It is what he wants, Martha.'

'Yes, but is it what you want?'

Rosamund turned her face away so Martha would not recognise her expression of bleak despair. 'I will not be used, Martha, bought and exchanged like some possession the king wishes to give to a faithful servant for services rendered.'

'So you believe that Sir Simon does not truly love you?'

'He is aware that I would prove a worthy prize.'

'But that could arise should the king grant your petition and find another husband for you—one not so acceptable, I might add.'

'Acceptable in what fashion? You mean some other husband would possibly treat me with even less consideration than this man, who is determined to force his attentions upon me?'

'That could very well be.'

Rosamund hesitated, then she confided, 'Arthur wishes me to wed Andrew Murton before we reach London and then—then beg the king's pardon.'

'A very dangerous proposition. Are you willing to do that?'

'Andrew is a good man, I think. Arthur likes him...'

'Arthur is not the one who is to marry him,' Martha

retorted bluntly. 'I would think very carefully indeed before embarking upon that course.'

'You disapprove of Andrew?' Rosamund was startled.

'I did not mean to imply that. The man seems reliable and pleasing enough but—' Martha shrugged '—he, too, is needing to fill emptied coffers. Marriage to you would be to his advantage, so of course he is willing to take the risk of enraging the king. But none of this is uppermost in my mind. I am more concerned and convinced that you are still deeply in love with Sir Simon and are deliberately trying to push that fact from your mind. I warn you, child, that if it is still true you will be unable to do so and, in the end, you will regret this action for the rest of your life.'

Rosamund turned a tear-streaked face back to her. 'So you are unwilling to accompany us?'

'Of course I shall go with you. Do you think your dear mother, who trusted me, will rest easy in her grave if I allow you two babes of hers to go on so perilous a journey without me?'

Rosamund ran to her nurse and threw her arms about her. 'Oh, thank you, Martha, thank you. I do not know how I could manage without you.'

Martha disengaged herself gently. 'Well, fortunately you will not have to. Now, let us set about finding you one or two suitable garments to last you during this journey and respectable enough for you to present yourself in when you reach Westminster. We must choose carefully because we cannot be over-burdened, obviously.'

Rosamund went down to supper in the hall that evening, as she feared that not to do so might excite suspicion. Both she and Arthur, as well as Sibyl, were present at the high table and Simon Cauldwell appeared halfway through the meal, excusing himself for his lateness as he explained that some business on the desmesne had kept him from table until then. Little was said save the usual pleasantries. Lady Sibyl attempted to keep the conversation light, though her efforts fell on fallow ground, and the atmosphere was chilly in the extreme. Rosamund and Simon exchanged not one word and Arthur answered in monosyllables when addressed. Brother and sister left the table hurriedly and Simon stood up courteously as Rosamund pushed past him. He looked weary and somewhat haggard, she thought, but he did not try to detain her, merely wishing her a quiet 'good night.'

She did not think that she would sleep, considering the problems that faced her in the morning, but, surprisingly, she did.

She woke later than usual to find Martha bending over the bed and shaking her gently. She started up and stared around her unbelievingly.

'I must have been wearied by all the doubts and uncertainties. Is it very late, Martha?'

'No, no. I have brought you some breakfast. Do not fret. We have plenty of time. Arthur and Andrew are, even now, in the courtyard, preparing to ride out. I have hidden our saddle-bag ready for them to find as instructed. Now eat. I know you do not feel like it, but you will need sustenance. Who knows when we shall next have an opportunity to eat well?'

Martha stood over her while she made a hasty meal and then helped her to dress in her plainest black gown. She and Martha had decided that, later, on the road, she should abandon her mourning dress, as searchers would be looking for a woman in deepest black. The day was warm, though not so much so that journeying would prove uncomfortable. Rosamund descended to the hall and found, after enquiring, that Lady Sibyl was in the solar.

Rosamund glanced meaningfully at Martha. 'I will go and inform her that the two of us will walk to the church.'

Sibyl sat with her favourite serving maid, sewing industriously at what Rosamund thought were to be small garments for when her expected child emerged from swaddling bands. She looked up, smiling, and Rosamund thought how much more cheerful her stepmother appeared now that the news of her pregnancy had been made known to the household.

Rosamund bent to admire the embroidery upon a tiny chemise. 'That is lovely. I am afraid my skill with the needle has never been good, even after my mother strove to make me as expert as she was.'

A tiny frown creased Sibyl's brow momentarily at the reference to her predecessor, but she forced a smile. 'My child will never know its father, unhappily, but I can provide for it as well as I can. God grant that the king leaves us all in peace here.'

It was a tacit reminder that Rosamund should do nothing to anger Sir Simon Cauldwell and her lips tightened.

'I intend to take Martha with me and go to the village church to pray near Father's grave,' she said somewhat coldly. 'I may go on then to visit one or two of the older women in the village.'

'Yes, do that. The air will do you good.' Sibyl smiled, then said quickly, 'You will arrive back here in good time for…'

'The betrothal ceremony? I have not forgotten,' Rosamund returned icily. 'Yes, I intend to be present, but as to what will happen then I make no promises. I have already stated my intentions very plainly.'

'Rosamund, please, you will not—'

'I will see you later, Sibyl,' Rosamund said hurriedly. 'Why do you not follow my example and go out into the sweet air of the pleasance later? It will not be too hot under the rose arbour.'

'Yes, I may do that. Say a prayer for me, Rosamund. I will go to visit the grave later in the week and we must talk together about a suitable memorial brass,' Sibyl said, her expression troubled. She could see that to tax Rosamund further about her refusal to accept Sir Simon's proposal would be useless at the moment, and watched her stepdaughter leave the solar, her doubts undiminished. It would be best to savour the peace of the present, for the evening's happenings were like to be troublesome in the extreme.

Rosamund joined Martha in the courtyard and prepared to leave as Sir Simon Cauldwell rode in. He drew rein and dismounted at once. Rosamund realised it would be impossible to avoid him and waited until he came close to them. His frowning gaze swept over the two women who were obviously preparing to leave the manor house.

Rosamund forestalled his questions. 'I have already explained to Lady Sibyl,' she said impatiently, 'that I am merely going to the village church to pray near to my father's grave. I trust that you have no objection, sir.'

His expression cleared. 'No, of course not. I see you are not mounted.'

'We intend to walk. The distance is but short and the weather is good today.'

He nodded and said curtly, 'Do you require an escort?'

Rosamund froze for a second. It would be impossible to accomplish their plan if Sir Simon insisted upon providing them with men-at-arms or worse, declared his intention to accompany her himself. She said quietly, 'That should not be necessary, sir. As I have said, the walk is but a short one and I have Martha with me, as you see.'

'You have remembered that we—'

'Yes,' she snapped impatiently, 'would I be likely to forget, sir? My reason to visit the church is to try to attempt to get my feelings in order before we meet later in the hall.'

'Ah.' His tone softened. 'Rosamund, I would have you come to our betrothal in a more willing frame of mind. I have no desire to force you...'

'Then release me, sir, from such an arbitrary arrangement.'

'You know that I cannot do that, Rosamund.'

'Then at least allow me to proceed and give me some hours of privacy before I have to come to terms with my fate.'

He bowed, his eyes glittering strangely, so that she was forced to blink rapidly; she felt that she was falling under a spell and being submerged into their blue depths. To her relief he saluted them and stepped back. She hurried past him and then, only when she reached the gate, did she turn briefly to look back at his rigidly stiff-backed figure as he remained still, continuing to gaze after her.

She quickened her step, Martha falling into place beside her, and she found that she was almost running along the road, both of them panting slightly.

'That was a close call,' Martha muttered darkly.

'Yes.'

'You have no doubts that you are doing the right thing?'

Rosamund knew that she had considerable doubts. Seeing Simon again, even briefly, confirmed for her her all-consuming love for him, which was threatening to tear her apart. However, for the present, she had to think of her young brother's needs and press on with this plan, even though her fear was growing steadily that this could all lead to disaster.

She found that the village priest was absent from the church, presumably visiting one of the villagers, and she and Martha went to the chancel, where they knelt for a while in prayer near Sir Humphrey's grave. Rosamund prayed that her father, if, indeed, he was watching over them, was heartened by her continuing care of Arthur and his soul was gladdened by the knowledge that his child would be welcomed at Kinnersley. She also prayed that she and Arthur would reach London safely and be successful in their mission. She rose at last, if not relieved, at least strengthened by the knowledge that her father would approve her effort to safeguard Arthur's interests.

She and Martha moved to the church door. Rosamund said thoughtfully, 'Perhaps it would be best now if you were to go out into the main street and make sure none of Sir Simon's men are frequenting the inn. I will wait here in the porch for your return and then, if the coast is clear, we will set off for the proposed meeting place near the ford.'

Martha nodded and set off briskly. Alone in the church Rosamund felt nervous and anxious now to set off, yet she knew it would be foolish to encounter any of the Cauldwell men in the village. If she were the least bit late, tales would leak back and pursuit would be sooner than Andrew Murton anticipated. She stood in the porch waiting eagerly for sight of Martha.

When she heard the sound of hoofbeats approaching from the direction of the manor house she drew back into the interior of the church, fearful that Sir Simon might have decided to follow and offer his escort home, in spite of his first acceptance of her refusal. She heard the faintest jingle of bells and was surprised to consider that the rider might be a woman. Only Sibyl Kinnersley rode a palfrey with bells attached to the saddle caparison, and Rosamund frowned doubtfully. What had possessed Sibyl to ride out at this stage in her pregnancy when she had been so careful of her health up to this day? Sibyl rarely rode out for pleasure at any time and she had expressed no intention of visiting the village during their previous conversation in the solar. Cautiously Rosamund opened the heavy door of the church just a fraction to see if she could catch a glimpse of the rider.

Standing in the shadows, she could barely see who had approached the church then, with a sudden shock, she heard booted feet coming along the church path and a familiar voice challenge the rider.

'Sibyl, what in the Virgin's name do you mean by coming here now? You know you should not be riding. You could endanger our child. I saw you from the ridge. I told you that you must wait at the manor for my return, however long it took me.'

Andrew Murton's voice, speaking in a far more commanding tone than Rosamund had ever heard him use before. Those two words, 'our' and then 'child,' caused her body to go icy cold as the full realisation struck her. She drew back even farther into the shadows, fearful lest the two outside could sense her presence.

Sibyl's voice in answer also sounded more confident than was usual when dealing with servants at the manor.

'I had to be sure that all was going to plan. Now it has come to it I find I am afraid, Andrew.'

He gave a harsh bark of a laugh. 'You were not afraid when I rode out to war with Sir Humphrey. You were sure then that I would find the means to dispose of him. I managed it without detection. As I told you, it was a simple enough matter to wait until we were alone, if only for a moment. I stabbed him in the neck as we reached the horse lines together in the rush before the Yorkist pursuit began. It was very quick; by the time others ran up, they were too much concerned for the safety of their own skins to bother about what I was doing. Then I had only to mount his body across the horse and wait until a suitable moment arrived when I could emerge from cover and enter Tewkes-bury. If I had so little difficulty in dealing with the father, do you think I will have a problem disposing of that brat of a boy?'

Rosamund leaned against the cold stone of the font, faint with shock and horror. She had to force herself not to cry out or rush from the church and confront the two, but some innate frisson of caution bade her remain where she was and listen to what followed, however terrible that discovery continued to be.

'But now the girl will be with him and—'

Again that harsh bray of a laugh came. 'Better and better for our purpose. I could not have arranged matters better. I had thought to wait for our next move until she was wed to Cauldwell and gone from the manor but now, if she were to die with the boy in some unfortunate accident, it could prove yet more convenient for us. She has some considerable dowry and, if she dies still a maid, your child will inherit. As we planned, you will be the grieving widow and bereft stepmother carrying Sir Humphrey's child. Who will wish to evict you from your home at such a sad time? I shall be there as your supporter, your late husband's loyal squire. Nothing could be sweeter.'

Sibyl said fretfully, 'You make it sound so simple. The whole plan is fraught with unseen perils. For one child to die accidentally is believable, but for two...'

'But a fire often claims the lives of more than one victim.'

'You intend to fire the house? But, Andrew, that could, just possibly, leave one or both alive to talk of what happened.'

'Never fear, I will do it only after I have already dealt with our two troublesome dependants. Now, Sibyl, I have arranged to meet Mistress Rosamund near the ford. You must not be anywhere in the vicinity. If someone should catch a glimpse of you, it could arouse just a fraction of suspicion. The girl herself would be surprised to see you here and, possibly, grow wary. Now ride back to Kinnersley at once.'

'I have suddenly thought—Andrew, what of the maid?'

'An added complication, I grant you, but I could hardly encourage Mistress Rosamund to embark on a long journey without a suitable chaperone.' He dropped his voice slightly and Rosamund found it difficult to catch his words, 'Leave this to me, Sibyl. Household servants have a way of proving unreliable. Who would be surprised to find that the elderly Martha had decided to leave her mistress part way, as the journey promised to get uncomfortable? She will merely disappear. No one will question my explanation. After all, you are the mistress of Kinnersley, when all is said and done.'

There was a trace of horror in Sibyl's voice. 'You intend to murder the old woman too?'

His reply revealed irritation for her revulsion at the proposed deed. 'I could hardly allow her to live and talk, could I? It might be best, on reflection, if she, too, were to perish in the Warwick house fire.'

'And you will return to Kinnersley with the tragic news? You have decided to confess that you had agreed to help Rosamund and Arthur to escape from Cauldwell?'

Rosamund fancied that she could see him shrug disdainfully. 'I will think of some tale of how I managed to survive, and the terrible consequences of my foolish promise to assist them.'

'But Simon Cauldwell is a redoubtable man. He frightens me, Andrew. Since he arrived at Kinnersley I have been afraid that he could wreck all our plans. If he should suspect… He is in love with the girl.'

'In love with her dowry, like as not. When she is declared dead he will lose interest and, in time, be recalled o serve Gloucester. These unfortunate rumours may serve our purpose. Gloucester's reputation has suffered greatly. He will need all his loyal supporters by him.'

There was a short silence and Rosamund craned forward slightly, fearing that, since they were speaking so softly now, she might fail to hear any further damning revelations.

At last she heard Sibyl ask, 'Where is the boy now?'

'At the blacksmith's. We discovered a loose nail in one of his horse's shoes. It needed to be fixed if he is to carry his sister pillion, even on the short journey into Warwick. I left him there and came to pick up Rosamund's saddlebag, which Martha hid for us to retrieve later.'

Again there was a little silence, then Rosamund heard a horse move fretfully and Andrew Murton said, 'You must return to the manor house, quickly now.'

Sibyl murmured petulantly, 'I worry lest you find young Rosamund more attractive these days. She is becoming quite lovely. Obviously Sir Simon thinks so.'

Andrew Murton laughed. 'You think I could ever prefer a little brown mouse to my beautiful, sleek pussy cat with the golden fur? Oh, come, Sibyl, I loved you desperately long before your father sold you to Sir Humphrey Kinnersley. We both knew our love was hopeless then and that we had to be patient until I could find a way for us to be together.'

Tears spilled unheeded down Rosamund's cheeks until she brushed them away angrily. These two had plotted and waited their time for well over a year, even before Sibyl came to Kinnersley, and it was now obvious that they had been lovers during her father's lifetime. She felt now an overpowering impulse to dash from her place of concealment and to confront them, but she knew, instinctively, that she must stay quiet and remain hidden while she thought this through. Finally she heard a sharp slap as if

Andrew Murton had slapped the rump of Sibyl's palfrey and her stepmother gave a little breathless laugh. 'Well then, I must go. Take the greatest care, Andrew. You mean everything in the world to me and, if you should be discovered…'

'Trust me. I did not fail with Sir Humphrey. Now there are greater stakes. Only keep your head and be patient, as you have done until now.'

Rosamund leaned, almost fainting, against the font once more. She heard the steady trot of Sibyl's palfrey as it made for home and she continued to wait, her hand gripping so tightly to the granite edging of the font that her knuckles were white with strain until she heard the noise of booted feet moving away. Then, and only then, did she allow herself to rest against her support while her hand pressed tightly against her mouth to suppress her sobs of panic and helpless fury.

Dear God, what was she to do? They were all in the most dreadful peril. There was no possible doubt that Andrew Murton meant to murder them all without a shred of conscience. And if she had not been present and heard the plot for herself he would undoubtedly have got away with it. She must hasten to the ford and warn Arthur. Though still faint with shock and horror, she forced her unwilling legs to move towards the door and then stopped abruptly.

No, at the ford she would have to deal with Murton. The man was a seasoned warrior and she and Martha would be totally helpless in his hands. Her warning, even if it were to be heeded, for Arthur had the utmost trust in his father's squire, would come too late. Murton would deal with the two women while Arthur would be unable to help them and then, if the boy tried to flee, he would pursue and kill him also. Somehow Murton would find the means to dispose of their bodies and their disappearance from the manor would not be questioned, considering the

pen hatred both had displayed towards Simon Cauldwell's rule at Kinnersley. No one would be likely to be at
the ford at this hour. She had deliberately placed them all
in peril by agreeing to run from Simon and the enforced
marriage. Simon! She gave a little moan of despair. She
must get word to him of Arthur's peril while she herself
went to the meeting place and tried to guard the boy. She
would keep silent even though the horrifying truth threatened to choke her, until she could find a means of warning
her brother. Martha must be sent back to Kinnersley to
find Simon.

He was her one hope. She prayed, silently, to the Virgin,
that he would come to them in time, for she did not doubt
for one second that he would come.

Chapter Twelve

When Martha arrived back at the church she found her mistress near the rood screen on her knees. Rosamund rose hurriedly as Martha entered.

'Close the church door,' she said tersely as she drew Martha farther into the interior of the shadowy little church. 'Did you see Andrew Murton outside? Was he in the inn?'

'Why, no, I thought the plan was for him to meet us near the shallow ford in the water meadow.'

'Was Sir Simon Cauldwell in the inn, by any chance?'

'No, there was no sight of any of his men either.'

Rosamund pulled Martha to the bench near the west side wall meant for the use of the sick and elderly during mass, and pressed her to sit down.

'Martha, I want you to hasten back to the manor house and find Sir Simon. Tell him he must come to Warwick immediately and look for a house near to the church.' Rosamund paused momentarily as she realised that there must be many and she did not know if Simon would have the authority to search or compel inhabitants to reveal whether she and Arthur were hidden inside. Naturally Andrew had given no description of the property. She added quickly,

'Tell him that Andrew Murton has owned a house there for some time, at least a year, or, if the house is not in his name, it may be owned by Sibyl's father, Master Trenton. He must make enquiries.'

Martha looked bewildered. 'I don't understand, Mistress Rosa. Is it that you now wish him to find you?'

'Yes.' Rosamund gave a great gulp of panic and hurriedly told Martha what she had overheard. The maid's eyes grew large with utter astonishment, then clouded with fear. 'Mistress Rosa, you must not go. You cannot risk…'

'Martha, I must go. Arthur is in the most direct peril. He is Kinnersley's heir. I have to be with him to warn him or, in the end, to try to protect him.'

'Then I should be with you. I could leave a message with the innkeeper for Sir Simon and—'

'No.' Rosamund gave a little determined stamp of her foot. 'You must do as I say. Simon will listen to you and realise the immediacy of the danger. I shall go to the trysting place and act as if I suspect nothing. Andrew Murton must believe that all is going to plan until I can get Arthur alone and tell him what I know. Somehow I must convince him of Andrew Murton's duplicity and get him out of that house, but I am afraid Murton will guard us well.'

'He could make his move far quicker than you anticipate,' Martha said, gloomily. She clutched at Rosamund's sleeve agitatedly. 'He could kill you both the moment you get to Warwick or even on the road and Sir Simon could come too late. He—'

'That is why you must waste no time in finding him,' Rosamund said breathlessly. 'I doubt that Murton will make any move until he gets us safely in that house. His whole plan, as I told you, is to make sure it will be believed that we both perished in the fire. I will delay here as long as I dare, for he must not suspect, and then meet him as planned. I shall tell him that you have cried off and

that I have berated you, but told you to leave me in a
temper or some such tale. There is no reason for Murton
to doubt the truth of that. He will be relieved that he has
one less person to deal with. Martha, you must convince
Simon of the urgency. He may decide to allow me to go
my own way. He may even refuse to believe in Lady
Sibyl's complicity. She is very beautiful. I have noticed
how much he admires her.' She gave a little broken-
hearted cry. 'Yet I believe that he loves me enough to
come. Dear God, he must.'

Martha rose to her feet and pulled Rosamund close to
her heart. Her eyes were streaming with tears. 'Oh, sweet
Virgin, I knew that no good would come of this. If only
young Master Arthur were not so stubborn... Nay, don't
you fret. I'll find your love for you, sweeting, and fast,
and I know he'll act. If I have any knowledge of men, and
I assure you I have, your man will not only come to you
immediately, but he will kill that black-hearted scoundrel
for you. As for Lady Sibyl! How dare she even call herself
that—' She checked herself quickly. 'No point in me
standing here ranting. It's action what's needed. You can
rely on me and—' she closed her lips together tightly
'—if that man of yours leaves you to your own fate I'll
be in Warwick as fast as I can fly there and have the
constable out of his bed, so there.'

Rosamund dabbed at her eyes and could not forbear a
tight little laugh at the thought of Martha setting about that
formidable, portly figure she had seen often in the town
when visiting with her father. In this mood Martha would
tackle Andrew Murton with her own bare hands and Rosamund, at this moment, felt that she, too, could tear him
to pieces like one of those Greek maenads she had once
read of. She pushed her old nurse gently towards the
church door. 'Go now, and God guard you, and grant you
success in your mission,' she murmured fervently, and

watched as Martha turned once to look back at her anxiously, then scuttled away down the church path towards the lych-gate.

Rosamund remained sitting huddled upon the bench until she believed that she had given Martha a fair start in her hurried dash back to the manor. She could only pray earnestly now that her maid would find Simon there and that he was not engaged in some business about the desmesne which might mean Martha taking some time to deliver her plea for help. She dared not delay too long—she could not risk Andrew Murton being in the slightest bit suspicious. Her one hope of saving Arthur was to manoeuvre him away from Murton and convince him that they were in mortal danger.

She rose reluctantly and slowly made her way out of the church and along the path leading towards the water meadow and the ford.

To her relief, both Arthur and Murton were already there awaiting her. Arthur urged his horse forward as she approached the ford, splashed his way to her and swung out a hand to assist her to mount behind him. Andrew Murton rode his horse alongside. He dismounted and came towards her.

'Where is Martha?' he enquired. 'I thought she had agreed to accompany you.' His tone was quite conciliatory.

She gave a little annoyed shrug. 'She twisted her ankle slightly soon after we left the manor. She managed to reach the church, but she was obviously in pain and grumbling so I thought she would be more trouble than help on this journey. She argued, but I insisted on her returning to the manor. She was still in pain so I gave her coin to go to the inn for a while. In that way she cannot be questioned too soon when she gets back as to where I was. She will make up some story to account for my temporary absence, which will give us time. I rely on her. She loves me well.'

Murton smiled sympathetically. 'You will miss her.'

'I will, but I couldn't insist upon her enduring more pain. If necessary we can hire some woman en route and I am amply chaperoned having my brother as escort.'

'Aye, that is very true,' Murton agreed. 'Come, I will take you up. My horse is used to carrying heavy weight when I am in armour.'

Rosamund shrank from the very thought of riding pillion behind the man, her arms around his waist, their bodies touching. She almost wanted to retch. She stared back at him, that sturdy, unassuming form, the disarming smile, all calculated to deceive, to inspire trust in others. She turned away hastily and reached up towards Arthur's outstretched hand. 'No, do not trouble yourself, Andrew. The two of us are lighter together for Arthur's mount to carry.'

Arthur swung her up expertly and cheerily. 'We did have some problem with a loose nail in his rear right shoe,' he told her, 'but the blacksmith in the village soon put that right. She will carry us easily and safely to Warwick and beyond if necessary. In the town we can buy a suitable palfrey for you.'

'Excellent,' she said as she tucked up her skirts and made herself comfortable behind her brother. 'I take it you managed to retrieve my saddle-bag.'

'I have it here.' Andrew informed her, touching one of two bags secured to his saddle. 'Well, we should waste no more time now if we are to reach Warwick before nightfall.'

Simon was polishing his sword with an oiled rag when Martha erupted unannounced into his gatehouse chamber. She was panting and dishevelled and clearly distressed. He rose at once from his bed where he was seated and lifted her on to it to rest as she stumbled on to her knees in her haste to reach him.

'Steady, Martha. Take a deep breath. Whatever is wrong? You are quite safe here. Where is your mistress?'

He signalled silently to Rolf Taylor, who appeared in the doorway to apologise for his failure to keep her out, to leave them for a moment and to close the door. Simon rose and went to his small travelling chest. He pulled out a metal flask and poured a measure of some colourless liquid into a drinking cup, which he pressed into Martha's hands imperatively. 'Drink,' he ordered brusquely.

She took a hasty swallow and broke into violent coughing. He waited for her to recover, tapping an impatient finger on the discarded sword hilt. At last she lifted a scarlet-flushed face to his and croaked, 'You must go to Warwick, sir. Mistress Rosa and Master Arthur are in the most terrible danger.' She clutched at his sleeve appealingly. 'I beg of you to waste no time, sir. He intends to murder them both.'

'Murton?' he questioned harshly and she blinked rapidly and nodded. 'How—how did you—'

'Never mind that now. What are they both doing in Warwick? Tell me while I prepare.'

First he opened the door and bawled out a harsh command to Rolf Taylor, who was lingering nearby, ready for his master's call should he need him. 'Rolf, go the stables and get them to saddle my destrier. Find my sergeant and tell him to round up a company of six men and follow me to Warwick. Tell him to rendezvous with me near the church. The men are to be armed and ready for combat and they must lose no time. Understand?'

'Aye, sir. Do I go with you?'

Simon hesitated for one second, then nodded. 'Yes, but we must ride like the wind. If you fall behind, I shall leave you. Now hurry, man.'

Rolf Taylor scuttled off about his message and Simon turned to Martha, who had recovered somewhat now and was leaning anxiously forward to catch his words. 'Now tell me quickly all you know,' he snapped. 'I must be well informed and ready for what awaits me in the town.'

Martha told her tale succinctly and he listened, while fastening on his sword belt, pulling on riding boots and reaching for his cloak from his clothing pole.

'So she wished to escape me,' he muttered and Martha reached up to touch his arm.

'The Virgin knows that she loves you, sir. She was thinking only of the boy's needs and now she has gone to join him, hoping to have an opportunity of warning him in time.'

'Aye, she would,' he grated, 'and you say you have no idea which of the houses near the church that it is.'

'No, but she believes that Murton lived there for some time before coming to Kinnersley and so is known in the town.'

He inclined his head. 'Never fret. I'll find it if I have to search every house in the vicinity and drag out all the inhabitants and, God willing, I'll reach them in time.'

She tried to scramble up. 'I would go with you, sir.'

'No.' He shook his head decisively. 'I know how your heart cries out to do that, but you can only impede me in my work. Stay here and pray for my success.' At the door he turned. 'Incidentally, keep your own counsel for the present. I do not wish Lady Sibyl to get a whiff of what we intend.'

Martha closed her lips tightly together. 'I will do as you say, sir. Bring her back safely…'

He forced a smile as he was about to leave. 'I will do it. Try not to worry about her, or the boy. She has spirit and grit and real courage. She will hold out somehow until I reach them.'

Martha thrust a hand hard against her mouth to prevent herself crying out her mingled fear and yet her relief that she had found him so quickly and that not, for one moment, had he hesitated before following his love. She moved to the window to watch him ride out with Rolf Taylor and heard the clatter and shouts of the sergeant and stable hands as he rounded up his men and their mounts to follow.

It was dusk when Andrew Murton and his charges rode into Warwick and he led them to a small house set some paces behind the churchyard of St Mary's. Rosamund scrambled down from Arthur's mount in ungainly fashion before Murton could dismount and move to lift her down. She could not bear the thought of his murderous fingers touching her body. She was shivering as he led them into the secluded little house, despite the warmth of the evening, and she knew that that was the stark fear she was experiencing. Still unaware of his peril, Arthur was chattering brightly as Murton lit two tapers and he gazed curiously round the small, cluttered room. Rosamund noted that, though there was some dust on the few rough-hewn pieces of furniture, the rushes on the floor were freshly spread and the place smelt clean, though somewhat musty, as if the shuttered windows had been closed for some days. Obviously Andrew Murton had been here quite recently and she supposed that he had made preparations for their arrival. He had most probably laid in food supplies.

She gave a little sigh of disappointment. He would be unlikely to leave them to go to buy provisions and she would lose the opportunity she needed to speak with Arthur alone. One thing he needed to do was stable their horses somewhere, and that might give her some little time at least, but her hope was frustrated when he requested that Arthur accompany him to some nearby stable he knew of. The boy went willingly, still chattering eagerly of his hopes for the journey ahead, which he saw as an adventure as well as a means to an end, that of freeing his sister from an enforced marriage.

Rosamund watched them go, waited for a few moments, then made a hasty tour of the property in hope of finding a possible means of escape. There were but two rooms, this downstairs one, which served as living solar and dining room, and a single bedchamber above, which boasted merely one truckle bed, a chamber pot, scrubbed clean, and a chest to store spare garments. She found bread, cheese and salted meat and bacon in a cupboard below and guessed that there was a well in the yard at the back, so there would be little need for Murton to leave the house again tonight. He would keep Arthur close at his side so, though she could leave at any time and save herself, she could not without leaving Arthur in peril. She must wait for their return and hope against hope that Simon would come to their rescue.

Simon rode into Warwick at a gallop, Rolf Taylor hard on his heels, much to the consternation and disapproval of the town watch, who was about to begin on his round of duty. It was almost full dark now and all houses and shops shuttered and barred.

Simon snapped at Rolf. 'Go and station yourself near the west door of St Mary's Church and wait for my sergeant and his men. Try to keep inconspicuous less the watch becomes more alarmed.'

Rolf rode off at once and Simon dismounted and led his horse along the length of the high street. When the watchman again appeared, he looked doubtfully at Simon's gilded spurs, recognising him as a knight who would take badly to being challenged. He stood back a little, lifting his lanthorn, his stance showing his concern and curiosity.

'Can I assist you, sir knight?' he ventured at last and Simon hitched his leading rein to a post and nodded curtly.

'Where are the premises of Master Trenton, the draper?'

'Is something wrong, sir? If so, I could call out a hue and cry…'

'I wish you to do nothing, fellow, but to point me in the direction of the Trenton residence. He is, I understand, the father of Lady Sibyl Kinnersley?'

'That's right, sir. She was wed just over a year ago. It's a sad business, for Sir Humphrey, he was killed at Tewkes-bury—'

Simon cut impatiently across the man's garrulous desire to chatter. 'I am in haste, fellow. Show me the way.'

The shop front was shuttered and barred, as Simon expected. He curtly dismissed the avidly curious watchman, who was inclined to linger, and banged imperiously on the shop doorway. It was some time before his summons was answered, and a couple of night-capped heads appeared at windows farther down the high street before Simon heard the sound of feet approaching the door and a voice grumbling loudly.

'All right, all right, what is it? Such a racket will awaken the dead in the churchyard. Don't you know it's almost time for decent folk to be preparing for bed?'

'Open the door,' Simon shouted and backed up the command with another fusillade of blows upon the stout oak of the door.

'Indeed, and why should I? Identify yourself, sir. I'll open to no fool who summons me for inadequate reason.'

'I am Sir Simon Cauldwell, seneschal of Kinnersley. I command you to open this door at once before I send for men to break it down.'

There was a muttered imprecation from within and what appeared to be a whispered exchange between the first speaker and another on the far side of the door but, at last,

Simon heard bolts being drawn back and the door opened only slightly. An elderly grey head was thrust towards him from within.

'What is it, Sir Simon? Is aught wrong at Kinnersley? My daughter, the Lady Sibyl—'

'Is well enough.' Simon thrust one booted foot between the door and the post and, grabbing the shoulder of the speaker, hauled him unceremoniously out on to the street. Master Trenton, for Simon supposed it was indeed his quarry, was still fully dressed and holding up a lighted candle to survey his unwanted visitor.

'You call at this untimely hour, sir, and decent folk do not wish to open up. My servants are afeared and—'

'You've no cause to fear. I need to know where is Master Murton's house in the town. Describe the property to me.'

'Andrew Murton's house?' Master Trenton blinked owlishly. He was a tall, spare man, probably about fifty years of age, his face lined and his expression troubled and querulous. 'Why, Andrew went to become squire to Sir Humphrey over a year ago, soon after my daughter was wed. As far as I know, he is still at Kinnersley Manor.'

'But he has lodging in the town?' Simon pressed relentlessly. 'Close to St Mary's, I understand. I need to contact him urgently.'

'Because of some accident at the manor? But, sir, you said my daughter was safe…'

'Where did he reside, man? I am in considerable haste. I've told you, Lady Sibyl is safe at Kinnersley.'

'Thank the saints.' Master Trenton turned to address a woman who pressed anxiously forward to his side from the corridor within. 'Well, I did not think that Andrew continued to keep up the house. It is small, near St Mary's, as you said, some paces away, edging the churchyard. It stands by itself, you cannot miss it, a poor place, plaster and lath, painted yellow.'

'I'll find it. My apologies for disturbing you, Mistress Trenton. There is no cause for alarm. My business is with Murton, who is absent from Kinnersley.'

Simon gave a hurried little bow in the woman's direction and turned from the shop. He retrieved his mount and led it towards the great church, whose tower he could distinguish looming ahead of him in the gloom, set back slightly from the almshouses, which he was now passing.

He found Rolf Taylor, as he had commanded, waiting for him just within the churchyard of St Mary's, behind the lych-gate where he could not be instantly espied by anyone passing on the road. Rolf came hurriedly to his side.

'Did you find out where the house you seek is, sir?'

'Yes, follow me. We will leave your horse and mine within the churchyard. We can tether the lead reins to some convenient bush. I will point out the house to you and then I wish you to return and wait for the troop.'

Rolf swallowed hard and fell into step just behind his master. He could feel in his bones that they were about difficult and dangerous business.

Simon spotted the house where Master Trenton had described it. Even now, in the deepening gloom, he recognised the distinctive yellow paint work of the plastering. He signalled silently to Rolf and moved around the house, keeping low and looking for any suitable entry. The windows were all fast shuttered, as he expected, and, as he moved by the downstairs window, he thought that he could just discern the sound of movement within and a faint glow of candle or taper light showed between the gaps in the shutters. He gave a satisfied little nod and withdrew to a broken fence by the side of the churchyard grave plot. Rolf squatted beside him on the grass.

'Go back now to the lych-gate and wait for my men. Tell them to leave their horses nearby, hidden if possible, and join me here as quietly as possible.'

'Sir. You expect to find Mistress Rosamund and her brother inside?'

'Yes, and still living, I hope and pray. Hurry, the men should be here any moment now and I want them in place and surrounding this property as soon as they arrive.'

Rolf slipped off quietly. Simon moved back to the downstairs shuttered window and prepared to keep a silent vigil until he had the reinforcements that he required.

Andrew Murton arrived back with Arthur, who was still clearly unaware of any problem. He told Rosamund cheerfully that they had stabled the two horses at a nearby inn and made a deal with the innkeeper to purchase a quiet mount for Rosamund.

'You can see it, Ros, and decide if it is suitable when Andrew decides that it is safe for us to leave this house and proceed further on our journey.'

Rosamund forced a smile of approval. 'That seems very convenient,' she said. 'We have sufficient funds.'

When Andrew Murton proposed to go to the well for water she hoped she might have one or two precious moments alone with Arthur but, again, she was frustrated as her brother opted to go with him, carrying a second vessel. She sank down dispiritedly on a stool to wait for their return. There was a nagging fear within her that Murton would not risk leaving the two of them alive beyond this night and every second counted now if she hoped to save Arthur.

She tried to imagine what was going on at Kinnersley. It was now many hours since Martha had left her. Surely she must have found Simon and delivered her message. For the first time Rosamund began to despair. Suppose he decided to leave her to her fate? She had treated him badly, doggedly refused to consider his point of view. If he loved her he would come, her heart told her but—did he truly love her? Was it only the lure of her dowry that had drawn him to her? Now that she had categorically decided not to wed him, why should he put himself out to come to her rescue when he might well be risking his own life?

She ached to see him once more, even if it was to be for the last time. She recalled the few moments of passion they had had together, the feel of his hard muscled body against her own, his breath, sweet and faintly wine-fumed, upon her cheek, the sound of his voice, clear, commanding, yet tender, when he chose it to be so. No, she told herself stoutly. He would not fail her, even if he knew that she would reject him. Even if he had not loved her so passionately as she had supposed, he would not merely turn away and leave her to suffer with her young and foolish brother.

She heard the sound of Andrew Murton's voice in the yard as he approached the back door with Arthur. It would be very soon now. Her hands gripped the sides of the stool as she forced herself to rise and greet them.

As she had surmised, Andrew Murton had taken in food supplies and he set about preparing an evening meal for them. Arthur came to her side, grinning happily.

'I told you everything would be all right. We are safe here. No one would think to find us in this little secluded house. Andrew says we have sufficient food to keep us comfortable and well fed for another day at least until he is sure Cauldwell's men will not look for us in the town, then we can set out again. I am sure the king will listen to your plea. He is gallant, they say, and looks kindly on women.'

Rosamund watched as Andrew Murton opened a cupboard and brought out platters and drinking cups. He placed a loaf of bread upon the table, several meat pies and some bacon and cheese. He turned his back on them while he poured wine and set three cups down again on the table.

'Come,' he said smiling, triumphantly, 'as the boy says, you are safe enough here. Come and drink to the success of our journey. Arthur, take this cup to your sister.'

Rosamund's fingers felt strangely numb as she took the filled cup from Arthur and he lifted his own high, preparing to drink.

She shouted a warning even as she still sat, partially frozen with foreboding. 'Do not drink, Arthur. Put it down. Do not partake of any of the food here.'

He turned, staring at her, bemused. His hand jerked and red wine spilled upon the deal table, marring its scrubbed surface as if with blood. 'Ros?' he asked awkwardly, 'What do you mean? What are you saying? You cannot think…'

She sprang up and went to her brother. 'He intends to kill us,' she said tonelessly, 'Ask him. Go on. He will not deny it, not now. His time is short. He cannot afford to wait. He will kill us tonight.' She held up the cup. 'The easiest way would be to drug this wine, render us unconscious, before he is forced to act. Isn't that so, Andrew?'

She faced him squarely, her breast rising and falling in her agitation and dread.

Arthur swallowed hard. He stared from his sister's accusing, grim countenance to that of the cold, impassive stare of the man he had thought his greatest friend and helper. Instinctively he felt a sudden chill of fear. He opened his mouth to try to speak, then abruptly closed it again.

'So you know.' Murton's voice was very cold, his stance and expression perfectly calm. 'Now I wonder how you can have discovered the truth of it? Ah, you must have been inside the church and near to the door when Sibyl and I discussed our plans. I told her she was foolish in the extreme to come there and risk discovery at the very last moment when our plans were almost complete. So you know—everything.'

'I know that you murdered my father and that Sibyl's child is yours.'

A terrible cry issued from Arthur's lips and he lunged impetuously forward, his wine cup spilling down Murton's leather jerkin as he aimed an ill-conceived blow towards the man. Andrew Murton caught the boy's hand in a vise-like grip so that he gave a sharp cry of pain.

'Steady, Arthur, there is no need for choler. As your sister says, there is a simple means of dealing with our problem. Drink the wine and you need no longer fear. Neither need Rosamund. You will suffer no pain. It will be quick and easy. You will fall asleep and know nothing more.'

'Ros?' Arthur, appalled by what he had heard, appealed to his sister for an explanation, while he struggled help-lessly in Murton's grasp. 'Tell me what all this is about. You said that he killed Father...'

'That's right,' Murton said suavely. 'I found myself temporarily alone with him, after the battle, just as we reached the horse lines. He had his back to me, reaching for his destrier's reins. I plunged my dagger into his neck between the gorget and his back plate. He gave no more than a strangled scream, then we were surrounded by men fleeing the field. They'd no time to think what I was doing. I mounted his body on his horse, waited in shelter till the main pursuit was over, and you know the rest.'

'But why? He was good to you.' It was an anguished cry from the heart and Rosamund ached to put her arms around Arthur and comfort him, but she felt rooted to the spot.

Murton shrugged. 'Why? I wanted rid of him. He stole my woman. Sibyl and I had loved for months before he came to Warwick and set eyes on her beauty. Her father sold her to him, seeing an advantage of having his lovely daughter as wife to a wealthy knight, and a grandchild born of a noble union. I had little or no support to offer her. I counselled her to obey her father and wait an opportunity. I took it at Tewkesbury and now I need to rid myself of his two brats so that Sibyl can continue to live in comfort at Kinnersley and I with her—and with our child, who will inherit.' He gave a grim smile and waved his free hand at Rosamund. 'I had thought you would wed Cauldwell and that he would take you away to the north, or to Westminster, to wait upon his lord, Gloucester, and that would leave me free to deal with the boy—accidentally. But you chose to run away with him and that serves our purpose better. Sibyl's child will inherit your manor as well as Kinnersley.'

'You will not get away with murder a second time,' Arthur shouted. 'People will suspect.'

'He intends to fire the house with our bodies inside,' Rosamund explained deliberately. 'In that way he can explain two accidents more easily.'

'And that is why you should take the easy way and drink the wine,' Murton said quietly.

Arthur had stopped struggling now. He had been so shocked by this sudden revelation of betrayal that Rosamund thought he was almost ready to accept his fate. She could think of nothing she could do. She could lunge herself at Murton, kicking and clawing, as Arthur had done, but she realised that it would be a pointless gesture. Even if he were forced to release Arthur and have two of them to subdue, Murton would accomplish that easily enough. He was a seasoned warrior, a strong man, made ruthless by a need to protect his own interest now. He could not risk the escape of either of them. That would doom him and he knew it.

While the desperate thoughts were going round and round in her mind Rosamund felt that time itself had stood still. They stood, the three of them, caught in a kind of deadly web, which even Murton seemed, for the moment at least, unwilling to break. At last Arthur blurted out, 'Let my sister go. It is me you need to kill. I stand in the way of Sibyl's child's inheritance.'

'And let her proclaim my guilt to the world?' Murton jeered. 'You are more naïve than I thought, young Arthur.' He tightened his hold on the boy and Rosamund feared that the moment had come when he would kill her brother before her eyes. His plan to lure them into drinking drugged or poisoned wine had failed and he could not afford to wait now. She uttered a swift prayer to the Virgin to save Arthur from experiencing severe pain and, even as she closed her eyes momentarily, she heard a sudden crash as the outer door's lock was splintered and the heavy wood thrust aside. She gave an incredulous cry, as the little room was abruptly invaded by the bulky figures of half a dozen armed men, who ringed the three silently, taking their places, as if on cue, around the walls. Into the centre of the circle walked Simon Cauldwell.

Murton turned with a snarl of rage. He released Arthur immediately, so that the boy fell to the ground and, reaching out, seized a startled Rosamund, forced her backwards to lean against his chest, so that she formed a solid bulwark between him and his enemies, and placed the edge of his dagger against her throat. She felt a faint, cold trickle of blood run down on to her gown's bodice, but experienced no pain.

Simon Cauldwell's chillingly calm voice cut across the dreadful stillness of the little room. 'Harm but one hair of her head, Murton, and I will cut out your living heart.'

'So,' Andrew Murton hissed, 'you came on to warn the boy and sent Martha back to the manor.'

'Yes, indeed,' Simon continued in that same cold, quietly menacing voice, 'and now I am here you will release my betrothed, instantly.'

Murton gave that oddly jarring laugh once more. 'And when I do, you will kill me.'

'You are doomed, and you know it.'

Murton's eyes roved the little room with its silent, waiting spectators, and narrowed like those of a hunted cat, but still he kept the dagger pressed tightly against the white skin of Rosamund's throat. She swallowed uncertainly, then said deliberately, 'Do not concern yourself about me, Simon. Kill him now and make sure that Arthur is safe.'

'Always the boy must come first,' Murton snapped and, without warning, he released his grip upon Rosamund and made a sudden lunge on Arthur, who was still, wonderingly, climbing to his feet, frightened and confused. Rosamund gave a terrible cry, fearing Murton would strike Arthur down with his dagger before anyone was able to prevent him, but before the boy could move, Simon Cauldwell had drawn his sword, stepped forward with the speed of a hunting leopard and smashed the dagger from Murton's hand. It fell to the ground with only the faintest tinkle and Rosamund followed its progress with startled incredulity. Andrew Murton appeared to have been taken totally by surprise and stood, rubbing his bruised wrist then, before he could move, two of Simon's men had captured him and drawn his arms so tightly behind his back that he let out a scream of pain.

Rosamund rushed to Arthur and drew him tight against her heart. 'Hush, you are safe now,' she whispered, nuzzling his rumpled brown hair with her lips. For once he made no childish move to free himself from unwanted attention, but hid his face against her bosom. She could feel the fast beating of his heart against her own and lifted her gaze to that of Simon, who was calmly sheathing his sword.

'Thank you,' she murmured huskily.

'Did you doubt that I would come?' His voice was harsh with rugged emotion.

'No, well, just once, when—when I feared that…'

He was making no motion to touch her and she realised that he was still working out in his own mind her reason for running from him against her desperate need to appeal to him when she and the boy were threatened. Had she wounded his pride beyond repair?

Arthur withdrew himself from her hold at last and said hoarsely, 'I have to thank you, sir, for saving both our lives.' There were distinct signs of tears forming on his lashes and he shook them away impatiently.

Murton's voice cut across the expression of gratitude. 'Well, Cauldwell, you managed to come to the rescue in time. There is little I can say in my own defence. I think you heard me clearly enough or discovered from Martha the truth of the matter. Make an end, now.'

Simon turned and regarded him dispassionately. 'I'll not sully my blade with the death of a murderer and one who preys on helpless women and children for gain,' he said contemptuously. 'As I see it, you have one of two choices. You can return with me as my prisoner and surely hang ignominiously, or you can make it easier for the boy, who has had some regard for you in the past, and drink from his cup.' He walked to the table, picked up Arthur's drinking cup and returned to the prisoner's side. He held the cup close to Murton's lips. 'I take it that you chose a merciful poison, or, at the least, the most merciful you could find, so I counsel you to drink it—now.'

Rosamund moved as if to prevent him from accomplishing his purpose and with his free hand he waved her back.

'Believe me, Rosamund, it is for the best,' he said softly. 'Arthur would not wish to go through the heartache of a trial bearing witness against a man he admired and trusted, nor the agony of seeing that man wriggle out an unpleasant and humiliating death at the end of a rope.'

Murton's eyes met Rosamund's over the rim of the cup and he smiled ruefully. 'Your lover is considerate of your feelings, Mistress Rosamund, and of that of the boy, and he is right. Try to ensure that Sibyl is treated with equal consideration.' He bent his head and swallowed while Simon tilted up the cup.

It took only minutes while the two men-at-arms held up the prisoner. Andrew Murton stood upright, then his body convulsed and his guards supported him to a stool on to which he collapsed. Mercifully they and Simon stood between the dying man and Rosamund where she stood with her brother. She turned away with a desperate sob and once more pulled Arthur closer to her. At last Simon came to them both, as they remained, tearful now, their eyes averted from the grim scene across the room.

'It is over,' he informed them. 'It was better this way.'

Arthur withdrew himself and turned to gaze at the body of the man for whom he had had a profound trust and affection. Murton was slumped on the stool, seemingly at peace, and Arthur drew a hard breath and looked back at his rescuer. 'Thank you again, sir. In spite of everything I would not have him suffer, at least for long.'

Simon inclined his head and looked intently at Rosamund. 'You are exhausted. I think you should remain here in the bedchamber for the remainder of the night. You will be perfectly safe with my men on guard.'

Rosamund gave a great shudder and swallowed hard. 'No,' she murmured, 'I cannot stay in this place. Simon, take me home—now.'

He sighed, then nodded. 'Very well. I will send my men to try to find a litter for you.'

'No, no, I can ride.'

'You will not,' he said sternly. 'I will not have that. You are too exhausted to stay safely in the saddle, and so, incidentally, is your brother.'

'Then allow two of your men to take us up pillion. Please, Simon, all I want now is to leave this dreadful place as soon as possible.'

He looked at her long and hard and slowly shook his head. 'Let it be so, then. You will ride with me…' he hesitated momentarily then added softly '…if you feel you can trust me and bear to be so near to me.'

She blinked back tears. 'Simon, please, do not castigate me, not yet, at least, though I know that I deserve it. I have suffered enough for my foolishness.'

His lips curved in a slightly bitter smile. 'Leave matters to me, then.'

She waited with Arthur while he gave instructions to his men, presumably about the disposal of Andrew Murton's body, for which purpose two of them stayed behind. He then returned to Rosamund. 'My men are preparing the horses. Arthur's and Murton's can be retrieved by my two men in the morning and returned to Kinnersley if you will tell me where they are stabled.'

Arthur mechanically informed him, his lips moving almost without his volition. For once he appeared to be totally vulnerable and made no opposition to any of Simon's orders. Simon made no attempt to touch Rosamund and, holding Arthur's hand, she followed him meekly outside. Simon's sergeant respectfully took up Arthur behind him as the men mounted. Simon sprang into the saddle of his own destrier and leaned down an arm to assist Rosamund to mount before him. Gently he drew her close to his body and she felt the warmth of him and the fast beating of his heart as she laid her head against his shoulder. Was that fast beat indicative of his continued love for her or of his anger at her betrayal of that love? She could only wait now and hope.

There was a full moon, which lit their path as the horses picked their way at a steady pace along the road. All Rosamund could think of was that she was safe and secure in her lover's arms. In spite of her rejection of him, he had not hesitated for one second to come to her help. She told herself fiercely that nothing mattered to her now but the acceptance of her love for Simon Cauldwell, not his loyalty to the Yorkist cause or Arthur's stubborn refusal to accept the possibility of their marriage. She needed him, they both needed him and, if he were prepared to overlook her foolish behaviour of the last few days, she would allow nothing to come between them. Arthur must be made to accept the situation as things stood. If Simon would marry her, after all that had happened, she would soon be gone from Kinnersley with him. She must trust him to find a protector for Arthur and pray that things would turn out for the best for the boy. He would feel all the more confused and distressed now at the betrayal and death of his former friend and mentor. Her heart ached for him but, despite all her misgivings concerning his immediate future, she was sure that it was safe in Simon Cauldwell's hands.

Simon's arm tightened about her and she relaxed against him with a little sigh. He looked down at her and she glimpsed a smile forming about that stern mouth.

'Comfortable?' he enquired.

'Yes. Simon, I am so sorry. I—'

'Explanations can come later. Let it all go now. You are safe.'

'Did you suspect…?'

'I felt that there was something strange in the relationship between Lady Sibyl and the squire, although they were completely careful when in the presence of the other.'

'She said—he confirmed it that…' she hesitated '…that the child is Andrew Murton's and that—'

'He murdered your father, yes. Martha told me.' He was silent for a moment, then he added grimly, 'Terrible things take place on battlefields, private quarrels settled—well, you saw something of the dreadful aftermath for yourself, one of the reasons why it is essential now that Edward continues to rule without hindrance.'

It was a tacit reminder to her of the reason for his un-questioned loyalty to the king and her abhorrence of what she feared was the murder of the late King Henry and she turned away to stare bleakly at the black trunks of trees as they passed. Stoutly she put the thought aside. These wars had set brother against brother, son against father, cousin against his kin. Like Simon she must pray that this peace would hold; the terrible grief that had overwhelmed her once more when she had heard of the terrible circum-stances of her father's death must be accepted and laid aside for all their sakes. He had made the mistake of loving an unworthy woman and paid dearly for it. She partly un-derstood too, now, that that arousal of love had been born out of his own desperate grief for the loss of her mother.

She gave another heavy sigh and Simon looked down at her quizzically. 'We shall be home soon,' he reassured her. She hid her face against the cold feel of his brigandine, while her silent tears wet the leather. Wherever home should prove to be in the future, for her it could only be a happy one if it were ruled by Simon Cauldwell.

Chapter Thirteen

The moment they entered the bailey Rosamund came to herself with a start. She had almost dozed through most of the way home, her head comfortably placed against Simon's shoulder. For the first time in days she had felt totally safe. Now she remembered that Sibyl would have to be faced. How could they break the news of Andrew Murton's death? No, worse than that, Arthur would never accept Sibyl's unborn child now that he knew its parentage; and could Sibyl be made to pay for her part in the conspiracy to kill their father? Rosamund's mind fought against the consequences of such a disclosure. There would be a terrible scandal and, in the end, Sibyl could hang after the birth of her child. All this would be dreadful for Arthur to bear. She swallowed hard and stirred against Simon so that he looked down at her curiously.

A groom came hastily up to the little group of armed men bearing a lighted torch though, already now, there were faint lighter streaks in the sky heralding dawn. The youngster looked very relieved when he saw his mistress and young master. Arthur sprang down though clumsily. He had grown cramped during the ride and events had

taken their toll of him so that he appeared drawn and almost haggard in the torchlight.

Tom lumbered up behind the stableboy and immediately
Rosamund saw by his expression that something was very
wrong at the manor. Gently Simon lowered her into the
old man's waiting arms and she steadied herself and turned
instantly to question him.

'What is it, Tom? Martha is safe?'

He looked up at Sir Simon as he was dismounting and
waited until he had handed his reins to the waiting boy
who led away the destrier. Tom glanced meaningfully at
the men-at-arms, who were dismounting and stood waiting
for orders. Catching Tom's mood of alarm, Simon dismissed them and watched, impatiently striking one hand
against his hip, as they dispersed in the direction of the
stables.

Rosamund touched Tom's arm questioningly. 'Tell us
what is wrong?'

'It's Lady Sibyl, Mistress Rosa. She's suffered an accident, like. She's in her chamber. Martha is with 'er,
but—'

'I don't understand,' Rosamund said impatiently. 'What
kind of an accident and how serious?'

Simon placed a warning hand upon her arm as Arthur
came to lean over his sister's shoulder, his young face
creased with an anxious frown.

'Where is the bitch?' he snapped and made to rush towards the hall steps until Simon dragged him back and
continued to hold tightly to his shoulder.

'Gently, young man, we want no further scenes tonight
to disturb your sister. Let us all go quietly into the house
and find out just what has occurred.'

Tom trotted awkwardly at their side as they mounted
the hall steps and entered the manor house. Rosamund
could feel that warning icy clutch to her stomach that fore-

told of further disaster and she stood still momentarily as the steward approached them down the length of the hall, his expression grave.

'Lady Sibyl is in her chamber, Mistress Rosamund. Martha and her ladies are with her. She is in good hands but—' he swallowed awkwardly '—after such a heavy fall from her horse we fear for the child. I am glad to see that you and the master are safely returned. We were concerned about your welfare so late and...'

'A riding accident?' Rosamund glanced back at Simon.

Arthur demanded roughly, 'What do you mean, an accident? Was she allowed to ride out alone and—?'

'No, Master Arthur, she refused an escort.' The steward glanced awkwardly at Sir Simon and wetted his lips nervously. 'She seemed very agitated when she saw you ride out with your men, sir. We thought perhaps that she had received bad news about you, Mistress Rosamund, and the young master. There was an altercation with Martha, who had only just returned to the house and she flung out of the hall, demanded that her palfrey be saddled and rode off at a gallop immediately her palfrey was made ready. She had, only an hour before, ridden in from the village and I thought it too soon for her to ride off again and alone. I was concerned for the child's welfare, sir, but I could not prevent it. I concluded that she was anxious about Mistress Rosamund and Master Arthur but, when I questioned her, Martha would not be drawn. She retreated to her own little room, saying that all would be made clear to us when you returned. About an hour later one of the woodsmen came dashing in, saying that he had found Lady Sibyl's mount riderless. He brought it back but could find no sign of Lady Sibyl, though he had called and searched about for her. He thought, as it was getting dusk, that he should seek help. I sent out four of the men to search through the wood and they found her. She was lying unconscious in the clearing near the stream. We think that her palfrey stumbled over a rabbit hole or some obstruction in the path and that she was thrown. The men brought her back to the manor on a hurdle and I have summoned a physician from Warwick, but it will be some time before he can come—' He broke off and took a hasty breath. 'Martha says that she fears that she will miscarry and needs help. She has remained with her, and two of the ladies.'

Rosamund stumbled slightly, shocked and dazed by the suddenness of this new disaster, and Simon steadied her while Arthur swore softly beneath his breath, fury revealed in his wide eyes. When he was about to speak again Simon warned him into continued silence with pressure upon his arm. It would be pointless to engage the house servants in speculation at this stage.

He said quietly to the steward. 'You have done well.'

Rosamund murmured, 'I will go to her.'

'No!' Arthur expostulated.

Gently Rosamund repeated, 'I will go to her.' She regarded her brother steadily. 'This is women's business, Arthur. Leave it to us. Wait here with Simon.' She turned to the steward, 'Bring refreshment for my brother and Sir Simon and see that Sir Simon's men receive an early breakfast. They have all ridden hard through the night.' She placed a hand on Simon's arm. 'I shall be quite all right with Martha. I will send to you when I have further news.' Then she moved purposefully towards the stair.

He inclined his head. 'I will see food is sent up to you. Do not tire yourself more than needful. I will see to Arthur.'

She forced a smile, then, turning once to look back at him and her brother, who stood, staring anxiously up at her, she continued to mount the stair.

Martha emerged from Lady Sibyl's chamber before Rosamund could lift her hand to knock upon the door. She must have been watching from the window and seen their return. She closed the door softly behind her.

'How is she, Martha?'

Martha shook her head. 'She has lost a great deal of blood. She miscarried, but I think other organs were injured in the fall from the horse. She has regained consciousness off and on. I do not think the physician from Warwick will be in time, nor do I believe that he could save her, even if he did. I have sent for Father John from the village. I was watching for him when I saw you arrive. Is Andrew Murton dead?'

'Yes. He took the poison he meant for us, monkshood, most probably.'

'That will have saved the hangman trouble,' Martha said dispassionately.

'Martha, how did all this happen? Did you tell her that I knew?'

'No, but she saw me talking with Sir Simon and he was riding off with his men. She cornered me in the hall and demanded to know where you were. I told her that you were visiting Dame Watkins in the village.'

'But she was aware that I was running off with Arthur and Andrew.' Rosamund sighed. 'She feared the worst and rode off to try to warn Murton.'

'Aye, that is about the size of it. She was never a good horsewoman. I suppose she was in a panic and could not control her mount. When they brought her back I saw that she would miscarry and did what I could but—' Martha shrugged expressively '—perhaps it is for the best.'

Rosamund considered that those words echoed those of Simon about Andrew's death and she had to agree, but, in spite of everything, her heart was troubled. Sibyl had been forced into an arranged marriage, which had spelt disaster from the start.

One of Sibyl's women, Joan, came to the door. 'Mistress Rosamund, Lady Sibyl is asking to see you.'

Rosamund hesitated. What could she say to a dying woman who had schemed to kill her? Could she find words of comfort? Would they be welcomed? Sibyl's heart must be full of bitterness and she was wanting to know now about her lover's fate. Rosamund sighed.

'Martha, wait and send up Father John the moment he arrives.'

'Of course, she must be shriven.' Martha's expression revealed how much she was of the opinion that Lady Sibyl was in need of confession and absolution.

Rosamund entered the chamber timidly. The older woman rose and came to the door. 'She has dismissed us. She wishes to talk to you alone, Mistress. She is very weak.'

Rosamund nodded and waited while the two women left. Joan was weeping and the other woman put a comforting arm about her thin shoulders. The room stank of blood and faeces and Rosamund was repulsed, nevertheless she went up to the bed and gazed down at her stepmother.

The women had done their best to make Sibyl comfortable. They had changed her soiled clothing and her clean chemise smelt of the lavender with which it had been kept in her clothing chest. They had washed her and combed her hair, which hung loose upon the pillow. Sibyl was as beautiful as ever, pale and clearly exhausted, but she appeared to be in little pain. Her lovely eyes were large and luminous and only her erstwhile full mouth was held in tightly, as if she was consciously holding suffering back by a real effort. She tried to lift her head and Rosamund hastened yet nearer and took the hand that lay loosely upon the coverlet.

'Is he dead?' The voice was faint yet eager and Rosamund bent closer and stroked back the tendrils of fair hair from the brow.

'Yes. It was very quick. I believe that he felt little pain.'

The pale lips moved in prayer and Sibyl murmured, 'I thank God for his mercy. He feared humiliation more than anything. I know that you can never forgive me, Rosamund, for you do know, don't you, what we planned?'

'Yes, but we must not think of that now. Give your heart peace.'

'I loved him so.' The avowal was so softly uttered that Rosamund could hardly catch it. 'It seemed the only way—to rid ourselves of your father—and the boy, and then you fell into our plan so suddenly. I never hated you, Rosamund, or even wished you ill. It was simply that I wanted him so desperately—and the child. When I saw Sir Simon leave so abruptly I feared—my only thought was to warn Andrew, and I failed.' She gave a little sigh. 'I take it that you heard us, hidden in the church?'

'Yes.'

'He told me how foolish I was to ride out to meet him. I could never bear to have him far from me. I doomed him with that foolish desire to see him before he rode out of my life for even a short time.'

The lovely eyes closed wearily. The limp hand within Rosamund's grasp quivered and tears started to Rosamund's eyes. She could not hate Sibyl, though the woman had been despicable in her scheme to kill a vulnerable young boy, yet she had been sinned against by a grasping father, who had valued preferment to his daughter's happiness. Had he known of her love for Andrew Murton? Perhaps they had kept their secret meetings from him.

There was a tap upon the door and Martha's head appeared around the gap. 'Father John is here, Mistress.'

Rosamund rose thankfully and went to join her. 'I think

she will open her eyes again in a moment and be able to be shriven. The women must stay clear for the present.'

She went sadly down to the hall. Arthur and Simon rose to greet her from table where they had been taking refreshment.

'How is she?' Simon asked.

'Dying. The priest is with her.'

Arthur gave a great gulp. 'I am—sorry that it happened, but—'

'It will be a relief to all of us in the end and for that poor woman,' Simon said gravely. 'There could be no easy solution to any of this. She could not be allowed to live and prosper. Now, finish your meal and then go to your chamber and rest, both of you. I will deal with matters here—and in Warwick.'

Rosamund sank down gratefully as Simon poured wine for her. She had been considering that the sheriff and the coroner must be informed and Andrew Murton's body disposed of decently and she could not bear to think of any of it at present. As ever, Simon had proved himself the solid, immovable rock on which she could lean and she thanked the Virgin for his presence. She could do nothing but smile at him in gratitude. He gave her that little half-bow of salutation and went out of the hall, leaving brother and sister together.

Arthur said little after he had gone. Rosamund knew that she must talk with him seriously about Simon, but this was not the time. Arthur looked up at her sheepishly and played with portions of bread. He stood up suddenly, scraping his chair across the floor.

'I would like to go to my room now,' he mumbled, 'if you will excuse me and—and you feel that you can be alone—'

'Yes, of course, Arthur.'

'I do not know what to say about—about our step-mother. If she lives—'

'I do not think that she will, Arthur, but, if so, we must try to find a way to avoid scandal. Do you agree?'

He looked away from her and then turned back and nodded. She thought there was a suspicion of overbright-ness to his eyes and she reached up and clasped his hand briefly. 'We must allow Sir Simon to handle this business as he thinks best,' she said quietly, holding his gaze steadily.

'You like him—a lot,' he murmured and she nodded in answer. He gently pulled his hand free and left her.

She waited until Martha came just after noon to tell her that Sibyl had passed away only moments before.

'She made a good confession, Father John said, and she has just slipped away. I do not think she was in any pain at the end.'

'I will help you to lay out the body and to keep vigil.' Rosamund rose to her feet, but Martha shook her head.

'No, best if you leave this sad business to her ladies. Father John will make all the necessary arrangements. Her parents must be informed. I will send a messenger to War-wick. What is to be done about—about the other business in Warwick?'

'Sir Simon will inform the coroner and a priest.'

'Good,' Martha breathed. 'And Master Arthur? He will take all this hard.'

'Yes. He will need to grow up very fast now.'

'And you—and Sir Simon? Dare I ask, Mistress, what you intend to do now?'

'He has said nothing of the marriage plans, thought it would be inappropriate, I suppose. I am prepared to do whatever he wishes, Martha. I think it will be best for Arthur in the end, for all of us.'

Again Martha nodded and, then, wearily, Rosamund
rose once more and moved slowly on stiffened limbs towards her own chamber. Later she would take her place
with the others in the prayers said for the dead by the body
of Lady Sibyl, but now she felt totally drained of all emotion and very close to tears. She would wait patiently now
until Simon came to her once more and she must pray that
he would forgive her for the humiliation she had dealt him
in running from the betrothal ceremony. She blushed with
shame as realisation struck her suddenly how much gossip
about her conduct must be circulating amongst both
Simon's own men and the members of her own household
concerning her precipitous flight from the manor.

He came to her chamber just before supper. Martha was
in attendance and Rosamund asked her quietly to leave
them. Martha went but, deliberately, Simon kept the chamber door open so that her maid could be close and observe
proprieties.

'I made my report to Arthur, since he is now unques-
tionably lord of Kinnersley. I told him that I have informed
the proper authorities. It is possible that you and Arthur
may have to be questioned, but there should be no difficulties since my men were present as witnesses of what
took place in the house. I have just been informed about
the death of Lady Kinnersley. I take it her parents will be
informed and come to the funeral?'

'Yes, messengers have been sent and a priest is here.'

He gave a heavy sigh and she indicated a chair. 'Please,
Sir Simon, do sit down. You must be very tired.'

'No, I am relieved that this is now over and that you
are both safe.' As he made no effort to sit but stood, still
and seemingly stern and unapproachable, Rosamund
moved a little uncertainly from one foot to the other. This

was undoubtedly going to be an uncomfortable interview and she moistened her lips nervously.

'You give the impression that you were suspicious of those two from the start.'

He shook his head slightly. 'A boy inheriting can always be extremely vulnerable and, since the second wife was so young and beautiful...' He left the implication unsaid and Rosamund blinked uncomfortably as she thought how despicably her father had been deceived.

He held her gaze for one moment then he said quietly, 'I have come to the conclusion that, since you were prepared to risk everything in order to escape what you considered to be an unhappy marriage, I must release you. I will send to the king and explain my reasons for withdrawing my request for your hand. Do not be concerned. I will not reveal anything in that letter which might embarrass you or Arthur.'

Tears started to her eyes and she longed to run to him, to break that little distance of ground, which appeared to be a terrible and insurmountable gulf between them, but her trembling limbs would not allow her to move. She made a little inarticulate sound and burst into sudden sobs.

Immediately he came close and took her hands within his own. 'Do not weep. There is nothing to be afraid of. You are perfectly safe here and I will remain until the king can provide a seneschal who will be more acceptable to you and your brother. Meanwhile I will keep out of your sight as much as possible.'

'Simon,' she burst out at last, lifting her face to his, tears streaming down her cheeks, 'can you ever forgive me? Of course I want to be your wife. I love you so—but—but everything seemed to be against it. Arthur is so hostile towards you and we cannot agree about the conduct of the king and the Duke of Gloucester. I know how deeply you feel a debt of loyalty to the Yorkist cause. Now—' she gulped '—nothing matters, only my love for you, my need for you. Please, please say that your feelings for me have not changed, that you still want me…'

He caught her close to his heart and nuzzled her soft brown hair, since she was wearing no headdress within her chamber. 'My darling,' he whispered huskily, 'if you knew what anguish it cost me to offer you your freedom you would begin to understand how much I want you.' He tilted up her chin with one finger and gazed deeply into her eyes, which were swimming with tears. 'We can overcome all difficulties, so long as we continue to love each other. I can leave Gloucester's household if that is your wish. He will understand and release me. As for Arthur—'

'No, no, you must not leave Gloucester's household. If you have such deep trust and affection for him, those ugly rumours must be false and I was foolish to give heed to them. In any case, affairs of the realm are beyond my comprehension though, one day, I hope that you will be able to discuss these matters with me freely and I can accept or reject your opinions without recriminations on the part of either of us. Arthur must also learn to accept the inevitable. You made a good start by reporting to him today, treating him with dignity instead of dismissing his rights as if he were still a young child and unable to understand what is needed for the good of the household. He loves me. He will understand that I must follow my heart.'

He released her for a moment, standing back to once again look deeply into her eyes. 'Then it is your wish that we should be wed—soon?'

'As soon as possible considering…' Her voice trailed off miserably. 'It seems that too often we are in mourning in this house.'

He considered. 'We must give it a little time. As you say, we must observe the proprieties. It is best if Lady

Kinnersley is buried honourably though, possibly, not too close to your father.'

Rosamund gave a great shudder and he continued. 'Since the priest must be knowledgeable—he heard her confession—he will suggest a suitable compromise. Neither you nor Arthur will want the neighbours to become aware of the deception of your father. That would be too humiliating. We will wait patiently. Meanwhile, perhaps Arthur and I can become better acquainted. He may learn to tolerate me though, I fear, there will always be a constraint between us. Our first encounter was too painful for him to forget. It was an assault upon his dignity.'

She hesitated, anxious not to prick at his pride. 'We could live on my manor—that is, when you are not in attendance at court.'

He smiled down at her. 'Certainly we can visit often. I hear it is quite near and you will see more of Arthur and your home here, but I will wish to take you north to see my mother and my home there as soon after the ceremony as possible.'

She smiled at him shyly. 'What will she make of me?'

'She will love you, as I do, and recognise your beauty and the strength of your resilience and nobility of spirit. But, most of all, she will love you simply because you are you, and my wife and heart's love.'

He drew her into his arms again and she rejoiced in the sweetness of his kiss, passionate, though restrained as it was, for, as yet, he dared not allow himself full reign to his overwhelming desire.

The days of summer appeared to Rosamund to crawl by. She was amazed by Arthur's composure during the funeral obsequies of Sibyl Kinnersley and his kindness towards her weeping kin. As Simon had promised, the enquiries concerning the death of Andrew Murton were mere formalities and she and Arthur were questioned only briefly. If there was talk about his disappearance from the manor, word of it did not reach her ears, and she presumed that Simon had uncompromisingly decreed it so. Work on the manor land progressed in a satisfactory manner with him in charge and there were no more outbursts of temper from Arthur contradicting Simon's commands. Rosamund watched them together and noted, as Simon had prophesied, that there was still a distinct coldness in the boy's manner though, outwardly, he deferred to Simon's rule. She sighed inwardly. Her heart ached that this should be, this antipathy of the brother she loved so deeply towards the man she adored.

She wished now that her marriage to Simon could take place soon, but she understood that Sibyl's untimely death required that it should not do so in too much of a hurry. Simon visited her manor and reported that all was going smoothly.

'Your steward and bailiff appear to be working well and seeing that the peasants stick to their obligations. The harvest should be good, which will bring in a steady income for you.'

She was pleased to hear this, but it stirred the one remaining doubt in her, of how much Simon's interest in her lands contributed to his love for her.

At the close of July a messenger rode in wearing the blue and murrey livery of the Yorkist court and the White Boar badge of Gloucester. Simon was closeted with the man for some time and then came to her where she was at work in the still room, his brow creased in doubt.

'My lord of Gloucester is on his way north on a punitive expedition against the Scots,' he told her, 'and, my love, I feel that I should be at his side.'

Rosamund dropped a bowl she was holding and looked

down, stupefied, to see a mess of pottery shards and ointment marring the clean swept stone of the floor.

'You will leave Kinnersley, before—before—'

He drew her close and kissed her. 'I must, Rosamund. Richard is in need of his friends around him just now. He has settled matters in London and takes Fauconbridge with him to the Border to keep a close eye on him. The man is his cousin, though illegitimate, and could still stir rebellion if not under guard. Also it is time that I visited my mother and saw to it that all is going well at my home.'

She nodded absently. She could not bear the thought of parting—and he was going into danger! She deliberately shied away from the fear that, like her father, he might not return to her. Could she lose him before she became a wife?

He was chatting on, informing her of the news the man had brought him.

'King Henry's body was laid out for all to see in St Paul's and is now finally laid to rest at Chertsey Abbey.' He gave a harsh little laugh. 'Rumour still has its day. There was talk that the corpse bled, proclaiming murder, which is nonsense, of course. Any army surgeon can confirm that corpses do not bleed, whatever the cause of death.'

'And the duke is well?' she forced herself to ask, unwilling to bring up again the cause of dissension between them, that Gloucester might have been directly involved in the late king's death. 'And is there news of the Countess of Warwick and the Lady Anne?'

'The countess is at Beaulieu in sanctuary and the Lady Anne is with her sister Isabel and Clarence at their London home at Coldharbour.' Simon frowned again. 'Richard informs me in his letter that he is concerned about that. He has formally offered for Anne's hand but Clarence opposes the match.' Simon gave a wintry smile. 'That is natural enough. He has no desire to share the Warwick inheritance.'

Again Rosamund experienced that little stab of doubt. Men put great store by such things.

Simon left early next day, leaving his men-at-arms with her under the command of his sergeant. 'I shall feel safer if they are here to swell the garrison and I will raise a detachment from my own home to ride with me to the Border. They are all well used to fighting in these skirmishes.' He cupped her chin in his hand at parting. 'I shall be home soon and we can be wed.'

She watched in desolate mood as he rode away with the king's messenger. Later Arthur found her weeping in the pleasance, where she had sought privacy.

He crouched before her on the path and took her hands in his. 'Do not weep, Ros. I can see how deeply you care for him. He will be back soon, if only to annoy me.'

She snatched her hands from him, her eyes blazing fury. 'How can you speak of him like that? He saved your life and you remain ungrateful as usual.'

He looked up at her, immediately contrite. 'I am sorry, Ros. I had no wish to anger you. That was merely a stupid joke made in an effort to cheer you. It is true that I have no great liking for the man, but I am well aware of the debt of gratitude I owe him.'

There was no news from the north, which seemed to Rosamund to be so far from her, in another world. She forced herself to oversee preparations for the autumn and coming winter, the slaughtering and salting of meat, the preserving of fruit and careful storing of apples. All was as it should be on the manor, as if the fatal combat had not taken place at Tewkesbury and everything was in waiting now for her betrothed to return to her.

* * *

In mid-August she was disturbed when a chapman, travelling south for the winter, was brought to her solar, since she was anxious for any news from the north. He informed her that he had been in Durham as injured men were brought in from the campaigning on the Scottish Border.

Her blood ran cold. 'What have you heard? Does the English cause go well? Is the Duke of Gloucester successful in his bid to restore order? Were…?' She hesitated then pressed on determinedly, 'Were there knights and noblemen of the duke's train among the injured?'

He glanced at her curiously, noticing the anxiety in her tone. He was puzzled to find a woman so alarmed about skirmishes that were happening so far from her Cotswold home.

'Aye, there were one or two. The monks took them in for tending.' He shrugged. 'It is always so on the Border. The Scottish reivers come down into Northumberland plundering and to steal cattle and are pursued.' He grinned. 'Many of our men do likewise. Women there are used to patching up their menfolk, aye, and burying some of them. It is a way of life. The duke hopes to put an end to it, for a while at least, to teach those poxy Scots a hard lesson.'

Rosamund dismissed him after purchasing some trivial gifts for the maids of the household, and sat on for a while, her hand pressed to her heart.

Dear God, could Simon be numbered amongst the injured, or worse, the slain? So far she had had no cause to fear for him in battle, because since Tewkesbury he had been occupied in guarding her and Arthur! Now she realised that he was in peril and the terrifying truth struck her that he might not return. He would be close to his lord's side throughout those engagements—in mortal danger. She thought that her heart would burst with the deadly fear of losing him.

Arthur, returning from a ride with Tom, found her there

and pressed her to tell him what had so frightened her. He listened gravely as she recounted what the chapman had said.

His response was truly considerate for the first time.

'He is a thoroughly experienced warrior, Ros, and comes from the north, so is used to this type of conflict. He knows he has much to lose and will take special care of his person, I am convinced of that. He loves you. He will come back to you whatever difficulties and dangers lie in his way.'

She looked up at him, then drew him down, pulled his face close to hers and kissed him, grateful for his understanding of her great need. Was he, she wondered, prepared to accept Simon as her husband at last?

Then, on one cold but overwhelmingly beautiful day in September, which appeared to her even more dreary and lonely, despite its autumn splendour, because she was without him, the man on the gatepost sent a message that three men were approaching the manor. She rushed to the entrance to see Simon ride in accompanied by two sturdy men-at-arms, whom she later identified as Yorkshiremen from their broad vowels and brisk, uncompromising manners.

She rushed into his arms and he kissed her soundly before them all, despite the presence of Arthur, who greeted him courteously but without great warmth.

'No, love,' he reassured her when she required of him anxiously as to his condition, 'I am unhurt and delighted to see you. I hope that all is well here, because I have stopped in the village to inform Father John that I wish him to wed us tomorrow. I'll wait no longer to possess my bride.'

She drew back, pink with confusion. 'But, Simon, I have no suitable gown and I am still in mourning and...'

He laughed heartily, throwing an arm around her shoulder to draw her into the house. 'I would wish to marry you tomorrow if you appeared in sackcloth, sweetheart. Tell me that you are as anxious for the ceremony as I am.'

She was scarlet with surprised delight and she lifted her face to him gladly. 'Oh, yes, my love, tomorrow is hardly soon enough. I have missed you so sorely.'

'Well said. I'll send for my sergeant later to discover how goes the world here. Everything is well at my home. My mother regrets that she cannot be present for our marriage but, after Christmas, when the weather permits, I shall take you north to be with her.'

'Was it hard, the campaigning?'

'There were one or two sticky moments, as always. The Scots are wily fighters but Richard, despite his youth, is an accomplished commander and we were able to force the Scots into compromises, which will please Edward well.' He frowned thoughtfully. 'In London all did not go so well for Richard. He discovered that the Lady Anne has disappeared.'

Rosamund sat bolt upright in her chair by the fire. 'You mean she has left her sister's house? But surely that could mean that she is in danger.'

Simon nodded grimly. 'That is what alarms Richard.' He put out a hand to take hers. 'I know that you distrust his motives, but you are wrong, Rosamund. Richard loves Anne as deeply as I love you. He suffered dreadfully throughout those months when her father married her to Edward of Lancaster and she was lost to him. Now his brother covets the whole of her inheritance and he is distraught. As you say, she could well be in danger if, indeed, she is not dead.'

'You mean that she might have been murdered?'

He gave a dismissive shrug. 'We have had experience of extreme greed and how it can threaten the vulnerable ones. I pray God that Richard finds her soon. He has his men combing all the dangerous areas of the capital, including the sanctuaries, where murderers and thieves take refuge.'

'Could it be that she has fled from all of them, trusting none of them?'

He sighed. 'Very possible. Anne must have been a very frightened woman from the moment she and Queen Margaret heard the news from Tewkesbury field and fled, then, later, even more so when she was captured and brought to the king. I believe, sincerely, that if Richard can find her he will be able to convince her that he means her well and that she will agree to become his wife, though they will need a dispensation, since they are cousins.'

'But so are her sister Isabel and George of Clarence.'

'Aye, that marriage confers even greater difficulties for Richard's hopes. He has loved Anne since they were children together and, knowing his determination, I am sure he will win her in the end if—' He broke off awkwardly and Rosamund realised that he, too, feared for the safety of the younger Warwick heiress. 'Richard has assured us that he is willing to forgo the greater share of the Neville fortune if he is granted Anne's hand in marriage. I know that he wishes to take her home to Middleham Castle in Yorkshire and withdraw from the intrigues of court life.'

Rosamund looked at him searchingly and read his affection and admiration for the young lord to whom he had sworn loyalty. Could a man inspire such unswerving devotion and be the villain rumour suggested him to be?

She spent a sleepless night, feverishly going over her plans for the morrow. She was both apprehensive and ecstatically happy to think that tomorrow night she would lie in Simon's arms. Arthur had been somewhat quiet and withdrawn at supper, but when they had parted at the foot of the stair he had lifted his sister's hand to his lips and smiled at her before mounting to his own chamber. He had accepted her decision, but he had not given her his blessing.

Early next day she visited her father's tomb in the church to pray, hoping that he would understand that her love for Simon was greater than the differences of loyalties between them. Simon had decreed that Father John would marry them quietly in the great hall at Kinnersley and that a temporary altar would be set up there. Rosamund was not disappointed that only her household and Simon's men would witness the ceremony. At this time she had no wish to be wed before the nobility of the district.

When she reviewed her gowns in an effort to choose something suitable, for she must put aside her mourning for this occasion, she sighed deeply. Rosamund had never been a slavish follower of fashion, but she did wish for this evening that she would look her best, so that Simon would be enchanted with her. None of her gowns met with her approval and she surveyed them all, where Martha had laid them out on her bed, her eyes narrowed in criticism.

There was a knock on her door and she called to Martha to enter, for her maid had left her briefly to find some special concoction of perfume in the still room. The door opened and Martha paused in the doorway. Rosamund turned to face her, a trifle irritably, and gave a great gasp of astonishment. Martha bore over her arm a gown of white velvet embroidered in silver thread at neck and sleeve cuffs—her mother's bridal gown, laid away reverently in her mother's dower chest since that joyful day when she had become the bride of Sir Humphrey. Rosamund had put aside all thought of taking it now for fear of antagonising Arthur, but suddenly he appeared in the doorway, gently put aside Martha and entered her chamber.

'Martha says she believes it will be a good fit,' he said awkwardly, 'or, at least, she can make it so. Mother would have wanted you to wear it, Ros.'

Impulsively Rosamund flung her arms round her brother, her tears of mingled emotion and delight marking his best doublet of green velvet.

'Arthur, this is the finest present you could give me today,' she murmured huskily.

Rolf Taylor appeared at her door soon after she had completed dressing and presented her with a nosegay of rosemary and roses, the last from the pleasance. Rosamund was amused to note than not one of the blooms was white. Martha extracted one or two which she twisted with a length of fine wire and white velvet ribbon to adorn Rosamund's flowing brown hair. When Martha showed her her reflection in the mirror of Venetian glass, which her father had once brought her as a present from London, she gave a little nod of satisfaction. The gown was very fine, despite the fact that it was slightly outmoded, but she believed that she looked well enough and that Simon would not be disappointed.

She descended the stairs with Martha in attendance, attired in her best gown of scarlet wool and found Arthur waiting at the foot. He smiled appreciatively at the sight of his sister and took her hand in his. She glanced at him wonderingly, but he shook his head determinedly and led her into the hall where the assembled household waited, ranged before the dais on which Father John had set up a temporary altar, which, also, was adorned with late flowers from the pleasance. The candles flickered on the silver plate of the candlesticks and the fine embroidered altar cloth, and Rosamund smiled with genuine pleasure that everything possible had been done to make this moment memorable for her. Shyly she lifted her eyes to her would-be groom.

He stood with his sergeant and Rolf in attendance before the altar. For once she saw him resplendent in a padded murrey-coloured velvet doublet over grey hose, his dark hair, usually unruly, combed into submission. A gold chain around his neck was fashioned with white enamelled roses between the heavy links and the device of a small gold well suspended from it, portraying his heraldic device, and signifying a play upon his name, Cauld Well. She gave a little gasp at the unexpected splendour of his appearance and he made her his habitual courteous half-bow of greeting.

Arthur bowed formally in answer and, taking Rosamund's hand once more, he laid it in that of Sir Simon, which was held out towards her.

'I wish to give my sister into your keeping, sir,' he said quietly. His cheeks were a little red with embarrassment, but his demeanour was calm and his voice steady. 'I know that you will treat her well and I want to wish you both every happiness.'

Rosamund's eyes were blurred with tears of happiness at this public announcement of her brother's blessing, so that she could hardly see the priest before her as she took her vows and felt the heavy gold of the marriage ring, which Simon solemnly placed upon her finger. Firmly he took her by the shoulders and kissed her before them all, which brought a hearty cheer from the members of the household and the soldiers of the garrison. She was his at last and nothing now could part them. She blinked away the tears of happiness and smiled into those startlingly blue eyes of her husband.

The feast, which followed, was a happy occasion though, afterwards, Rosamund discovered that she could not remember much about it. Simon announced that he had appointed Rolf Taylor officially to be his squire and the young man beamed with his newfound happiness. He had stood beside Simon as his groomsman throughout the ceremony.

Rosamund was glad when only she and Martha retired to the bedchamber, which had been her father's and mother's, and which, surprisingly, he had not used after his marriage to Sibyl. Arthur had declared that it was right and proper that the bridal couple should occupy it for their marriage night and, again, Rosamund was pleased by his acceptance of the match. During the feast he had been a little withdrawn, but apparently happy that his sister had wed the man of her choice.

When Martha left her, having strewn the marriage bed with traditional herbs to encourage fertility and murmured her good wishes for her mistress's happiness, Rosamund lay in the bed, excited and apprehensive. She knew that this was to be expected but, since she had been impatient for this hour to arrive, she could not understand now her own reluctance to admit to herself that she was afraid.

She sat up anxiously as there came a tap upon her door and she called permission to enter, which she had to repeat, because her voice had at first deserted her. Rolf Taylor and Arthur accompanied Simon into the chamber but, although they offered, as Martha had done, the usual expressions of goodwill for the future happiness of the newlywed couple, there was no bawdy talk. Arthur approached the bed and kissed his sister tenderly upon the cheek.

'Be happy, Ros,' he murmured and she reached out and squeezed his hand gratefully. He had not let her down in his behaviour or made this day uncomfortable for her. She watched wistfully as the two men left, then turned to her husband. He was attired in a brocaded bedgown having, apparently, disrobed in some other chamber nearby and he closed and latched the door before approaching the bed.

She was sitting, upright, clutching the linen sheet almost to her chin and he perched upon the side of the bed and grinned down at her.

'It is both natural and proper for a maiden bride to be fearful,' he assured her as he reached out and stroked her flowing brown hair.

How beautiful she looked, even though he could see only her head and ivory shoulders and the shining white bones of her hands beneath the skin, proclaiming her panic in the way she had clutched at the concealing sheet so tightly!

'Simon?' she whispered nervously, and he bent and kissed her gently.

'All is well, sweetheart. It is true that I find it hard to hold myself in check and have done for months since I first laid eyes upon you in my tent in Tewkesbury. I want you, Rosamund, so much that it hurts, but I am willing to woo you gently, my love. There is no need to fear me.'

She watched mesmerised as he slipped off his bedgown and she glimpsed his manhood for the first time. She swallowed fearfully, despite his assurances. But she need not have been troubled. As he promised, he was very gentle with her, deliberately holding back his own responses until she was ready and the first experience was not unduly painful. He had caressed her body until she was fully ready to receive him and, afterwards, she lay in his arms, content, having known an ecstasy she could not have believed possible.

He sat up in the bed and regarded her smilingly. 'I love you now, Rosamund, my rose of the world, and I shall always love you. Tell me you return my love.'

'Do you have to ask?' she said anxiously starting up beside him. 'Have I not proved that? Did I not please you?'

'Aye, sweetheart, as I knew that you would. That first time in the tent when I almost took you—entirely by mistake, I might add—I knew that our bodies were meant to become one, that your passion would match my own.'

She looked shocked and demanded, 'Are you saying that you thought, even then, that I was wanton?'

He grinned broadly. 'Well, just let me say that I informed my mother in my letter that I had found the partner of my dreams.'

She flushed rosily. 'I hope she will like me.'

'Like you? She will adore you.'

'Arthur behaved with dignity today...'

'Aye, he did, but, my love, we will not speak of Arthur tonight.'

He took her again and she lay in his arms content, as the first spears of dawn light pierced the gap between the window shutters. She loved him so deeply. She had committed herself to him utterly. It mattered not that he wanted her dowry or that they could not agree about court intrigues, nor even that he was bound in allegiance to the young duke whose honour she doubted. She was his wife, the woman to whom he had given his love and his name, and that was enough.

Chapter Fourteen

Rosamund looked apprehensively at Arthur, who was staring out of the window at a group of boys in the tiltyard. They were standing outside the presence chamber at Middleham Castle in Yorkshire. It was early March. The icy weather had broken and Simon had declared that they would leave Kinnersley and travel north at last to his home near Aysgarth. Rosamund had looked forward to this during the long winter months following her marriage in the late autumn of last year, though with some sense of trepidation. It had been a wonderful time of fulfilment for her, learning to know and love her husband even more than she could have believed possible. The icy weather had marooned them within the manor for most of the time, making it difficult and treacherous either to venture very far from the house or for visitors from the neighbourhood to come to them, so that nothing had intruded upon her quiet happiness. She had dreaded the moment when that privacy would be shattered and she would be forced to meet Simon's mother and his companions of his childhood for the first time. Although he constantly assured her that she would be welcomed with open arms, the doubt nagged at her that his mother, whom she knew he adored, would

have preferred him to choose a wife from those she knew
well and of the same persuasion. They had received one
letter following the ceremony wishing them every happiness and assuring Simon that all was well at home before
the weather had closed in and messengers had not travelled
south again.

Life had progressed normally at Kinnersley. The harvest
had been excellent and gathered in and stored without
problems. The manor household had worked well under
Simon's benign yet firm rule and the only thing that had
disturbed Rosamund's peace was the stark loneliness she
had read in her brother's eyes. She knew that, despite his
knowledge of the man's betrayal, Arthur missed Andrew
Murton sorely. Now that he had inherited the lordship of
the manor, the boys of the village no longer regarded him
in the same companionable way. There was a barrier between them that could not be crossed, and Rosamund could
recognise that her brother had grown up suddenly very fast
indeed.

Simon kept him busy, talking with him of manor affairs,
arranging a continuation of his lessons with Father John,
who visited the manor house most days. Rosamund was
pleased that he insisted that Arthur learn to read and write
well, as he himself had learned to do at Middleham. He
talked enthusiastically of how Gloucester had met the master printer Wiliam Caxton during his childhood exile in
Burgundy and how his brother the king wished to foster a
knowledge of books and printing in England, in the hope
that he could lure Caxton into setting up a shop within the
capital. Rosamund had also learned to read and enjoyed
the romances her father had acquired, especially during the
bitterly cold and inhospitable days of the winter when
Simon was not at her side and occupied in the business of
the manor. He himself had spent some time in the courtyard with Arthur, practising his skill with the broadsword

and at the archery butts, and Tom had ridden out with the boy whenever the weather had broken sufficiently to allow it. Yet Arthur needed youths of his own age with whom to hone his martial skills and Simon spoke of arranging a place for him soon as a squire in some noble household.

Rosamund had been doubtful about Arthur accompanying them north and even more so as, now, Simon had announced his intention of waiting on the Duke of Gloucester at Middleham Castle on the way. How would Arthur be received by the powerful duke whom he had once publicly insulted? Rosamund doubted the wisdom of this decision and, glancing again at her brother, could see by his expression, that he, too, was deeply troubled.

Richard of Gloucester had, at last, been granted the hand of his childhood sweetheart, the Lady Anne Neville, and had been married at Westminster in February. A messenger had ridden north to inform Simon of the joyful tidings. The Lady Anne had been discovered hiding in a cook shop, even doing menial work in the kitchens, and Richard had discovered her there, rescued her and conveyed her for safety into the sanctuary of St Martin le Grand. There he had persuaded her to trust him and they had finally been wed. Now the Duke and Duchess of Gloucester had established themselves at Middleham, the favourite castle of her father, the late Earl of Warwick, and Simon's party was now awaiting an audience.

Simon had been chatting with one of the young men of the household. Rosamund thought that she remembered him as Sir Richard Ratcliffe, with whom Simon had served as page and squire at Middleham.

She said anxiously, 'Do you not think it better if Arthur waits for us out here, Simon? The duke can hardly receive him graciously after what happened when he came to Kinnersley.'

Simon threw back his head and laughed. 'My lord Richard is not so petty minded as to take exception to the thoughtless words of a boy, especially one who happened to be under great stress at the time.'

Rosamund lowered her voice to a whisper, keeping a careful eye on her brother from a safe distance. 'But you know what he has said about the duke. What if he should insult him here? That would be calamitous. Have you spoken with him about suitable behaviour?'

Simon shrugged. 'Certainly not. The boy is no fool and has matured a great deal recently. I expect faultless behaviour from him.'

'I still think it advisable for him not to be admitted to the presence chamber.'

Simon grinned down at her. 'I have informed the duke in the message that I sent in to him that I would be bringing Arthur.'

'I see,' Rosamund murmured apprehensively as the great wooden doors opened and the duke's steward emerged, carrying his white wand of office. The man appeared so formidable she was almost afraid of him, let alone the constable of all England into whose presence they were about to be conducted. She nervously smoothed down the burgundy velvet gown she had donned for the occasion, hoping that she was presentable, for, even now, she had only recently fully emerged from her mourning garments. Simon was wearing a green velvet doublet and Arthur his best brocaded one. Though Simon's appearance was fine, he could never be termed elegant and she wondered that he had not fussed more than he had over this audience. Certainly the duke had been accustomed to seeing Simon in his soldier's apparel, but now that the wars were over she thought that if he were to attend court at Westminster, he would be wise to give more attention to his mode of dress.

He looked at her appreciatively and smiled as she

smoothed back one of the gauzy folds of her veil and wondered if her truncated hennin headdress was quite straight. Martha had assured her that she looked her best. Her maid had accompanied them north and was hovering anxiously behind them, near to the screen doors.

As the steward approached, nodding to Simon, he held out his hand imperiously to escort his wife into the presence and turned his head slightly to beckon to Arthur to fall in behind them. For the first time in months Rosamund felt that her stomach did not belong to her as the steward preceded them up the length of the presence chamber towards the dais, on which were seated the young duke and duchess. Behind them stood friends of the duke and the duchess's ladies, who were all chattering merrily until the newcomers were admitted. Then they fell silent and Rosamund swallowed, knowing that she was the centre of their critical appraisal. Simon approached the duke's chair and bowed low as Rosamund sank into a deep curtsy. She prayed that her legs would not let her down when she attempted to straighten again.

Already Duke Richard was on his feet and holding out his hand in greeting.

'Simon, it is good to have you with us once more. And Lady Cauldwell, allow me to offer you felicitations upon your wedded state and to welcome you to Middleham.' He turned impulsively to the woman seated just behind him. 'Anne, let me present the former Mistress Rosamund Kinnersley. You will recall, I think, that her father served at one time in your father's company.'

The duchess rose and came forward, as welcoming as her husband, and offered her hand to Rosamund. 'Simon has spoken of you to Richard many times in his letters. I am delighted to meet you at last. Please come and take a seat beside me.'

Rosamund found herself handed up on to the dais and

escorted to a chair next to the two chairs of state provided
for the duke and duchess. As she sank down obediently,
she looked round in a panic for Arthur, who still stood, a
trifle bemused, beside Simon, whose hand lay warningly
upon his shoulder.

'And this, my lord Richard, is my brother-in-law, Arthur
Kinnersley,' Simon was saying.

The duke laughed. 'Indeed, I recall meeting this young
man very well indeed.'

Rosamund looked down at her brother and felt that the
blush mounting upon her cheeks was as deep as the scarlet
diffusing his throat and cheeks as he shuffled nervously
from one foot to the other.

The duke had once more seated himself and was leaning
forward. 'So you have brought him, as you promised,
Simon,' he said, in that pleasant, low voice Rosamund remembered. 'Well, Master Kinnersley, I have been learning
something about your progress since the dark days following Tewkesbury. Your brother-in-law has kept me informed. He tells me that it is quite time that you entered
service as a donzel. What would you say to the prospect
of entering my service here at Middleham? My master-at-
arms is a stern, but fair, teacher and there is none better
in Europe, I assure you. He taught me and Simon, too, and
our opponents have had cause to remember our skills in
battle. Mind, though, lad, he will not spare you when you
fail to come up to his high standard. You can bear me out
in this, eh, Simon?'

Rosamund felt that the silence, which followed this offer, stretched to infinity. She dared not look at Arthur.
What would he do now?

As if from a distance she heard his softly uttered reply.
'I would be deeply honoured indeed, your Grace.'

The duke laughed again. 'Well answered. Later my
steward will take you to Jehan Treves, my master-at-arms,

and you can make the acquaintance of the other lads in service here. Sir Simon will see to it that your manor lands and estates are well governed during your absence.'

Later, while Simon was in talk with some of his former companions, the duke drew Rosamund over to a seat in the oriel. He was dressed in a doublet of dark-blue figured velvet, overlaid with a massive gold chain bearing his personal device of a white boar in jewels and enamel work. She thought that he looked much younger than previously, for after Tewkesbury, when she had seen him on those two occasions, she had hardly thought it possible that he was still only eighteen years of age. The responsibilities of command and the position of his role of Lord Constable of England had fallen heavily upon youthful shoulders. Now he glanced back towards the dais where his young wife sat chatting happily with her ladies. Rosamund had never seen either of the Warwick daughters before and she was struck now by the beauty and fragility of the Lady Anne. The duchess was dressed in a gown of blue and silver brocade, which hung heavily upon her rather thin young body. The eyes, which had looked at her kindly earlier, had been deep blue and luminous and the hair, which had peeped from beneath the butterfly hennin, was fair and lustrous. There was a flush of colour now upon the ivory cheeks and it was obvious that the duchess, also, was happy to be home and wedded to her childhood companion. Rosamund thought that she had endured much suffering over the two or three years preceding her second marriage and she hoped, fervently, that the Lady Anne would find as much happiness as she had herself with Simon.

The duke said, 'You are thinking that she still does not look well.'

'I think that her Grace appears to be truly happy, my

lord, and that my father, who served hers, would have been glad to know that.'

He inclined his head gravely. 'And you, are you happy, Rosamund?'

'Yes, my lord.'

'You need not be concerned for your brother's welfare. My master-at-arms is hard but also kind, and he will find true companionship here, as I did in the company of friends like your husband.'

He was looking at her intently and she looked down somewhat unnerved by the scrutiny. Was he aware of the differences between herself and Simon, which concerned her husband's allegiance to him personally?

He said quietly, 'I hope that Simon will bring you often to Middleham and that you will become one of my wife's ladies and a true friend. I had no hand in her first husband's death, Lady Kinnersley, though, perhaps in my heart, I wished him dead. He was killed in the retreat and by another hand than mine.'

She looked back at him, colour flooding her cheeks. 'My lord, I made no such accusation...'

He sighed. 'Not openly, though I well know that others have implied it, as they had implied other, more heinous crimes.' His grey-green eyes regarded her steadily and she swallowed.

'Rumour should not be heeded, my lord, particularly false rumour.'

'Aye. It is true that I have profited from the Warwick inheritance by my marriage, particularly by the acquisition of this castle and the one at Sheriff Hutton, but they were both dear to Anne's heart and I wanted to bring her home. Simon understands that.'

'Yes, your Grace.' Her reply was whispered.

'You will be living at the castle near Aysgarth for much of the year, I hope, so Simon and I will be close once

again.' His lips twitched. 'You will adore his mother
though, as a child, I found her formidable. She writes that
she is awaiting your arrival with a mixture of pleasure and
apprehension. I hope that you will deal well with each
other. She has longed for a daughter over the years.'

Rosamund stared at him blankly. 'The castle? Simon
lives in a castle?'

'Indeed, yes. Has he not told you about his principal
home?'

Again she echoed his words, somewhat stupidly. 'His
principal home?'

'Why, yes, Simon has lands here in Yorkshire and in
the south and the Midlands. His mother has overseen the
work at Aysgarth, but he will want to travel to the others
soon now, I take it, and show you off to his households.'

His eyebrows rose at her expression of complete bewilderment.

'But I thought— I believed that Simon was almost penniless,' she blurted out, at last.

His lips twitched again. 'You thought that he had wed
you for your dowry? Oh, no, Lady Rosamund, Simon is
very wealthy indeed, possibly more wealthy in real terms
than either I or the king. His great-grandmother, I think it
was, brought enormous wealth into the family. She was
the daughter and sole heiress of a rich merchant. Other
lands have been acquired by inheritance. Simon's mother
brought further holdings. You will rule over several great
households, my lady, and will do well to learn from
Simon's mother, who will be delighted to teach you, I am
sure.'

'But he has always dressed and behaved as if—'

The duke laughed merrily. 'Simon has never been one
for extravagant display, nor has he ever boasted of his
wealth and influence. When I came here to Middleham as
a child of eight years, he was my superior at arms. He

befriended me for, believe me, Lady Rosamund, despite the fact that I was the king's brother, I was greatly in need of companionship, as is your brother now. I value your husband's friendship highly and will always do so.'

Rosamund was almost too choked to reply. He bent and took her hand. 'Be very happy, Rosamund. There will be hard times ahead but, with love and courage, we will weather them.'

Later, as they prepared to ride out of Middleham, leaving a surprisingly contented Arthur, who had already found companions, Rosamund looked lovingly towards her husband, 'Why did you not tell me of the splendour of your home?' she questioned softly.

He chuckled and bent to kiss her. 'I had no wish to be wed for my fortune,' he commented and she reached out to cuff him lightly. He restrained her by seizing her hand and conveying it to his lips. 'Tonight we shall sleep at Aysgarth, where my mother waits eagerly to greet you. Do not fear, my love, we will visit Kinnersley often, in Arthur's best interest. All will be well, as I promised, if only you continue to love me through the years to come.'

She blinked back tears of joy. 'Believe that I always will, my heart's love,' she murmured.

* * * * *

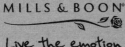

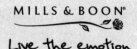

FREE!

2 Books
and a surprise gift!

We would like to take this opportunity to thank you for reading this Mills & Boon® book by offering you the chance to take TWO more specially selected titles from the Historical Romance™ series absolutely FREE! We're also making this offer to introduce you to the benefits of the Reader Service™—

- ★ FREE home delivery
- ★ FREE gifts and competitions
- ★ FREE monthly Newsletter
- ★ Books available before they're in the shops
- ★ Exclusive Reader Service discount

Accepting these FREE books and gift places you under no obligation to buy; you may cancel at any time, even after receiving your free shipment. Simply complete your details below and return the entire page to the address below. *You don't even need a stamp!*

YES! Please send me 2 free Historical Romance books and a surprise gift. I understand that unless you hear from me, I will receive 4 superb new titles every month for just £3.49 each, postage and packing free. I am under no obligation to purchase any books and may cancel my subscription at any time. The free books and gift will be mine to keep in any case.

H4ZEE

Ms/Mrs/Miss/Mr ....Initials...............................
                                                                                                                BLOCK CAPITALS PLEASE

Surname..

Address...

....

....Postcode ....

Send this whole page to:
UK: The Reader Service, FREEPOST CN8I, Croydon, CR9 3WZ
EIRE: The Reader Service, PO Box 4546, Kilcock, County Kildare (stamp required)